MW01038426

Fields of Asphodel

ALSO BY TITO PERDUE

The Sweet-Scented Manuscript

Opportunities in Alabama Agriculture

The New Austerities

Lee

Fields of Asphodel

TITO PERDUE

THE OVERLOOK PRESS
Woodstock & New York

This edition first published in the United States in 2007 by
The Overlook Press, Peter Mayer Publishers, Inc.
Woodstock & New York

WOODSTOCK:
One Overlook Drive
Woodstock, NY 12498
www.overlookpress.com
[for individual orders, bulk and special sales, contact our Woodstock office]

NEW YORK:
141 Wooster Street
New York, NY 10012

Cataloging-in-Publication Data is available from the Library of Congress

Book design and type formatting by Bernard Schleifer
Manufactured in the United States of America
ISBN-10 1-58567-871-6 / ISBN-13 978-1-58567-871-6
10 9 8 7 6 5 4 3 2 1

Inscribed to

Christopher Clark

1911-1985

ONE

"I DIED," (HE SAID), "I FEEL QUITE SURE I DID," WHEREupon he groaned twice, very loudly, and began then to crawl off toward where he hoped the pines might hide him for a certain time from buzzards and other things. And if it were bad enough that he had fallen off to sleep in cold weather (and it was), so much more the worse was it to awaken into this, in which the temperature was also worse. "Frozen corpse!" (he said), "*that's* the state to which I have now been reduced, the reward, one must suppose, for integrity and all those past efforts of mine. I see. And so then why, pray, am I still producing thoughts, hm, why? Goddamn it!" And then, speaking further: "But I'll not say anymore just now, no, nor look any longer on those pines, if that's what they are—whatever they are, they're dead—nor crawl, nor anything, not until I've had some explanation for all . . ."—(and here he indicated around with his free arm at the landscape, a bleak terrain with sky and trees and not much else)—". . . all this." Accordingly, he now rolled over and, eyes squeezed tight, tried again, but all in vain, to sleep.

It was all in vain—he had known from the beginning that it would be. Two minutes passed, perhaps more, during which he tried to call up memories of warmer periods in history and in his own personal experience. Whether he was decaying or whether not, or whether he should go on talking like this, eyes squeezed tight . . . Suddenly he leapt up, cursing wildly and striving to shrug off his suit which, incidentally, appeared to be of better quality than the one in which he had originally been dressed at the time of his death. And that was when he saw that he *had* in fact opened both eyes and *was* in truth looking off across a low, level field, empty in the extreme, that *did* seem more or less representative of his own personal condition while at the same time conforming in large measure to the reading that he had sometimes done on this particular topic.

Very little did he see here to remind him of the once-lovely South—a few acres of pine, their branches mostly missing, and beyond, a grey, dead, coagulated lake scintillating in the afternoon light. All things now had the appearance of old photographs, a rule that applied as well to the sun; taking out his glasses and focusing upon the object, it seemed to have mired down in mid-flight, its assorted beams not quite reaching all the way to earth. But was this in truth the sun? Pointing to it, he groaned out loud and began casting about in wild despair for his walking stick, appalled by the mere suggestion that he might have to go forward in this new world without it.

Fortunately for the good of his welfare, he found some twenty rods to the south-southeast, there where it had been driven up to its neck in the sand. It needed all he had, as strengthless as he had lately become, to draw it forth and inspect it at length and, using his scarf (a silken affair that he had never before in his life laid eyes upon), to burnish the thing and thrash about with it, making it hum in mid-air. Well-balanced still, he could have identified it from among hundreds of its kind. Comforted now to have it once more in his keeping, he thrashed again, lurching wildly, which is to say until he caught view of his own shadow dancing thus preposterously across the plain.

He decided to press forward. Of cigarettes, there were but three in his vest, none in his coat, and only a very partial box of matches, always the most essential of his equipment. Discovering a chit of paper at the bottom of his pocket, he learnt that the man who had owned this suit had attended the performance of a certain opera whose cast, however, was not listed within the microscopic text that concerned instead the rights and duties of the ticket holder. Twice he read it through, forbidding himself out of old punctilious habit from handing it off to the breeze once he had finished with it.

Money, too, he had, even if not in the amounts (and tightly-rolled little cylinders) in which he was wont to carry the stuff. Searching all three pieces of the suit, he found trivial bills only, not even so much as fifty dollars worth. Dismayed, he next examined the tawdry little billfold (manufactured out of cardboard, poorly sewed) that held, in addition to money, a document of some description bearing the photograph of a young but highly unintelligent-looking man shown in profile. He marveled at all of it, the money, the knife and pistol, the photograph, the two sets of eyeglasses and five prophylactics in golden foil, apprising himself of each of these before then returning them one by one to his pockets and then, again, drawing them out for a second and a third and sometimes even for a fourth inspection.

He knew this much already, that he had left home with two books and several hundred dollars, but only to finish up in a place like this with under fifty in bills and nothing worth reading but an old, fading, pink-colored chit that once had admitted someone to one of the lesser operas of one of the eighteenth century's most over-regarded composers. True, yes, his wardrobe now did comprise a fine brown suit, double-breasted indeed and boasting some of the broadest lapels that he had ever yet seen—*this*, at least, gave him no grounds for complaint. And shoes—he examined them anew, confirming that they were black, heavy, two in number and with perhaps 500 miles of unpaved travel remaining in them still.

It was while he was congratulating himself on this (and while taking out, and then changing his mind and returning to his vest one of the precious cigarettes), that his attention strayed down the path to an ant mound that was so perfectly formed and so much like a miniature volcano that when he began to approach it, he did so with considerable circumspect. Even an ant was life, and up till now he had seen no life anywhere.

Five minutes went past while Lee, constantly changing glasses, waited with growing impatience for one of the little animals to come forth or even just show a face in any of the innumerable little channels that ran down for great distances, as he believed, into the substrate. But when the minutes were up and no single ant had let himself be seen, Lee, his gorge high, got up off the ground, let down his pants, and began to urinate with accuracy direct into the opening. That it was an authentic sun overhead (and not just a photograph), he could attest to it in the way his own shadow continued to lengthen, clouds to gather, and the far-away lake sparkled redly each few seconds before always turning back to grey again. He could feel a chill coming in, an unfavorable indication threatening bad weather for someone of his age (quite old) and possessed neither of victuals nor, so far as he could see, of any sort of shelter in which to defend himself against the night. He who had always fled from human company, *now* was he swept with self-pity to see himself like this, an old man still waiting in a panic for but one single ant—he did not ask for words—a single ant to cheer him forward in this new world.

It was well along in the afternoon when he descried what at first he thought to be another of the mile-markers, human size limestone tablets with platitudes engraved on them that he had come to expect at certain intervals along the trail. Even so he took the precaution, first, of changing over into his long-distance glasses and then, secondly, of fumbling about in vain for the .32 caliber weapon that in recent years he had accustomed himself to carry wherever he went. Huge was his surprise when he recognized the "tablet" was instead a human individual, a mature person apparently (his hair was white), who stood by the trail with his hands in his pockets while peering up into the sky. Lee stalked nearer, halting again when he perceived that the man was fitted out in a woman's coat, a dark brown garment all of fur that gave him the appearance of an orangutan with, however, the aforementioned white hair.

Moving *with* the path (but against the desert's grain), Lee pressed forward. Already he had determined that he would not himself be the first to speak, no. For he much preferred to go on in ignorance of things than to chance his dignity with a person who had been loitering here for no one knew how long in woman's clothing. Accordingly Lee began to travel with more speed, approaching and then passing the fellow while keeping his gaze fixed upon a particular location in the hollows of the blue-grey hills that loomed ahead.

"Ha! Ha!" the man said. "Ha. And so you're really going through with it—strolling past like that. As if you didn't have a thousand questions—look at you—a thousand questions you'd like to ask. Well! I can see *you* haven't changed."

Lee spun on him. "What's that you said just now?"

"Thousand questions."

"I don't have any questions! Not for someone of *your* sort anyhow." (He glanced to the man's coat, finding it belted with two lengths of rope joined together with a shoestring.)

"Oh you're a grand one, you are. No, I've seen some grand ones in my time, but *you*!"

Lee had no intention of responding. Instead, he turned to his short-distance glasses and, after some little trouble with the case, fitted them on in time to witness the other man doing the same. They both now scanned each other up and down, both wearing bifocals, both with their heads tilted back.

"Gad!"

"No, I've seen some types in my day. But *you*, oh my goodness—I just don't know."

"Woman's coat. Nothing will ever persuade me that that is anything else in this world but a . . ."

"Which world did you say?"

". . . but a woman's coat. The muffler, too."

"So grand, aren't you? I do hope you'll remember this conversation, Dr. Pefley, when you lie freezing tonight on some barren hillside." (He pointed toward the hills.) "The first thing you're going to have to learn, 'sir,' is that all those old courtesies you're so proud of, that they don't apply over here, they just don't."

Lee snorted. He was looking at a man who had stolen a coat—he was as certain of that as that the fellow now was casting jealous glances at his own two good shoes. (The man's shoes were deplorable. Lee could point to at least three places where the hose, and in one instance an actual toe, were sticking through.)

"Stay! I have something for you, Pefley."

Lee groaned and then, calling upon his patience, which had been under considerable strain during the past few minutes, answered with as much politeness as he was able to summon at that time. "I guess you just didn't hear me. I said I wanted nothing to do with you. *Nothing*!"

"You never said that. I would have remembered if you had. Anyway, I have something that will interest you."

"I doubt it." (He did however come two paces nearer and

begin to squint with new interest into the person's face. He had seen this before—the pained look so characteristic of those who had gone through a greater number of years than of books.)

"And so if you'll just step this way, 'sir,' I'll try not to waste *too* much of your oh so valuable time."

Lee did follow. Above, the grey sun was shuddering all too conspicuously, as if in dread of the night to come. Keeping one eye upon it at all times (and the other on the man in front), Lee began to question whether he ought not take that fur coat for himself, the muffler, too, and never mind that they might sort poorly with his brogans, his stick, and his personality.

"Ah me, endless plains," he said, whispering to himself as he trudged at a safe distance behind the man in the coat. "Or steppes, rather, that seem to continue on to perpetuity. And me as old as I am, and a sun like that." (He touched it with his cane.)

"Yes, I can just imagine the quality of nighttime in this place"—he was close to tears—"to which I've come."

The other man said nothing. Trundling hurriedly up and down the furrows, he was apt to disappear from time to time, but only then to climb back into view a moment later, always within two cane lengths of Leland.

"Winter, is it? Lee asked. "Or can this be merely fall?"

This time the man did utter something or another. But Lee couldn't hear it.

"Fall, you said?"

"That's twice you've asked that question. Tell me—no, I need to know—do you want to stop here and chat for a few days, or do you want to see that body?"

Lee jumped back. "Body!"

"Why, yes. It'll be dark soon."

"But my God, man, what sort of . . . *Body*, you said?"

"Because it'll be picked clean by morning; oh, you can count on that, yes, sir. Roaches, don't you know. And whatnot."

Lee followed, his mind in part upon the body and in other part upon the man's fur coat. Together they now entered a quarter-acre swatch of pines that looked as if it might have been snipped out with giant scissors and set down in front of them on the otherwise empty plain. Here, moving on tiptoes, they soon arrived at the heart of the grove, a place where very little sunlight entered.

"He must have been traveling at high speed, Dr. Pefley, dragging that old stick behind him. I can say that with some confidence based upon how the straw... Ho! Look there, there where he tossed away a cigarette!"

It was true. Lee waited as the man dashed forward and retrieved the thing.

"Naked, too—he must have been in a great hurry to arrive at the place to which he thought he was going. Wait! See there? No, no, not there; *there* is where he is, by Jove, lying just yonder with one eye open. Most peculiar grin, that. 'Rhapsodic vision'—is that how it was?"

They came from widely-separated approaches, Lee and the man. Already the corpse lay partly covered in debris and pine needles, and already the ants had gathered. Lee's memory flashed back to when he had still been able to take pride in the form and the figure that once had been his—hale, well-shouldered, taller than the average.

"Taller than average. It was your privilege, was it, to go through life that way?"

Lee nodded.

"But oh, those *scars*! Makes me ill to look at it. Now just why would a person want to do that to himself I wonder? No, that does bother me, really, when I have to see that sort of thing."

Lee blushed. "But the head, consider the head."

"Yes?"

"Doesn't that strike you as a head that had 'more than the average' in it? And doesn't he get credit for that?"

"Hm? Oh, I don't know." And then: "To be perfectly honest with you, doctor, I don't see anything in that head that is *remotely* like those '12,000 volumes' you're always going on about, not at all, no. A few dozen. *Maybe*."

"Why you great ass! Just look at that . . ." (And here Lee knocked three times, tapping emphatically at the cranium with his cane.) ". . . bony structure!"

"Imagination pure and simple, and contaminated with egotism. I see nothing here but the residue of a vain old man who had been mistreating himself."

"Ah? You say that to me, do you?"

"And see here, this other eye. Why, it's as vacant as a cow's!"

"That was a good eye, blast you, in its day. But will you *kindly* stop probing about in the poor devil's mouth with that . . . What is that, pliers? That was a full set of teeth he had in there, all the way till sixty-three!"

"Yellow gold—I'll have those."

"You'll have nothing of the kind!" Suddenly Lee pushed him with his shoe, causing the man to teeter and then go tumbling some distance down the slope. But Lee had not credited the man's tenacity; right away, he was back at it again, again trying to carry out the operation. This time Lee sent him all the way to the bottom, where he sat huddled-up and weeping bitter tears.

"*Everybody* gets *everything*, except me. Me, I don't get *nothing*. And I'm the one who found it!"

By the time they had returned to the path, both men were tired. It made Lee uneasy, to have this person traveling so closely behind; finally, he turned and, still moving forward, expressed his concern.

"Again you're following very closely. Why?"

The man grinned guiltily but then did allow some inches to open up between them. This required Lee to walk backwards if he wanted to keep the fellow in view, and made it necessary for him to enunciate his words more distinctly and at higher volume than was his ordinary wont.

"How cold, I say how cold does it get in these parts?"

"'Old?'"

"Nay, nay. *Cold*, how cold?"

"Ah, 'cold.' Yes, 'cold,' you said. Well! You'll soon have the answer"—(he waved his free hand around at the sources from which he expected the night to gather)—"the answer to that, won't you? Just pray it doesn't rain."

Lee opened to speak when, that moment, he bumbled into another of the extinct ant castles that interfered so much with travel and disfigured what otherwise had been an ordinary field eventuating in mountains east and west. He staggered, listing dangerously as he tried to reach out and take hold on nothingness. And that, of course, was when the man came rushing forward, his eyes glittering with excitement at what must have appeared to him the best opportunity he was likely to be given. Lee had presence enough and agility to find his balance and then, cane lifted on high, to face the man.

"Back! Stay back!"

"Me?"

"Back!"

"I was coming to your aid."

They proceeded anew, Lee scanning the path with one eye and with the other keeping constant surveillance on the man. The dead sun, previously so low on the horizon, had climbed to a position where it was immune (if only temporarily) from the many sharp peaks and jagged hills; apparently, it was retreating *away* from the earth (he still believed it *was* the earth) at the breakneck speed characteristic of such things and was in process of turning into but one more star of which it would be difficult to say which star it was. In any case there was almost no warmth reaching down to them from any portion whatsoever of the sky. Addressing the man, Lee, using his hands to form a "horn," began to call out the list of questions that had been cumulating in him:

"*Is* this the world?" he asked, and: "Are we indeed in some sense still alive?" And: "What happened to the ants?" (He blushed, realizing too late that he had many questions more crucial than this last one.) Now, allowing the cane to dangle from his belt, he again cupped his hands and asked the most important of all questions: "Hast seen a certain woman, quite short, who 'came over' some years ago in a bright red jacket and ribbon in her hair?"

"Gibbon?"

"No, no, no, no; I'm talking *ribbon,* man! Ribbon. My guess is that it had come undone, that ribbon, and was streaming out behind her as she ran."

But the man was no longer responding to questions. Getting into his other glasses, Lee realized that although the person continued to face forward, in fact he was stepping backwards, getting smaller, and returning, apparently, to the same glade and same corpse from which they both had so recently come. Seeing this, Lee remained in some bewilderment until . . . Until the person drew a set of pliers from his fur coat and flaunted it.

"Blackguard!" called Lee. "And all for a couple of rotten teeth with very little gold in either of them!"

Twenty minutes later, cursing still, he began the tedious ascent. Already night was pouring down upon him from that self-same hatch in the sky through which the sun had so recently absquatulated. As to the "ascent" called "tedious," certainly it was steep enough and the path sufficiently bestrewn with pebbles as to give him considerable trouble indeed. But mainly it was the chill he dreaded, chill and frost, the possibility of wind and a life of coldness never ending. "Judy!" he called, his gorge rising as time continued to go by and still she refused to fly to his side.

But now the trail grew steeper still. Soon enough his old man's strength, such as it was, began to falter and he found himself bending to within a beard's length of the hillside. One single pine he saw, but when he reached for it, expecting to snare it with his cane . . . Lo! It was further than he thought. His eyes and everything else, yea, and even his glasses as well, they all were an old man's, too. Lee cursed. His hemorrhoids, too, were coming back, no doubt about it, returning in great force while trailing clouds of glory. But even more fundamentally than that, he was beginning to guess at what he might find at the summit of this present hill—whether it might not perhaps be tenanted already and he himself caught by night perforce in company with the dead.

In actual fact, it proved empty both on the ridge and in the adjoining woods. He spent a minute on each knee, and then a third such period flat on his back while he waited for his stamina to return. Well pleased was he by what he saw—a dell of long-leaf pines (not all of them dead), and on the floor a considerable deposit of those same needles in which he expected very soon to be bedding down and, hopefully, soon to be sleeping. No reading material. And yet he considered it a dispensation that on this his first night he was to have for company nothing more obnoxious than an owl, a small but indignant personality who, apparently, imagined he had a pre-emption on the place.

From this elevation he could see far, Lee, and what he saw was the trail itself, a precise line sketched in, as it seemed, by a cartographer using dew in place of ink. Considered as a line, it dashed back and forth (this way and that), before, suddenly, running off into the hills where it vanished, reappeared, and then petered out altogether before coming back and continuing on out of range of Lee's ordinary glasses. Was that *snow* tonsuring the upper crests? Whatever it was, it was giving off fumes.

The moon, too, he saw, his own favorite star. The other stars—and now he did change into his more powerful glasses—they were too numerous by much and too unstable, as if those responsible for bringing them forth and hanging them in place, as if they had been carried away by their enthusiasm for the project. And in short he was suspicious of everything that he could see. He, too—was it still *Lee* inside this fine brown suit? Yes, he believed that it was. Something in the irritability and hemorrhoids told him so, not to mention several other things as well. That was when he jumped back in great surprise, astonished to find a sod-built settlement sheltering about two hundred feet beneath him at the bottom of the hill.

Shielding his eyes against the shrinking sun, he leaned out at full extent over the canyon. At this remove the village looked to him more like a collection of toy buildings arranged by a child than like anything familiar to him from his own experience. Was it due to the clatter of the windmill, or was it his own sudden movement that had sent the hamlet's one unsleeping hound off into his long spree of desultory barking? These things were smart, dogs, and this one had already no doubt divined Lee's baleful shade spying down from the crest whence he might have spit into any chimney of his choice. Certainly his silhouette was large enough, Lee's, and sharp as flint; coming nearer, it enveloped the community and, with a vulpine profile that needed only a long pointed beard, scanned the tundra for hundreds of leagues. And did these villagers, intellectual innocents, did they tremble in the pitch-black night, doubting not but that some new-arrived danger even now was hovering over the town? Lee chuckled (his shade chuckling along with him), whereon the dog whimpered twice and then turned and crawled hurriedly beneath the nearest house.

Moving off to one side, Lee urinated twice and then, coming back, began gathering armloads of pine needles, expecting to fabricate a "mattress" along with "sheets" and "blankets" that, in truth, refused to hold together. It put him in mind of the recommendations of his late grandfather, a provident man who had himself once been caught in the out-of-doors on just such a night as this one.

"Gather the leaves thickly!" the old man had urged. "But draw them *gently*, as it were, even to the chin."

"Otherwise, they don't stay together," said Lee. "See?"

"And lie without moving, if you can."

Lee nodded. He was alone, the stars innumerable and cold weather moving over as he lay face-up, the cane crowding at his side. It failed to surprise him when he observed "faces" materializing in the sky, enormous configurations representing personages from English literature. Some, to be sure, were simply too stereotypical for modern taste, whereas still others were perhaps typical of nothing whatsoever. It pleased him that he could identify so many of them, that is to say until the characters became less and less identifiable and the literature more and more obscure, falling at last outside his province of knowledge. He was *not* asleep, not yet. And now, groaning (for he had been putting it off all day), he took one of the matches at last (but not for purposes of reading!) and used it in his accustomed way.

TWO

Come morning and dawn, Lee leapt up much refreshed and proceeded to shake the needles out of his hair. Dreams of happiness had regaled him all night even if he could not now remember what they were. Again he yawned and stretched and was in process of reciting out loud certain pieces of conversation from the more notable of those dreams when, suddenly, he recoiled in huge astonishment to find that yet another old man had bedded down next to him at some moment during the foregoing black night and now was grinning up toothlessly while waiting for Lee to continue with the recitation.

Quickly Lee gathered his possessions and, using for that purpose his yard-square kerchief of fine silk, made a hasty bundle and hung it from his stick. All his worldly goods, his cash and coins (one of them from Canada), his book of matches and his wee pen knife, all of it together added up to such inconsiderable luggage that no matter how much he looked at it from various angles he still wanted to cry. The other man, meantime, had gotten into a sitting position and was fighting valiantly to rise.

"Now you take a person like me," he said. "I consider a person like you to be lucky, what with all them *things* you got there. In that there little *pouch*, I mean. You looking for a partner?"

"No, no," said Lee, "not really, no. No, actually I . . ." (He had gone off to finish urinating and was striving to hurry the process.) "But thanks all the same."

"Shit, I could carry all that stuff for you, and shit, why you wouldn't have to carry *nothing*." And then, in a somewhat darker voice: "They won't take that Canadian penny. Nobody will."

Lee hurried. The "sun," more dead than alive, had only just that moment snapped the last thread still holding it to the horizon and, lifting a few centimeters, had finally begun to throb under its own power. Lee looked for, and found, a small clutter of dark clouds rushing up too late to forestall dawn from taking place. Always it was the same—he could see so much more clearly at this time, and farther, than by night, and what he mostly saw was a sight that any historian could envy—a walled village (the gate was open) with hens and children running in and out. Bending nearer, he could also see an adamant cock strutting dictatorially atop the gable of one of the more prosperous-looking cottages.

"Medieval Ages! Or something very like it."

"I wouldn't know," said the man, who had given up on trying to rise and now was lying flat, his hands behind his head. Lee could barely hear what he was saying: "That's right, and now he's got his goddamn little pouch all nice and neat, got his goddamn little shoes, got his penny. Oh, you bet he does! Me, where's *my* penny, hm? Hey! I got to be quiet or he's liable to hear me."

Lee hurried. Already he had descried what looked to be a human couple wending slowly toward him down the trail, hand-holding youths they seemed, one of each gender. "Suicidists, I'll warrant," said Lee, his indignation rising high—until he recollected how his own career had ended. So poor was their rate of speed and so regularly did they pause to consult with one another, he saw little danger of having to speak with either of them, now *or* later.

Coming down the hill, Lee tried to slow his momentum by grabbing at the vegetation and, all in all, ended up by sledding the last fifteen yards on his palms and brisket, rousing the village dog! In all his many years, never yet had Lee been able to go anywhere, neither into homes nor cities nor neighborhoods, nor yet into the open countryside without dogs gathering to hoot at him, their hair standing on edge. This time he tried to patronize the thing, even going so far as to smile affectionately and then get down on one knee, as if he had trekked all this way for the specific enjoyment of stroking this one dog. He accepted it, of course, the dog did, but would not for that reason alone leave off baying into Lee's face. The barking got noisier. So old was Lee, his trousers so much too short, ankles so thin, socks so flaccid and smile so sly . . . And that was when he perceived a woman's face looking out at him worriedly from a cottage window.

He stood, smiled, entered the house in dignity and after sniffing at the various nice aromas coming from the kitchen, slapped his cane down smartly across the table. Here inside it was more accommodating than he would have imagined, cozy to a degree, and with a highly satisfactory fire in the clay-built hearth.

"Coffee," he said, drawing his chair nearer to the fire. "Yes, and eggs too, if you please. Well-fried. And bacon as well."

She stood in one place, the matron of the house, while plucking nervously at her hands. Lee had noticed the giant wooden ladle hanging from her belt, the symbol, as he had to suppose, of her position within the community.

"Coffee?"

"Why, yes. And the other things as well."

"Yes, sir, I'll bring some coffee—I don't mind. But this is *not* a restaurant, or anything like that. Never has been."

Covered with embarrassment, Lee leapt up in horrible confusion and immediately began blaming himself. "Ridiculous of me, stupid, stupid!" (Twice he smote himself on the forehead, both times flinching.) "I shall of course leave at once."

"No. No, it's all right, I reckon. Since you're here."

"Cream, too, if you please."

It needed some time before she could bring the water to a boil, valuable minutes during which he was able to remove both socks, wring them dry, and then hang them up in front of the fire. No bacon, nothing of that sort; he had to be content with hot coffee, three cups, which he paid for with conversation and news from the "outside" world.

"And do they still . . .?"

"They do, madam, and other things even worse than that."

"Tsk, tsk, tsk."

"Voters, madam, yea, and sports fans; they come together in great masses, paying money to hear bad music. There's not a dozen departments of classical studies still remaining, they say, in all those universities of theirs."

"But do they . . ."

"They do. And yet, those pleasures are highly over-rated, ma'am—we both know that."

"Oh, I don't know. I sure wish *I* could . . ."

"Over-rated. The decay of literature—*that's* where you should have fixed your attention, when you still could." He rose, stretched and then, barefooted still, padded on into the kitchen where, in truth, he found almost no foodstuffs of any kind, not even so much as a peach or grape, or late tomato ripening on the sill. "Absolutely void!" he said. "But tidy, I will give you that." Suddenly he yanked open one of the cabinets and, finding it dark, began to probe about inside it with his stick. "Ah, but is it also tidy . . . here!"

"You shouldn't be going in there. My husband, he . . ."

"Fine man, your husband." He opened the pantry, uncovering a few tools and light bulbs, a broken churn and several vials of pharmaceuticals—he kept one—whose prescriptions had all long ago expired. "No bacon. And yet, I myself have seen hogs wandering at freedom in this land."

"Would you like more coffee?"

"Certainly. And especially so if that's all I'm to be given in return for the information I've brought. Ah, well."

She never accepted his Canadian penny and when, after having arrived at the edge of the village and having turned and come back for his socks, she passed them out through the window in preference to letting him back inside. The sun was high now and enjoying smooth sailing; changing into his other glasses, it looked to him as if the surface of the thing were infested with worms driven insane by the heat. That he was himself being stalked by blackbirds, he attributed it to their natural curiosity about the little golden pouch that dangled from his cane. He stopped and smiled at them, hoping to woo them with charm alone in order that he might seize one. For he had not fingers enough, nor toes, to count the hours he had gone without . . .

And that was when a small blue lizard scampered across in front of him and, hesitating just long enough to make a judgment about Lee's character, raced forward into the desert.

It carried Lee further from the road than he wanted to go, and when at last he pounced upon the thing (never asking whether it might be venomous), and looked into its tiny eye, finding anguish there, and observed how the creature appeared to be starving too (but still had managed to change into a bright green "suit" by means of which he thought to dazzle the old man), and saw that its infinitesimal ribs were dilating wildly, *then* Lee took out his knife and set about the tedious work of removing the viscera, a trivial possession which, however, the animal seemed to cherish above all things in the world. The entire organism, such as it was, was not much larger than one of Lee's own fingers; accordingly, he choked it down in a single bite, calling his Will into play. And why (if asked) had he not bothered to roast his meal? Because he would have had to search for miles to fetch the fuel.

Two hours later, his mind rummaging back through time and certain old-world opera tunes, Lee went off to one side and manured. Ordinarily a blessing, this time he yelped out loud three times in acute pain. Hemorrhoids! he never went anywhere without them. But worst was this—to know that he was being evaluated by hundreds of eyes from the encompassing hills.

By early afternoon his limp had begun to tell on him, reducing his efficiency. Cursing, scratching, taunting at the sun with his stick, he caught sight just then of a disturbed-looking person hobbling toward him at high speed. Quickly Lee shifted over into his better glasses and then, bending forward at the waist in order to reduce the distance between them by a few inches, verified that this, too, was an elderly man, or "mature person," as he preferred to call it, and that he, too, was furnished with a cane.

"Pefley," said Lee, coming forward with his hand outstretched. "Of the Alabama Peflies, don't you know."

Never pausing, the man brushed past without a word. Lee had to run after him and even then had trouble catching up with the person. "You there!" he said. "No, this is *outrageous*, simply to stride on past in this way! Can you not even at the very least . . .?"

"Back, go back! Bad, it's bad; go back *now*!" And then: "No, no, not *that* way. *This* way!"

Lee paled. The man was old, his condition awful, and Lee could not stay even with him. He had time enough to call out just one question, which he did in his strongest voice:

"Hast seen a woman in a red jacket, uncommonly short? And scarf?"

No answer. The man, hobbling at high speed and leaving behind odd marks in the powder, already he was out of hearing.

By mid-afternoon Lee began to feel that he was getting tired again; even so he continued to push forward against the grain of the desert, drawing closer and closer to the promise and the threat of another night without benefit of shelter. "Ah, me," he said, "I see no shelter anywhere, neither here nor there nor over yonder." Ahead were hills, highly detailed, and all but one of them sown to evergreens that had grown to precise heights—only once before had he seen anything so utterly *summoning*, so like the engravings seen on certain old world postage stamps. He longed to go there, knowing that it would need two days of hard travel across unmarked lands. Even so, he persisted in thinking about it, grievously tempted by that faint far-away and grainy blue-gray texture that had always, as it were, spoken to him personally, his own favorite hue. Thus Lee grinned therefore, stroking his whiskers and wetting his thumb and harkening to the mile-wide fissures in the hills that told him all he immediately needed to know about the geology of this place.

Two miles further he passed a smattering of skeletons, cow bones with no flesh whatsoever adhering to any of them. Ahead, he began to make out what at first he took to be a depôt of some kind, or caravanserai, laid out in higgledy-piggledy fashion alongside the highway. His natural impulse was to fly to it—he could smell food, hear talk, see three bright fires with human figures standing about. Instead he caused himself to move more slowly, especially as he approached the bend and, with head held high, drew near to the perimeter. He saw no reason to give any further heed to these people who, in any case, did not appear to be of the highest type. He did note one particularly bedraggled-looking woman bending over a kettle and stirring in it with a long-handled spade. But here, too, he chose to give no further attention to her or to the strange song she was so loudly singing. Soon he had rounded the bend, had strolled the whole length of the bivouac and was heading out of town when one of the men called to him:

"Gosh! Aren't you even going to stop and chat for a little bit?"

Lee spun on him. "What's that you said just now?"

"Stop. Chat."

There were other men as well, gaunt people in boots and overalls and bits and pieces of business suits; they stood, two of them warming at the fire, a third bringing fuel (dried manure, to judge by the fumes), and the fourth man, the speaker himself, who came forward now with his paw (which might be soiled), extended far out in front of him. Seeing that he must shake with the person, Lee groaned and glanced heavenward and shifted the cane over to his other hand, which in any case was much the stronger of the two.

"Pefley," he said. "Alabama branch."

"I'm pleased, sir. Myself, I . . ."

"Good, good. Now can you tell me how far—and I don't expect accuracy, not anymore—how far to that low-lying swath of tufted uplands"—he pointed—"just yonder?"

"We don't know."

"No, I dare say not." (He started to move on.)

"Hey! Won't you even have some stew with us?"

"'Stew?'" (He could not but snort at that suggestion.) "I shouldn't think so, no." And then: "And what manner of 'stew,' exactly, might we be talking about here, hm?"

"Well surely you'll come and *warm* yourself for a bit? Look, I'm just trying to offer a little elementary *hospitality*, if you'll take it. However, if you . . ."

A second man now spoke up, a tough-looking individual with a bandana of some kind twined about his head. "Shut-up, Steve. Let him starve, for Christ's sake, since that's what he seems to want."

"No, no," said Lee, conceding to them at last. "No, I recognize the importance of keeping up with these things, sharing and whatnot, et cetera." He followed. "Far be it from me!"

It *was* a jolly fire, manure-fueled or not. And a ravenous scent that evanesced from the kettle, rushing headlong to the nostrils of the mind. Lee saw things therein—peelings, a rib cage that was too small for a cow's but too grand for a mouse, also some third element that breached the surface every few seconds to take a new breath. Twice he tapped at the cauldron with his stick, commenting upon the contents, the stink, the generosity of those who had brewed even so poor a solution as this.

"'Pefley,' he calls himself. Seems he dudn't want any of our concoction."

"Good!" said the fifth man, a bald-headed pot-bellied

little troll whose whole responsibility, seemingly, began and ended with the fuel.

"Ah, well," said Lee, stretching, "I don't suppose I'd refuse a *taste* of it."

"You already have. And by the way, now that we're talking about it, what's that you're always carrying around in that goddamn little *pouch* of yours? I don't like that."

"Yeah, me too—I been wondering the same thing. Ever since I saw him coming around the bend, moving real slow."

Lee looked at them. The troll had slumped into a "chair" assembled out of stones, thus placing himself at serious disadvantage should Lee elect to aim his blows direct upon the man's head; indeed, he saw just the spot for it. Instead, listing badly, he got down on one knee and began untying his bundle, knowing full well that it contained nothing to inspire jealousy in such men as these. They gathered around, competing for space.

"Oh Lord, another one of *those* things. What, from Canada? That's going to be real useful out here, oh yeah."

"No, he has every right. It's *his*, after all, and not *ours*."

"Claude?"

"Yes?"

"I'm getting pretty tired of you. We all are."

"He does have a knife."

"But see how wee it is!"

At that, Lee could not but smile. "I do not, gentlemen, rely for my protection upon this tiny knife. No, not for so long as I am accompanied by . . . this!" (Having unsheathed the cane, he flashed it back and forth for several moments in front of their eyes before then grounding it and wiping it with his kerchief. Its girth, too, he made manifest, demonstrating how even his own considerable fingers could not reach all the way around it.) "Yes," he said, "we've come far, my stick and me, oh dear yes, very much so, him and me. I am minded of a certain nasty little *troll* who once ran afoul of us both."

There was a long, still, and very profound silence during which two of the men drew back some distance and began to occupy themselves with unnecessary tasks. The others, the ones left over, they pressed closer, hoping to hear more about Lee's story.

"What happened?"

"Hm?"

"The fellow who ran aground."

"*Afoul*, ran afoul."

"Ah!"

Evening now began to fall, Lee drifting at hazard among the fires. Of the women, most were broken down by the travel and the weather, their prior-world vanities having been mostly (but not entirely!) cast aside. Seating himself nearby, he watched a hump-back woman hovering greedily over an expiring blaze that had burned down to a few last coals that looked like little smiling faces. To him she almost resembled someone he might have known at one time, judging from her deformity and unmanageable hair. Stepping forward, he caught himself just in time before committing the awful mistake of tapping at her hump.

"Ann?"

She turned and smiled—she had invented a substitute for lipstick but then had used such quantities of it that he thought at first she was deliberately playing the clown—turned and smiled and began lifting and lowering her eyebrows in a manner so lewd that it made Lee want to turn and flee. Thus they stood, Lee aghast, the other grinning whorishly. And yet, even here, he could read in her that eleven-year-old who once, when still the world was good, had been so adept at running and jumping and doing all her homework. She was old now, older than Lee, older than anyone, and her hump was even older than that.

"Very good. At first I thought you might be . . ."

"Ann?"

"Yes."

"I ain't her."

"No." (She had eased her hand into Lee's front pocket and was exploring in it.)

"I can do anything what Ann can do."

"Yes! But I can't."

"Got himself a little *sack*. Carries it around with him all the time. You're cute, honey."

Lee was appalled. She had gathered his nose between her thumb and finger and was pulling it playfully, even forcing his whole head over to one side. Must he indeed lash her about the hump and shoulders in order to get free? No. His nose was not really so much of a handle, and after a struggle, he managed to take it back again.

With night coming in, Lee's habitual nervousness began visibly to increase and soon he could be seen running up and down in search of an unclaimed blanket, or even just a vacant place near to one of the fires. He who herebefore had always adored the night, had respected afternoons and been an idolater of twilights, now he dreaded the departure of even so dubious a sun as this current one, which seemed to toggle off and on every few seconds, giving no warmth at all. Quickly he ran through the crowd looking for a quilt or bed—and he would have settled for anything—or just a plain simple tarpaulin in which he might cocoon himself in semi-comfort against the worst hours of the on-coming night. Finding nothing, and with the sun falling rapidly now through clouds and mist and approaching ever nearer to the time when it must forever disappear, Lee went running back to the original man who previously had been so courteous but now seemed measurably less so.

"Still with us?"

"So it seems!" quoth Lee, laughing and scoffing at himself and then pointing off into the cold that even now was migrating straight for them, a "wall," as it seemed, blue about the edges. "Promises to be chilly tonight."

The man said nothing. He was in process of making up his own pallet, a fussy procedure that entailed a layer of newspaper, a pillow devised out of a pair of trousers filled with grass, and *two* blankets, one of them so nearly new that it was still shedding some of its superfluous nap.

"*Two* blankets!" said Lee, probing at the pillow with his cane. "And one of them so nearly new that . . ."

"Dr. Pefley?"

"Yes?"

"Let me do you a favor."

Lee agreed to it at once. "Most kind of you, really." And that was when, while reaching for the better blanket, he suffered an access of bad consciousness and took the inferior one instead. The man grabbed it back.

"Let me save you some time and embarrassment, doctor, if you will allow me—*there is not the slightest chance* that anyone will be giving away a blanket on a night like this. No! that's just the way it is. I *am* sorry. I am. Truly I am."

"I can pay."

"You cannot pay."

"Can."

"Can't. All the money in the world won't buy a blanket now." (He pointed to the on-coming night.)

"But . . . But, but . . ."

"*Soooo* dignified, weren't you? And look at you now. Oh, I don't know; you people, you come over here bringing all sorts of stuff—puppies, photographs, old love letters, everything except what you *should* bring. No, no, put it away, I don't want your penny."

"But . . . But, but . . ."

The man went back to work.

He was still going back and forth, still testing with his cane the arrangements of other people when, that moment, and to the accompaniment of wide-spread shrieking, the dense black night began to pour down upon them from out of a source in the sky. Lee, not wanting to spend his whole time in the slums of the encampment, turned and paced back hurriedly toward where the personnel, it seemed to him, showed signs of somewhat higher refinement. One entire family, man, woman, child and pets, had bedded down all in a heap, affording warmth each to each. Lee, smiling, came nearer; he understood, of course, that there was no *real* chance for him to slip in amongst them—they would have noticed it at once. Instead, he began bouncing up and down, flailing himself about the shanks and withers in an effort to stir up the blood and keep it moving. It cheered him only fractionally to see two others, old men both, both of them also flailing and jumping in far parts of the camp.

He smoked, he sang, he tried several times to call his Will into play. The dark was not twenty minutes old and already the cold was so chill, the night so thick and the chill so cold, he doubted anyone's Will could have prevailed against *this*. And that was when he observed two grey wolves narrowing in grinningly upon the camp, their golden eyes glancing at everything except at what to them was most truly interesting. Lee now showed the cane, whereupon the greyest and most evil of them did in fact retreat by an inch or two. What wouldn't he have given, Lee, to disemburthen both of them of their glossy pelts! marvelous vestments with so much more insulating power by far than even the nappiest of blankets. He smiled and beckoned, at the same time probing for the little pen knife that was supposed to be in his front pocket. And meantime, east and west and everywhere, he still had in front of him a solid nine hours of utter blackness before the return of a sun that he had come to deem as nearly worthless. Figments of world literature flitted through his mind along with thoughts of his own late beloved wife. He was too old, too weak, his Will too blunted and bent over for him not to wish that she might come to him from out of the good place to which she had gone and make him warm again.

Not until nearly midnight and after a spate of vomiting on his part, (vomiting from the cold), did he take a sheet of cardboard from among certain other litter and, with the use of this rather sorry material, strive to get into a sleeping position. More importantly, it let him turn his attention to the over-sized stars that seemed, many of them, to be fading out of existence even as yet brighter ones leapt jubilantly to life. It was, of course, their numbers and outlandish size (some of them actually competing with the moon), that gave him to understand that he had somehow dropped off to sleep after all and that these "stars," so-called, in fact they were printed on his lids and were the products of his mind.

Old age and bad weather! Could any combination be more unfavorable for a person of his kind? He had been allowed perhaps forty minutes of mediocre sleep, enough to pre-empt the balance of the night. Accordingly, he rolled over onto his good side and lit a cigarette. No one durst come near him nor try to snip his laces and make away with his fine shoes, not while he lay unblinking, his left eye stretched wide. Bringing his Will into operation, he was close to sending himself back to sleep again, that is to say until it registered on him that the fuel-gatherer had been gone for a very long time and was not likely now to be coming back again. And yet the wolves (and he could count a full half-dozen of them), abhorred the fire too much to venture into camp itself. Suddenly Lee made as if he were about to rise and go lurching after them, whereon the nearest of the animals yelped out in dismay and darted back into the night.

Lee now rolled over onto his original side and began humming softly from, first, the music of Scriabin, before then lapsing into an old opera tune that required higher notes than he could supply in his current posture. He was cold and old, old and cold, and his throat was sore, too. "Oh good," he said, "I seem to have an illness coming on. And why not? After all, it's *always* possible for things to get worse. They always do, don't they?" Suddenly, he groped deep into his underwear, there where new-world insects had set up an infestation in the second-to-last place where one would wish to find it. The earth might very well have thousands of miles of surface and yet provide no defense at all against the cold when old men take to lying out-of-doors. He tried to focus on the stars, hot ones endued with warmth. These *true* stars, to be sure, were less theatrical than those conceived in dreams; nevertheless, he was able to single out one that seemed to him particularly sweet and, indeed, rollicking with light and chromatic seas. It was here his late beloved wife waited for him still—*these* were his thoughts when he detected someone hissing at him, a white-headed man with a confetti beard whose sleeping paraphernalia appeared not much superior to Lee's. The person lay beneath a winter coat that covered, at best, the seventy percent of his person that most concerned him at any given time.

"Yes?" said Lee, putting on his glasses and glaring back with severity.

"We're old, you and me. That's why we can't sleep."

"'We?'" (The man looked to be a good seventy-five years into his age, perhaps further.) "'Old?'"

"It's hard, when you get to be our age."

"I sleep very well!" said Lee. "Or used to. Yes, and could again, if only it weren't so . . ."

"Cold?"

"That, yes. Along with other things."

"Want to chat?"

Lee had to crawl the whole distance, a concession to the other man's greater age. Thirty yards into the journey he passed two women lying back-to-back beneath quilts and shawls and, on top of those, a comforter that Lee might almost have taken for his own use, had not a third woman been watching him so fixedly. Came next a dried-up little man who had actually lapsed off to sleep with a dagger, or more probably a letter-opener, gripped threateningly in one hand. Lee experienced no temptation to try and make away with *his* quilt which, in any case, bore a much too cute pattern of bees, hive, honey, and a naughty little bear. Finally, dragging his cardboard with him, Lee pulled up next to the man who had called him and, after looking him over, drew back somewhat in order to get into the right glasses.

"Want to chat?"

"Possibly," said Lee. "I shan't be able to sleep anyway, not till the sun, if that's what it is, until it comes back up again."

"We leave at dawn."

"Leave! Where are we going?"

"We don't know. But first, you're going to have to speak *much* more softly than that. After all, we don't want to wake all these people, do we now? Look at them."

Lee looked.

"*Whisper*. Like me." (The man now began to give a demonstration of whispering, a patronizing display, it seemed to Lee, in which he started in at the beginning and then reiterated all the words that had passed between them up until this moment.) "Want to chat?"

"Possibly."

"Because you shan't be able to sleep anyway, not till the sun, if that's what it is, not till . . ."

"Oh Christ. *All my life* I've had to deal with people like you. And now . . ."

"And now your life is over."

"Oh? Oh? And what, pray, do you call *this*?"

"We don't know."

Lee could feel a headache coming on. To return to his previous place—it would require a larger effort than he wanted to invest in it at this time. And then, too, the man was clutching tightly to the edge of his cardboard mattress.

"Say, that's an awfully . . . *sorry* sort of situation you've got there. What is this, cardboard? You ought to be more like me. See? *I* brought a coat."

"Yes. And it shouldn't be too terribly difficult to take it away from you either, I shouldn't think. Not at *your* age."

There followed a long, highly awkward, and somewhat nervous silence.

"Please don't."

They consulted into the late hours, the other man giving Lee to understand that he, too, had been a student of things, a perpetual learner, acquainted with books.

"Always, beginning from age sixty-eight, I have regretted the coming of the post-modern world. Regretted especially that ever it was decided to put down pavement everywhere, covering trails and routes."

"Why, that makes you even more reactionary than me!"

"You simply *must* keep your voice down! We have no authority to wake these people, none!"

Lee hushed.

"Let *me* do the talking. After all, I've been talking, so to speak, or so to whisper, since I was sixty-three."

Lee replied, doing so in a whisper too soft to be heard.

"I look at you, doctor, and I look at me, and I say to myself, I say: 'This is how reactionaries end up—a place like this.'"

But here Lee stopped him. "No! No, no, that's not it. No, I've been studying these people. No, these are *egotists*, plain and evident. And that's why we travel in this herd, you and me."

"Egotists!"

"Quiet! Yes, ego people. See them yonder, each man and woman of them hoarding their blankets so greedily? Where's *our* blankets, hm? I put it to you."

"And yet, if one were to add up all the blankets that *you've* had in your . . . What? Eighty years?"

"It's true I'm reactionary," said Lee. "It started, I think, on that day when I saw for the first time that I had more past than future." And then: "Eighty!"

Lee's voice, harsh at the best of times and mixed, as it were, with "broken glass," had obviously frightened the man. At once he vanished beneath his coat, but only to reappear a few seconds later looking renewed and fresh. "There may be something in what you say."

"Certainly."

"Egotists."

"Precisely. Each and all. You and me." (He reached across, shaking cordially with the fellow who, to Lee's mind, had a certain *simian*, or saurian, or possibly an ursine . . . No, simian quality, as if of one descended from chimpanzees in lieu of the usual great apes. Further, the man exposed a little silver medallion on his lapel that Lee could not instantly interpret, given the glasses he had chosen to wear.) "Alabama branch, don't you know. I'm looking for my wife."

"Really! I'm trying to stay away from mine."

"Red jacket. Quite short, last time I saw her. You couldn't possibly mistake her, not with the sort of person she is, and that nose. She used to . . ."

"Egotist, is she?"

"What's that you say? Be very careful."

"Well! You can't expect to find her here, can you? Unless she's one of us."

Now was it Lee's turn to hide beneath the cardboard, where he lay suffering for a considerable time. Finally, coming out part-way, he posed the question that most troubled him, and awaited the answer he most dreaded:

"Where could she be?"

"Likely she's on some other trajectory altogether, if she was good."

"And is it warm there? Reasonably pleasant? Answer, goddamn it!"

"Steady on, man! I was only a Latin teacher in my day, not a prophet for goodness sakes."

Lee jumped back. "Lat . . . !"

"What's the matter now?"

"I have always respected the Greeks."

"Gre . . . !" He drew off, dragging his coat behind him. A third man had meantime come hurrying up to join them, an almost bald sort of person who, to judge by him, had crawled a very great distance in hopes of witnessing a fight. Having recovered some measure of calm, Lee enunciated his next sentence in a tone that was as grave and as full of certainty as if he had been reciting from a book of laws:

"My Hellenes, the worst among them had more mother wit on their sorriest day than *your* best day among the . . . Your worst Latins . . ." (He saw that he was getting lost.) ". . . bad!"

"Hey! You ain't going to let him git away with *that*, are you?"

"And your divine wife, no doubt she's even now tripping among the goats and dales of hilly Arcadia—is that what you think?"

Lee reached for the cane.

"Dining on olives and all those dates! *My* wife now, she'll be sitting down to roast oxen at just about this hour. *Roman* ox, well-basted."

"Ay, and weighs twenty stone by now, I'll warrant. Little wonder you prefer to keep away from her. *My* wife still fits quite adorably into that same red jacket in which . . ."

"O, blast you. Blast her, too, and blast all Greeklings everywhere!"

Lee paled. He had found his cane and had taken a pretty good grip about the neck, which he could identify in the dark by the five notches cut there with a carving knife.

"You speak of my wife?"

"I do."

"And how many men—no, I want your best guess—how many haven't I already slain for much smaller offenses than I've had from you?"

"And how many—no, I want your best guess—how many of those you slew were dead already, like us?"

So passed the night. For full two hours they lay several yards apart, each boasting the literature, the women, wars, and general achievements of each's own favorite moment in history. Finally, toward four, with the cold colder, the wolves bolder and the bald man sleeping, they relented somewhat and began more truly to "chat," not this time about Homer and his imitators in inferior tongues, no, but rather of philosophy itself, and of the intrinsic nature of the place to which they both had come.

THREE

"THE PLACE TO WHICH WE BOTH HAVE COME, IT HAS," said Lee, "a certain inherent nature."

"Well sure!" the third man said. "It's hell."

"Intrinsic," the Latinist said.

"Hm?"

"*Intrinsic* nature—that's how this conversation started. Forget 'inherent.'"

Lee, however, waved both of them to silence. "What we have here, gentlemen—and I've been thinking about this in some rather considerable detail—is a recapitulation in cold weather of man's progress on earth. This long and awful tundra, it's here that we are to reenact the rise of our species, all those battles with wolves" (he glanced to the wolves), "and" (he looked to the teacher), "chimpanzees."

"No, no, no, wrong, wrong, wrong," said Latin Teacher.

"Hell—that's what it is."

"The glorious promise of all that was destined to come—women and iron-smelting, literature, the invention of cities."

"I told him what it is, but he doesn't listen."

"And our job, gentleman, is to start afresh with it, a new development, better than the last, with nobler music and a more exquisite grade of . . ."

"Twaddle. No, what you see here is precisely what it is and nothing more—a parable of life. Unhappily, *this* parable has a barb in it."

"Oh shit."

"Here, life's general badness has been *cubed*, to match our own great badness."

"Yeah, but what about life's *goodness*?"

"Halved. However, there are those who say we're simply being put through a trial."

"And why not? Everything else has been a trial, and so I don't see any reason why . . ."

"Hell is what it is."

"And so I don't see any reason—no, this is what I was in process of saying before I was prohibited from finishing—no reason why . . ."

"That's the third school."

"What?"

"'No reason why'—that's how they explain it."

Lee could feel a headache coming on. "I see. And so each time we die, our general badness gets multiplied by three."

"*Cubed*, Pefley, cubed. It has nothing whatsoever to do with 'three.' Forget three."

"Now just hold it right there!" the third man said. "Now you've been doing a lot of big talk about 'school,' and 'the third man,' and so forth and so on, and now you want us just to up and forget *all about it*, forget we ever heard about 'three,' and all. I reckon next you'll be wanting us to forget about 'four,' and 'five,' and all them other ones, too."

"No, no, no. *You're* the third man."

"I know that! And I knew it a *long* time before I ever got hooked up with you fellows!"

Lee groaned. It needed his full patience to explain how, according to his theory:

"This is but a staging ground, as it were, a chance to prepare for our next insertion into history."

"Again with that? It doesn't get any better, does it, listening to you? A minute ago we were recapitulating The Old Stone Age, and now . . ."

"Nietzsche knew it. Theopompus understood it particularly well. I don't recall that any *Roman* had much to say."

"No? But then you wouldn't, would you? Very difficult, Pefley, to remember *what you never knew*."

Lee sat up. "What's that you said just now?"

"Said you never knew—that's what he said. Says you don't seem to know much of anything."

For a moment Lee thought seriously of gathering up his cardboard and of relocating to some other spot within the circle of sleepers. One single fire was burning still, and doing it so prettily and with so bright and protean a flame that it tended rather to draw the wolves than to send them away. He had heard many theories this night, the most original of them issuing unpremeditatedly out of his own mouth, and he wanted to think each of them through to its end. For although he remained at all times confident and highly logical to utmost degree, the words that somersaulted animal-like in the cage of his mind as finally he dropped off to sleep (a thin sleep hardly worth the bother), those words were "cubed," "school," "squared," and, as morning came, "all good things halved."

FOUR

DAWN, DEVELOPING WITH UNBELIEVABLE SLOWNESS, made his gorge begin to rise. He stood, threatening back at it with his stick until at last the furniture (furniture of the sky, including sun, rays, clouds, mist, and some of the higher mountain peaks), until these had assumed their right positions and he was able to go back to sleep again.

He could hear groaning on all sides. Finally, needing to pee, he rose again, but only to find that the morning had *not* worked out as he had expected and, as dim as it still remained, that he must use his best glasses and bend down close to ascertain that the Latinist was sleeping still, sleeping well, and had recently been dreaming (if Lee were any judge), of sleep itself.

There were further humiliations to follow. Ordinarily Lee was accustomed to micturating six times each day whereas now, although he might go on jumping up and down and spinning around and listening astutely for distant rivers, rain, or waterfalls, now he could come out with nothing whatsoever. And then, too, he had taken the general sickness and was coughing as much as anyone. Headache, throat, an exhaustion that came from more than just an insufficiency of strength. Hemorrhoids, too, although he didn't care to speak about it; it sent him hopping and skipping throughout the camp, as if in this way he expected to outrun the condition.

"Ah yes," he said, "charming, charming. Goddamn it! Why, this is no better than life!"

And so Lee wandered among the dead, drifting between the two-blanket aristocracy on the hillside and some four or five acres of old people on the plains who presented such a sorry array that he yearned to cane the whole lot of them. He saw where a man and woman had actually come together beneath two thin sheets, but whether it was in order to conjugate or simply keep warm . . . He wasn't so sure. Twice he prodded with his stick, but then finally opted to let them go on snoring.

They were sorrier than he knew, a nation of cold weather geezers who moaned, suffered, wanted someone to take care of them, and refused to harken to the sun. Not that it commanded any huge respect, this "anti-sun," far from it! Just now the thing had twisted sidewise, and glinted like a razor in the sky.

He moved on, scattering cats in all directions as he probed amongst the people and their possessions. It appalled him to come upon the suicidists, adolescents locked in sleep, their faces proving how horrified they were to have arrived in a place so much worse than the one they had left. Egotists, these? No. No, he would have to uncover some other explanation, would Lee, to account for why these two were here. Accordingly, after taking his seat and removing one shoe and adjusting his sock, he bent and whispered into the boy's ear:

"Pride?"

At once the youth opened his eyes, blinked, and then turned and stared at Lee in anguish. "Sir?"

"Lechery then. No, I can understand that, all things considered." (He indicated toward the girl who, however, seemed to be enduring bad dreams while at the same time blowing bubbles in her sleep. Long time since Lee had kissed an eighteen-year-old upon her face; he bent nearer. "I don't blame you, son, really I don't. But everything in moderation, no?" He chuckled, nudging the boy in the ribs and slapping him on the back while grinning continuously in friendly fashion. "No, you'll go far, you with your youth and me with my cane. Want to be partners?"

"Sir?"

The girl, too, now came awake, but then immediately made provision to hide the gunshot wound that had wrought such grievous harm to her erstwhile beauty. Lee now lost all wish to kiss her on the forehead.

"Gad."

"Please, sir, she's not dressed."

"Oh, for pity's sake, I'm not trying to steal a glimpse of those wretched little breasts of hers! Jesus!"

"Now sir, I'm asking you kindly . . ."

"Yes, it's a great consolation, carnal youth. Never freezes. Nor will it matter very much if we find ourselves condemned to go on trudging ten thousand miles or more, or even further. Lust endures."

"Sir?"

"Yes?"

"Now sir, I'm asking you just to go over there, right over there where you used to be, and us, we'll stay right here. And we won't bother you, and you won't bother us. O.K.?"

"'Bother,' you say. I see." He stood. "And yes, that *is* the way of youths—to scorn what they most stand in need of. Wisdom. Now *I*, for instance . . ."

"Sir?"

"Yes?"

"Please."

Lee abandoned them. Already the fuel collectors had arisen and, employing dew, had splashed themselves awake before tiptoeing out with extreme precaution into that same grim plain where but lately the wolves had been coming to within spitting distance of the tents. Very soon new-built fires would be springing to life and with them, he hoped, a better grade of porridge than yesterday's. One woman indeed, an angry-looking quantity, had come out with a burlap bag of turnips and was slowly and emotionlessly shaving off their skins (and skins only) into a copper pot of about the size of a human head. Lee right away went and stood next to her.

"My!" he said. "And how did you manage to come into such a copper little pot, and so conveniently-sized, too!"

"Where'd you git them shoes?"

"I don't know."

"Then shut up."

Lee looked at the shoes. "It's true that these are not the shoes in which I . . . fell off the world. A gift of the gods, one must suppose."

"And you figure I 'fell off the world' wearing this stinking little pot on my head?"

"Ah, madam, it wouldn't matter much what you wore. It's your . . . *Je ne sais quoi*. Sticks out all over you."

She went on shaving. "Well, bring some fuel then. If we don't eat 'em all up, why they're liable to rot."

Lee ran off, grinning. He had perceived beforehand a lode of desiccated manure near to an outcropping of shale that ordinarily would have interrupted the horizon, had not horizon and shale both participated so closely in the same hue of grey. Unhappily a younger man had seen it, too, and was loping forward at a speed that Lee could never hope to equal. He had to content himself, Lee, with leavings, which is to say the leavings of leavings, mere fragments of the sun-dried stuff that, seemingly, had been discarded hundreds of years ago by migrating camels.

The turnips needed another hour, Lee's contempt growing by leaps as the old people bestirred themselves and washed and pissed, all of them moaning betimes and complaining non-stop. He did identify one rather nice-looking woman who somehow had maintained herself in hose and heels and make-up, and whose face and methods reflected such a high social level that Lee at once resolved to stay well away from her. The last thing he wanted at this point in his career was to be noticed by a person of that sort and made responsible for stirring up lusts that he was in no condition to appease.

High above, the sun-wheel now began to grind in clockwise fashion, giving off a hum. Coming nearer, he believed that he could read the first twelve Roman numerals chiseled in its face. Hot weather it promised, although Lee knew by now the degree to which such promises were usually honored. Cheered in spite of it, he tugged at the sleeve of the man next to him, an old time farmer who carried a pail with perhaps half an inch of unclean milk in it.

"Spring, I reckon, will soon be coming in."

The man went on chewing. "No spring."

"No summer neither," said the farmer on the other side.

"And this ain't even winter!"

They mustered in the highway, a tatterdemalion crowd of some half-hundred former souls who, some of them, possessed almost more than they could carry. Others, by contrast—and Lee was chief among these—owned so little that they could have transported all of it in a kerchief fixed to a cane, like Lee's cane, and like his kerchief as well. Quickly he ran to give assistance to the turnip woman who had been so good, even allowing Lee to feed himself out of her best spoon.

"You have so much," he said, "so many pots and things that you're liable to make a great clash and clatter while moving on the trail! Shall I try to find someone to help you?"

She turned to him, a mule-like woman in many ways. Or rather, she was like one of those Andean beasts who, though heavy-laden, look forward complaisantly out of mild eyes with very long lashes. "I reckon not," she said.

"It's that bronze kettle—must weigh thirty pounds! And oh my word, those galoshes of yours. No good." He went around behind her and began to assist with the many straps and cords wherewith she had striven to attach her cooking vessels and other things that continued to collide and chime each time the breeze came up. Of course, he could only guess at what those bundles (bundles wrapped in plain brown paper) contained, (apart, that is to say, from the old-fashioned typewriter whose covering had blown away). To this unfortunate woman Lee now bowed sweepingly, even lifting his hat and following it with some of the most courtly words in his whole inventory before then excusing himself and hurrying up toward the head of the column where the men, but especially those with small cargoes, were contesting for the leadership.

"No, I'll just go on ahead," said one, a gruff-looking sort of person in a black beard. "I'm used to it."

"No," said another, "I think we should have a vote."

"No, let Smathers do it, if he's so cocksure of himself. After all, he's brought us this far."

"Oh, you like this, do you? The place to which he's brought us?"

"Hey! How about the old fellow?" (It surprised Lee, to hear himself talked about in this way.) "He's got nothing to lose, not at his age. And look, he doesn't even have to carry anything!"

"Well I reckon not! Not since he talked that pore old

woman back there into carrying it for him."

Lee snorted. He was about to explain himself when the Latinist stepped forward and began to speak. Of the classicists that Lee had known, most of them had generally been reticent men.

"Friends! Give me your ear!"

Groans. "Oh Christ, it's that monkey again," Lee heard someone say.

"No longer can I stand apart, avoiding responsibility as if I were a reticent person or something of that sort. No, let me offer myself, if you'll permit it, to go marching out ahead. You know me, friends, and how I am. Now *this*, for example"—he motioned around grandly, scanning the narrow terrain with a gesture and world-historical eye—"this might almost be ancient Dacia itself!"

(Lee wanted to puke.)

"Dacia! Well that explains it then," the farmer said.

"Yes. Therefore I'll just . . ." (He tried to step past the gruff man who, however, refused to give way to him.)

"Fools," said Lee.

"What? What did he say? What did you say? No, I really want to know what he said."

"*I* know what he said. And look, he's climbing up on top of that ant hill there to tell us something, I guess."

Lee cleared his throat. Why was not his wife here when he needed her to see him standing up in front of a group of people and humiliating them? "This has the appearance to you of Dacia, does it? Hm? Full of rivers, is it? Where? Where!"

"He's right."

"It's a mystery to me," Lee went on, "how *anybody* who has read his Xenophon . . ."

"You're too old to go marching out ahead."

"He *is* old."

"Really, he ought to be in the rear, along with the luggage."

For a moment Lee thought that he might actually faint. Of the six men hungering for the leadership, he could point out two, and possibly a third, whom he could have thrashed easily, and one he could have settled even without using his cane.

"'Old,' you say. And yet I see here three men older still than me. And that one over there, great God A'mighty look at him!" He pointed directly at a fourth man whose face was the weakest, not to say most evasive, in the whole crowd. They ended up, Lee and this person, glaring hatefully at each other. It shocked Lee, and hurt him, when they settled upon the gruff man after all, an unlettered sort whose sole credential was vested in his eye, his beard, his instinct for dangers, his strength of body and many years experience in forest and hills.

Even so, they set out in good-enough order, each man maintaining a prudent distance between himself and the individual just in front. Far in the rear—and Lee in spite of himself was impressed by their tonal quality—the women had joined together in a medley of popular songs dating back to the 1950s. Last of all came the farmer, a lanky man who from moment to moment spun around and went marching backwards, as if in his extreme pessimism he still expected wolves or even worse to unfurl an attack upon the column in its blindest part. Himself, Lee shortly abandoned the path altogether, preferring to march in parallel with these people than to be *of* them, or even just *in* them, and subordinated to uneducated leaders. Here, together with the wolf or, to be technical about it, the dog that had taken up with him, he could stray sometimes a full hundred yards or more from the line of march, ignoring the calls of those who ordered him back again.

There was much to see—two horizons, fore and aft, strange

prints in the powder and, later, an almost indecipherable trail that came up drunkenly out of nowhere, hesitating, as it seemed, before then plunging across the highway toward what might once have been a grove of highly deciduous trees but now was simply an agglomeration of long-dead stumps broken off at various heights. If ever this district had been endowed with moisture, all of it long since had blown away, leaving man, woman, and lizards in constant peril of dehydration. Lee therefore thought of himself as in some measure obligated to look for sources of water. His cane, of course, was not a dowsing rod; nevertheless, he did at one point allow it to float out in front of him and, with eyes squeezed tight, allowed himself to follow whithersoever it led—which is to say until the women began hooting at him again.

So passed the morning. Behind him were hills, smoke coming off the summits, and in the extreme distance a ship, or giraffe, or mayhap simply another solitary traveler bending against the currents of the horizon. Hastening into his heavier glasses, he found this giraffe, ship, or traveler being chased by a small black dog, a mere dot more minuscule even than the punctuation mark that ought to finish the sentence that told about it

At a little past noon, he went to rejoin the main body of the group. However, after moving in concert with them for a short while, he came back out again and took up a position on the western flank. Truth was, he disliked having to hum his old-world opera tunes in competition with the trash music of his colleagues, a simple-minded people, many of them, whose whole repertoire was so small that it had only four songs in it. Far from the crowd, Lee could swing his stick back and forth, could suck on one or another of his cigarettes—he dare not waste them—could curse and think and spit and talk out loud about the people he was traveling with. He was not unhappy. Nor was he ever unhappy when he thought that he was *going* somewhere. And then, too, he had a rigorous stride, excellent shoes, loose socks, and the West's most practiced cane. Suddenly, believing himself to be drawing nearer and nearer to *her*, he burst out into one of the wildest scenes in all of Moussorgsky—till the women began hooting at him once again.

It was near to mid-afternoon when he heard an uproar, including shrieks of outright jubilation coming from the mob. At first he thought someone might have come upon a watering hole; instead, he saw it was simply a lizard, a green one with glistening scales. It was the humpback woman who, apparently, had pummeled the thing to death with her umbrella and now was holding it aloft to the general applause. Lee could not but grin. For unlike the others, he knew the effects upon the human digestion of this especial species.

They moved on. The chill was growing chillier—it did so each day at this time, exactly when it *should* be getting warmer—and meanwhile the jagged hills continued to retreat into the distance even while the souls trundled forward to meet them. Lee noted then how one of the women had lapsed off far to the rear, out of hailing distance. And observed how the farmer had set down his pail and gone back to fetch her.

"Ah, yes," (said Lee), "very touching, this. They're both liable to be taken, if not by wolves, by red Indians then. And see how the 'leadership,' such as it is, has bogged down almost to a stop, marching 'in place,' one must suppose. Is that wise?"

He moved on, thinking deeply. Some other common thread must surely hold this group together apart from egotism and old age. But if so, he didn't know what it was. Nor was he so confident that his own intellectual processes, as decayed as they were, that they would give him to understand what thread it was precisely that tied that thread together, yes, and tied him, too. *These* were his sluggish thoughts (for he was very tired and was strolling by rote alone), when he caught sight of that same silver and unwrinkled lake that he had first descried two days earlier.

He resolved to move in that direction. In any case the lake was full of leaves and had a scum on it. Lee therefore veered back and forth, sometimes broaching up near to shore and then, sometimes, coming away again before finally making an approach toward what appeared to be a little cove on his left hand side.

The pool and its contents were not as salty as he had supposed, or otherwise those ducks who stood some dozen rods off shore, they would not be gargling with the stuff. Lee smiled, beckoning them (unsuccessfully) nearer. He mistrusted his ability to swim that far wherefore, instead, he began casting about for stones, or coconuts, for lumps of fuel or indeed anything with which to assail the things and get himself a meal.

All such efforts proved absolutely useless—the ducks had only to lift up their skirts and tiptoe a few yards further from shore where they settled in great smugness, wagging their tails at him. Cursing, Lee now reached out irrationally, as if to snare one of them in the hook of his cane, an impossible business that amazed both birds and the man. And that was when it came back to him that fowls such as these were often in the habit of making *eggs*, and sometimes were prone to *hiding* them, and more often than not doing it *poorly*, too.

He now commenced his tour of the lake. His was a dignified figure, or so it would have appeared to himself had he been watching from the opposite shore. And if his socks were loose, and they were, and if they gathered at his ankles and if his pants were short, nevertheless he used his cane with delicacy and reserve. No one had more dignity than Lee, or a smile as crafty as his. Toads and minnows raced to get out from under his shadow. Flailing at them, he succeeded only in splashing himself about his trousers and exposed ankles mentioned above. Nor could he deny that his left shoe was slowly filling with water. He spied one single trout, green but cynical, who right away began backpedaling into the depths where Lee could by no means get at it. He cursed, realizing too late that he had trod direct upon a trove of . . .

Eggs! Brown beauties, testicle-sized, delicately speckled—*this* is what he had demolished with his clumsy ways. He wanted to weep. And yet, three eggs did remain more or less intact. Hurriedly, before anyone could hear of it, he carried them to higher ground and, elevating the most speckled of them to a position above his wide-opened maw, permitted the exquisite matter to ooze quite naturally down his perforated gullet. Immediately his wonted cheerfulness began to return. Now was it *Lee's* turn to vaunt it over the ducks, he who had consumed three of their progeny, repositories of so many fond hopes. He grinned, smacking his lips at them as he discovered each succeeding egg to be tastier than the one before. Most appreciated of all was the *vitelline*, a stuff the color of gold; even after it had long disappeared, still he lay thinking about it. Albumin, too.

Today the clouds looked like certain old-world philosophers, each going through a series of facial expressions. "I see you!" shouted Lee, pointing to his favorite. It pleased him that if anyone was to be memorialized in this way, that it should be these. "But no composers?" He saw one only, and not his favorite either.

Peering further, he began to make out other things, strange and interesting sights such as, for example, a rural scene from what looked to him like the sixteenth century, a rose-tinted image that, however, soon vanished forever behind one of the philosophers. Themselves, the ducks had flown. Lee scanned the whole undifferentiated sky in an attempt to locate them, but found the area mostly vacant. One single wren had been caught in the pull and, rotating helplessly, was being drawn on ever so slowly toward the huge yellow wall of the sun.

He moved on, probing with his stick wherever the land seemed marshy. But had not gone much more than a quarter-distance of the lake's circumference when he began stepping through hills of broken pottery, small sherds, most of them, most of them unvarnished. What wouldn't he have given now for even just one of the archeological manuals in his former cabinet! *Minyan Ware*, this? Hardly. No, it was far too crude for that, as crude as Huron work, if not indeed even more despicable still. He was almost ready to label these the most primitive of peoples, and would have done it, too, had not then he happened upon a broken tower, twice taller than himself, that up to now had stood in perfect camouflage among the kudzu and the pines.

For a long time he stayed just outside the entrance, daring not to set foot within the place. It consterned him that the structure was as tilted as it was, and as old, not to mention so ancient and squat. And how that on a certain bad day in history the upper stories had toppled off into the lake itself where now the barnacle-enshrouded hulk provided tenement to the breams and eels. Lee speculated upon the scene, his mind reaching back quite easily into those remote and remoter than remote times when those who had given rise to the Elamites still were young, whereupon his historical understanding came to a complete stop. Itself, the tower appeared empty.

He entered, brushing to one side the strings of hanging beads that provided only a symbolic sort of barrier against the weather and people like him. No books—he saw right away no books, no shelves, no furniture neither, nor curtains nor paintings in oil nor any of the other accoutrements he liked to find in quarters that he might wish to convert to his own usage. A score of cannon balls, bright red with rust, stood neatly-stacked just next to the embrasure whence, no doubt, the cannon itself had long ago been hauled away by marauding tribes. To that awful day Lee's mind now returned, which is to say until the sights and sounds, women screaming . . . Until he elected to think about other things.

He made a quick tour of the area, measuring for curtains, shelving, and the rest of it, but especially for a roof. The sunbeam in which he had chosen to stand was suffused with dust particles of outrageous size; coming nearer (and putting on more suitable glasses), he tried to track one speck in particular, surrendering finally when he had to admit that the thing was simply too erratic for any eye of his. It was while he was folding those glasses, and then again snatching them out and polishing them as well as he could with what he had—he had not much—*that* was the moment he discerned a little heap in the corner, rubbish, he assumed, that had been folded up in a blanket and . . .

Blanket! he raced for it, congratulating himself both mentally and in actual words before then lifting one corner of the thing in order to shake out its contents, namely a human embryo, quite pink really, somewhat larger than a bread box but . . .

Embryo! He groaned, reeled, ran outside and, congratulating himself now in somewhat more ambiguous tones, came back and began to inspect the object in closer detail. He had read of this—the parlous condition of the human fetus in the moments following birth. Other readings had told of how these things, festering in the dark for certain months, how they recapitulate (it was said), the whole history of life's progress, from tadpoles to frogs and back, the impatient little baby wishing to try out *every sort of possibility*, no matter how base. Coming still closer, he attempted to get a better look into the rascal's face which, however, was veiled with a milk-colored membrane that discouraged any too-hasty judgment as to what quality of child this might prove to be. In any case Lee had already determined that his own need for the blanket easily pre-empted . . . *Its*. But who was it had laid the creature here?

"Gad!" said Lee, "and smiling, too."

He must make time, if he hoped to overtake the geezers before nightfall. Fortunately, he had now a cloak (or blanket rather) which, when deployed rightly, caught up the currents of the wind and augmented his forward progress. Long ago he had learned to use his cane as if it were an oar—seventeen beats per minute. Soon enough he was doing actual damage to the desert floor and leaving behind such unmistakable marks in the powder that no one who had been acquainted with him in other realms could doubt who it was that had come this way.

Lee smiled. The wind in his teeth, the sun that gave no heat—even here there was beauty of a kind. All his life he had been tracking Beauty to its lair, even unto *this* place, where . . . Suddenly he stumbled, catching himself just in the breath of time to go spurting forward at tremendous speed and covering, with the assistance of his oar, his sail and loose socks, a tremendous distance with almost no effort whatsoever. Ahead were hills (fog and smoke enshrouded), the bluest of them growing taller even as he gazed upon them. More than once he had seen boulders breaking off from the canyon walls and then tumbling as slowly as cotton to the desert floor where they rolled for a mile or two before sinking up to their necks in the dust, there to present a problem to all future geologists.

Shrewdly, Lee threaded among and between those giant pebbles, never permitting any of the new-arrivals to catch him by the toe. But it was when he emerged from all this (having actually been flirting with danger), that he detected, and then caught up with, and then passed, the humped woman, tipping his hat.

From this and other indications he knew that he had drawn to within jogging distance of the main body of pilgrims, who continued to hew only too single-mindedly to a trail that might more likely be pointing them on to some new doom, to badness cubed or coldness emphasized, than to anything warm or good.

It was late afternoon when he entered into a series of low-lying hills joined with connective tissue as sharp as paper. The red sun had turned out to be an unenthusiastic eye gazing down upon the hills through veined and puffy lids. Lee bowed sweepingly to the object and then turned and oared northward with the wind in his teeth. Phrases of Grecian literature redounded in his head and then, coming up against calcified walls, bounced back again. Hemorrhoids sped him on his way, putting him in danger of over flying the cold-weather geezers now wending through the valley half a mile below.

A sorry bunch were they—stragglers, children, unshaved men, all of it followed up by a tattered wolf who seemed actually to prefer the society of egotists to that of his own genus. And all this time, forever, the women continued to chant in unison, a ballad from the 1950s that in *their* mouths had come to sound like wretchedness in motion. It was difficult for Lee, who had prided himself on his general hardness, not to snort out loud at these people, a caravan of quarter-educated mediocrities, all of them (save one) devoid of knowledge or Greek or any of the higher learning altogether of any kind. But instead of snorting, Lee now took out a cigarette and began smoking sputteringly while urinating spatteringly, even to the last drop. Certainly he could take very little pleasure from this particular cigarette; it was too short and the blaze too near to his nose.

He lay that night beneath his blanket, grinning in the warmth. He had *his* way and he would have possessed dozens of such things (blankets), more by *far* than any other single geezer. And finally, as he rolled off to sleep, as very quickly he did, he began to dream that his blankets were *hundreds* and that no one else had any, a dream that fell apart all too soon when he awoke five hours before the sun and began calling for his wife.

Why had she not already flown to his side? "Judy!" he yelled, much irked to find that the Latin professor had sidled up closer than Lee fained and was striving to avail himself of one of the cardboard sheets that Lee utilized in lieu of a mattress. A long time they glared at each other, till at last the man weakened somewhat and his eyes began to water and finally he pulled back.

"I saw something," said Lee, "today."

"Oh?" (At once the man came hurrying back, once more taking possession of some of the cardboard.) "What did you see?"

"Something."

"You can tell me."

"Maybe not."

"But of course you can! We're thinking people, aren't we, you and me, both of us? Was it something evil?"

Lee tried to go back to sleep. That was when he realized that the other man, working with subtlety, had gotten possession of the cane and had put himself in a position to use it.

"I want to know about the evil, and by God I *shall* know,

too!"

"Thinks he wants to know about the . . . about what I saw. Great fool." And then, in full voice: "Things are a lot worse"—he pointed to the ambient night and plains—"than you know."

"I know that!"

"Says he knows."

"Will you tell? Or not?"

"Will you give back my cane?"

He had to fight for it. Finally, his walking stick restored, Lee told his story of the "ruined tower athwart a poisoned lake covered over in silver algae."

"Hmmm," said the Latinist, "algae. My mind is trying to remember whether I've seen algae like that in my readings."

"Broken tower—it was there I found my blanket."

"Tower with bedding in it. But my God, man, why didn't you fetch *all* of them, those fine blankets? No, this is outrageous. I mean!"

"One blanket, one only. I found it and now it's mine. Nothing else that I saw in that tower would have been of the least use to either of us."

"You say that."

"And cannon balls turned all red with rust, nothing more."

"You unstacked that artillery, of course, making certain it didn't hide a hatch in the floor. Always a favorite hiding place, or for the military mind anyway."

Lee said nothing.

"Great Caesar! You never touched that pile, did you? No, this is what steams me. And you wonder how Greece and people like you fell under Rome and people like me."

"Now just you hold on for one goddamn moment!"

"Yeah!" said the third man.

"I was distracted, *sore* distracted."

"By the evil?"

Both men came nearer. Lee now could read much more clearly the little silver medal fixed to the lapel of the classicist, that simian fellow, and how it referred back to a certain Latin prize awarded him in his fourteenth year.

"I was distracted," Lee went on, "by what I saw—a blue-gilled baby embryo giggling in that shattered tower."

"Ha! *Now* he admits it!"

"Ha! He admits it *now*," the third man said.

"Encapsulated and laminated, and yet inhaling, too. Floating in his own liqueur. You can imagine my distraction when those vast blue eyes snapped suddenly open and . . ."

"Don't stop."

". . . the monster smiled."

"Ah! Yes, hmmm, interesting, interesting. 'Blue,' you say. It follows. And the sac, you claim, it was all of a piece with no conspicuous seams, as it were, and no leakage worth talking of—you're willing to adhere to that?"

"It were as smooth, that thing, as glabrous and impeccable as glass."

"Yes, I doubt it not, no. No, I seem to see it too, even as you rave. But why do you insist on characterizing it as evil?"

"*I*?"

"And how are you so certain this was a *human* worm, and not a heifer's or a shoat's?"

"*Human*, goddamn it! I know it because of . . ."

"That smile. Alright, I'll take that. Now let's move on to the covering it was wrapped within—what do you have to say about that?"

"Blanket," said Lee. "*This* blanket. I found it and it's mine."

"And all endued with blood, I wot, before you troubled to clean it off. Placenta and the like. Gore and stuff."

"It were as fresh and as clean, that thing, as a jelly bean."

"Hmmm. But you've told us nothing of its general *size*. No, that's important—girth, heft, and width."

"Not so long as my cane," said Lee, drawing it out and measuring with it. "But on the other hand, much, much fatter."

"Well I reckon!" the third man said. "*Everybody's* fatter than that old stick."

"But I'm surprised at you, Doctor, that you haven't divined the meaning of all this. Me, I divined it ten minutes ago."

Lee, struggling to divine it also, retreated deeper into his blanket where he could permit his facial expression to reflect the puzzlement he was actually experiencing at this time. "Ah, ha!" he said at last.

"Yes?"

"No. No, that couldn't be it."

"Think, man!"

Lee now concentrated in full. "This child," he said (although he was actually thinking about his wife, his mind having veered off into that direction), "this baby child is but one more newly-arrived egotist just now coming over from the old world. Right?"

"Oh, great Jupiter and Jove, you've got it all backwards again! What you saw . . . You're going to suffocate for sure, Pefley, if you don't come to the surface once in a while. What you saw, as I was saying, was one of *us*."

"Not one of *me*," said Lee. "Not what *I* saw."

"Starting anew. Going home. Born again. To gladden some poor wife."

Lee squinted at him, allowing the words and the huge meaning that lay behind them to be gathered up slowly, but also permanently, by his old man's mind. "'Starting anew.'"

"Just so."

"Gladden . . ."

"Some poor wife."

"Wish *I* could start over," the third man said.

"Yes, we're all growing younger here, even you Pefley, minute by minute. Why, I predict you'll make an adorable little boy, Doctor, what with those foot-thick glasses and absurd little hat."

Listening to him, Lee began rifling furiously through his own theories. It was not in his habit to give credence to people, and absolutely not his habit to be growing younger day by day. "This is pure speculation on your part," he said, "mere theory, and a very dubious one, too."

"What's *your* theory?"

"Shit, he don't even got one! Look at him."

Lee had nothing to say. He knew what he knew, and knew among many other things that the weather had turned unfavorable, wind rising, wolves near, moon transparently thin. In former times he had carried on some of his best thinking "beneath the quilt," so to speak, and especially in cold weather when he had had as much to think about as in those days he had. "And so," he said, "I think I'll say goodnight," and did.

F I V E

HE WOKE TWICE DURING THAT NIGHT, BRIEF INTERLUDES during which he thought, first, that he was young again, and then secondly, after throwing back the covers, saw that he was not. Dawn, when it came . . . Never had he been able to describe such dawns in real exactitude. This one came while he was dreaming.

They set forth in good order, the women shouldering their luggage with but small complaint in weather as zesty as this. Soon they were singing in parts, the bottom voices taking the harmony. These were, to be sure, mournful verses, and seemed to relate to the hard fate that had always lain in wait for women and girls. Not that there were any number of young girls in that crowd—on the contrary! No, these were mostly mature females, worn-out wives and the like, hefty people with incommodious hips—Lee resisted the temptation to go about kicking them—badly designed for long-distance trekking. And yet, he had far more lief go traveling with these, far more so than with the postmodern girls back on earth, copulators, and careerists wearing aggrieved little faces of perfect discontent. Thinking of them, he suddenly broke out of rank and slashed five times wildly with his cane, a whip-like gesture that made the air wince.

By noon the file of women began to fray at various points along the route. Smathers, the man who had arrogated the leadership to himself, was by now so far out in front that Lee was beginning to entertain hopes of never having to look upon him again. That was when the quondam whore came racing up after, apparently, a bad night with no sleep along the trail. Lee slowed, consenting to walk side by side with her for a certain distance.

"Possibly you've not given much notice to these shale-like outcroppings that seem to run parallel with us everywhere we go." He stopped then, laughing at what was probably her interpretation of those rocks. "You're thinking it's the trail that runs parallel to the shale, aren't you? You're right of course. But still . . ."

"I'm dying."

"Hm?"

"How can you stand it? How!"

"Ah. But then this isn't so awfully unlike the life I was living already, eh what?"

"I can't *stand* it. Can't!"

"Steady on, old girl! Someone might be listening. 'That old whore,' is *that* what you want to hear? 'Old whore with that big tangle of preposterous hair? Uses charcoal in lieu of eyebrow pencil?' You don't want to listen to that."

She quieted. Though much the worse for wear, and although she had added to her luggage by collecting every stick of fuel and each cow pat that lay along the route, even so he believed she had a few hundred miles left in her still, enough to take them . . . Where? To that city, that town or village or altar-in-the-dell toward which throughout history all roads have tended?

"You've done a spate of walking in your time," said Lee. "But remember this, that there is no road nor boulevard nor avenue but that it must eventually empty out upon some town or fair or altar-in-the-dell. We know this to be true from what we have read about such places. And such trails."

She brightened, though only slightly. "Fair?"

"And why not? And why should there not also be gambling there, and drinking places, and numbers of men with unsatisfactory wives? No, no, I wouldn't advise you to give up *all* hope, not yet."

"And maybe they'll have libraries and such, and books and . . ."

But here, chuckling, Lee held up his hand to stop her. "And concert halls? Nay, nay, don't strain yourself." And then: "What sort of books?"

They went on. Up front meantime the gruff man was continually halting every half-minute to point out the way and, as often as not, to deliver informational commentaries—(Lee yearned to cane the very daylights out of him)—concerning the weather, the cacti and shales.

The day darkened, bringing atrabilious clouds that looked like little children with their tongues sticking out. Lee darkened too—he had left off singing an hour ago and had again gone back to his wonted line of march, mid-distance between the geezers and the outcropping. In this way he could sometimes actually move out in advance of the gruff man who looked at him with displeasure, waving him back. But Lee had seen what the others had not, namely that they had come into a region of very different lizards, silvery creatures of a plumpness that explained itself only in reference to the large number of depopulated ant mounds extending in all directions. As slow as he was, and old, Lee yet had no difficulty in chasing down one such lizard, slaying it with his cane and then, after throwing on his reading glasses, scaling the thing with his wee pen knife. It was when he got into the entrails and, jumping back, saw how truly awful the whole business was, and how that the reptile's emerald eyes continued to watch with intelligence and curiosity, *that* was when he hung the trophy from his cane and allowed its tongue to trail behind him in the dust.

Lee's mood now darkened further. In front, the column had begun pressing into a gorge that was so constricted (and so perfect a place for being ambushed) that some of the more heavy-laden women had perforce to turn edgewise in order to squeeze through the narrow places. One such person, the heaviest in the whole group, would obviously be accompanying them no farther; here she sat, her back to the wall, dropping bitter tears. But all this was as nothing when compared to what Lee saw at the top of the defile—some half-dozen lines of prose in foot-high cuneiform, a more immaculate inscription than any he had seen in books. Too agitated to speak, he ran to the Latinist and began pounding on him.

"Calm you!" the man said. "Yes, yes, I see it." And then: "Oh!" And then finally: "The workmanship!" adding: "And what a poor speller, too!"

Lee agreed. As to the spelling, he knew no more about that than about a number of things connected to the period before the Greeks. "What does it say?"

"Say?' The man turned slowly, smiling sweetly. "'Say?' Surprised at you, Pefley. Why, you have only to open your eyes and to read!"

Lee opened, making both eyes three times larger than they were and then switching over quickly into his thinner glasses which, however, were smeared with something or another. This much he did understand, that the engraver had been endowed not just with a jeweler's eye alone. He had also been endowed with wings.

The Latinist went on smiling. He had taken out his chap-book and bit of chalk and was transcribing the stuff in a hand that was too small by far for any glasses of Lee's.

"But what does it *say*," Lee asked again, lifting the cane. "What!"

The man went on smiling. He had written it down in full and had stored it away with great smugness in the pantry of his mind. Lee wanted to throttle him.

"Someday you may come into a *Greek* inscription," said Lee, "ha!, and *then* what will you do?"

"I read Greek very well, Dr. Pefley—if you *are* a Doctor. But are you?"

"Oh, I see. Things have dwindled down that far, have they? That you could put a question like that to a person like this."

"Call yourself 'retired.' Tell me, Pefley, what are you retired *from*? Oh yes, you talk so airily. And yet we still haven't been told where you took your degree."

"Horace—you actually read that stuff?"

"Hey! You ain't going to let him git away with that, are you?"

"The degree, Pefley, *where did you take your degree*?"

"I'll say this much, that I lost all respect for Dante when he took Virgil to be his man. Me, I took Poe."

"The degree, Pefley. *Where*?"

Lee lifted the cane to smite him. Unfortunately, the lizard was too heavy and made unwieldy what once had been a highly effective lever, good for killing professors.

His mood, which had been darkening all day, began now to show other symptoms as they proceeded between canyon walls embellished with the portraits of devils engaged in pornographic acts. Very few of the travelers could bear to look upon it.

"Gad!" said Lee. "Why, this puts even invertebrates to shame. See there?" (He tapped twice with his cane, there where something especially unspeakable seemed to be going on between several of the creatures.) "Now what would you call that, what they're doing there?"

"Shut up, Pefley."

"And there, that business with those tentacles?"

"I guess you didn't hear what Beasley was saying. Shut up, is what he said."

Puzzled by it, Lee climbed out of his glasses and, coming to within a nose of the wall itself, discovered what appeared to be a number of modern American names drawn with ballpoint or, in one notable instance, the author's own blood, as Lee surmised. Right away he began scanning for Judy's name, reminding himself that she could not have reached above a certain height.

Ought he to leave his own name, using lizard's blood? No. No, he had no posterity chasing after him, no followers, no readership neither, nor brush nor quill to dip or fill with lizard's blood.

He continued to darken throughout that afternoon. Far away in the west he thought that he could see mobs of crows, maliciousness made manifest, thousands joined together to form a cloud. It was true that he had finally managed to foist the lizard off onto the humped woman, who seemed oblivious to the weight. He could now travel so much more easily that his mind began to darken at a slower rate than at any time since that morning. Accordingly, he resumed singing again from his favorite opera, a cautionary story in which an elderly man had played the noblest part of all. It was a dry noise Lee produced, and resembled the sound of a desultory southern breeze pushing through crisp and shriveled leaves of long-ago corn. He had only just arrived at one of the best arias in the whole work when, suddenly, he collided into a large man, a vendor of some kind standing by the roadbed in a clown's apparel. Lee jumped back, cursed, raised his cane, and then came charging forward.

"Blackguard!"

"Want to buy a balloon?"

Indeed the man had dozens of them, helium-filled affairs in all the colors.

"No, no, I have no use for balloons, never—think about it, man!—not at *my* age. What do you want for that yellow one? And look, this one has a picture of President Truman on it!"

Others now came running up, including especially the deformed woman, the lizard slapping at her shanks. Already the vendor had unfolded and had set up his display table and was arranging and rearranging to best effect the assortment of watches and earrings and silver busts (stolen objects, Lee averred to himself) of a certain famous basketball player.

"And I have postcards, too," he said, "with pictures on them."

"Of course you do! Pure filth, I'll warrant."

"Pictures of . . ."

"Yes?"

"… other places."

"'Other places?'"

"Other people, too."

"You mean to say . . ."

"Other people on other pathways. Don't tell me you never wondered about *them*."

Lee was staggered. The geezers, too—they stood glancing

around at each other in amazement, horror, and poorly-feigned indifference. Already the engineer, a silent man usually, had taken out his wallet and was thumbing through his considerable money.

"I'll have those pictures," he said. "I will."

"My father," said the Latinist, "you wouldn't have a recent shot of *him*?"

And then, turning to Lee: "You're familiar, of course, with his edition of Plautus. Ah? No, on second thought, probably you're not."

But now the crowd was pressing all too violently upon the clown. Again he tried to sell off some of his balloons, even knocking down the price to a ridiculous fee until, finally, with the crush growing insupportable, he released them altogether, whereupon they surrendered straightway to the pull of the faraway sun.

No one was more frantic than the whore, she who (he learned later) had lost a daughter and hoped to find her among the photographs. Lee, too, he could have mentioned any number of people he would have wanted to locate, some of them dating back to the Late Bronze Age, and one soul in particular, a contemporary of his. Accordingly, on this one occasion only, he was willing to coöperate with the Latinist; together they lifted the vendor, who had fallen to the ground, and restored him to his feet. The geezers pressed forward:

"The pictures! Mine, mine!"

"Kill him!"

"No, let the whore have them!"

"Hey! You ain't going to let him . . ."

"No, *me*!"

"No!"

It was quite hopeless. Lee found that he, too, was on his back, his one hand reaching ever so desperately toward the vendor's satchel, his other stretching just as uselessly toward where the engineer had dropped his wallet. A general mêlée now ensued. Among it all, Lee caught glimpses of the gruff man striving mightily to pull the people apart.

And succeeding. Lee had time only to give the classicist a single stroke with the butt of the stick and then, leaping up, go chasing after the woman with the photographs, who fled direct to the humpback and the whore. Together they held everyone at bay, which is to say until they had gone through each and every one of those pictures and then had dashed the whole stack of them to the floor.

"Why, there ain't nothing here but niggers and chinks!"

"Not so," said Lee, rescuing the things. "Here's a landscape scene." Quickly he went into his other glasses and then, after holding the scene up to his eye, walked off some distance in order to study it in more detail.

To study it in more detail, Lee needed light, time, and quiet; accordingly, he now trundled off toward the shales and found a "chair" for himself among the stromatolites that flourished there in such numbers as to supply bleachers enough to seat the whole population of an ordinary town. Soon enough, however, he relocated to another of them, a much better-padded and more comfortable piece of furniture by far. He still possessed two cigarettes, of which only one remained in respectable condition. Choosing the one that was bent, he lit it in a sudden gesture of high resolve as he took up the photograph, which also was highly resolved, and began to go over it in minute detail.

In fact, the scene was empty. Yes certainly, it did show mountains in the distance (smoke coming off the summits), and some few pines in the foreground with, yes, a burnt house that had collapsed into ashes about the surviving chimney. Nothing else was to be found within the four borders of that print; indeed, he could not think why anyone would have squandered the film. Intrigued nevertheless, Lee looked again and then, while striving to transpose himself, as it were, *into* the scene, lifted his glasses and brought the picture up to within a centimeter of the more reliable of his two eyes.

He very nearly fell off his stromatolite. There seemed after all and in spite of everything to be a small and apparently very shy person peeping from behind the ruined chimney, an unsteady pile that, according to Lee's best guess, had been teetering there since circa 1864 or 5. He groaned. What would he not have given just now for a magnifying glass, or even just better sight, or that she might be twenty times nearer than she was! Or let her but step out into open view and then let Lee, let him miniaturize himself by force of Will and, letting a great deal, let him set foot in that abandoned field. Or let *her*. Or, or, or.

He groaned, very loudly. The picture was a recent one, judging from its general freshness, the above-mentioned resolve, the milk-white paper that bore a lavish watermark and this morning's date inscribed on the verso. Groaning still, Lee slumped deeper into his chair, near to crying. To his surprise he had altogether wasted his cigarette, leaving him with nothing to do but toss it away. It was not a good moment—his wife was small and in hiding, his cigarette wasted, and this country was no good either, a mere field with endless cold breezes, he hated it. Thus blubbered Lee, each fruit-sized tear breaking into a thousand pieces as it hit the floor.

As old as he was, he soon ran dry however and began scratching at his hemorrhoids, using for that purpose the end of his stick where the bark was roughest. It was while he was engrossed in this rather ungraceful proceeding that he became aware of a small child, the tiniest in the whole camp, who had taken up on one of the stools and was watching him with curiosity. Lee turned upon her, lifting his cane and putting on a grotesque expression. It frightened her not at all, she who had perhaps seen too much already.

"Dr. Peffy?"

Lee growled.

"How'd you catch that ole lizard?"

"Liz? Why, here am I, a ruined old man weeping his heart out, yes and scratching, too. You talk of lizards?"

"Can I have him?"

Lee stood and glared at her, but then did finally sink back down again. "Its flesh," said he, "will be bitter, and the hide as heavy and cumbersome as a crocodile's, owing to all those scales. Besides, he might still bite."

"Dr. Peffy?"

"Now what?"

"How come you . . ."

"Because I'm an old man, *that's* why!" And then, somewhat more tolerantly: "What, child?"

"How come you . . . ?"

"Talk funny?"

No, that wasn't it. Lee waited for the underlying question which, however, she appeared to have forgotten. She was adept at rotating at high speed on her stone chair, enjoying it. Lee refused to look, lest he lose his own equilibrium.

"Nay, child; gives me a headache."

"What's *that*?" she asked. (For he had been sketching in the powder with his cane.)

"That? Judy, of course."

"Oh. But why . . . ?"

"Because I don't draw so terribly well, that's why! And neither would you, if you had my… ailments." (He scratched.) "But it *is* Judy all the same. See that nose?"

She came forward, reading it with care.

"Nose?"

"Curse you, child. And a lovely nose it was, when I was young and knew how to draw."

Better was Judy's hair; he had construed it out of the most delicate of strokes, allowing it to spread, Achaean fashion, far out over the sands.

"Judy, loyal wife, the last of her kind; she consorts now with Andromache and Penelope, and one or two others whose names long ago were forgot." (But not even they could stand next to Judy in terms of the delicacy of her light brown hair.) "And look here, see how she moves? Ah child, she was like unto an anemone in mild currents, deep currents reported by divers who used to glean for treasure in The Vermillion Sea!"

The child was thrilled.

"And two brown eyes. But I never complained, not when she came to me that morning and explained how she, too, must grow old someday in obedience to precedent and life's behests. Would she had grown as old as me!"

"But where . . . ?"

He inserted them now, teeth and lips and the rest, mere lines and dots in the medium of the sand. The girl clapped hands and twirled around. It was not too awful a child; he predicted for her a future as a goose or hen, to reckon by the shape of her head and the mien that had been inflicted on it.

"A swan was Judy," said Lee, "envied by geeses and hens." And then, suddenly, the anger rising in him without warning: "Go! Leave me! Or otherwise I'll . . . !" He lurched toward the girl, his cane lifted on high and his loathing unfeigned. "Never come near me!"

She fled screaming, racing back at breakneck speed to her appalling mother, an alcoholic who stood listing stupidly in pools of warmthless light.

* * *

When came dusk, it rendered the day not very much darker than it was before; marching forward against it, he took out his last cigarette, kissed it and put it back. He was not unhappy, not with night moving in. Instead, he began whistling a wry tune that left a faint smile in the hollows where once he had boasted a set of ordinary cheeks. *This* was his predominant expression as they drew within ken of, and then passed through, a ghost city of false fronts with a papier-mâché cowboy standing on one of the roofs with drawn gun. It led to a grove of breadfruit trees that had grown up in the roadbed itself, a hindrance to traffic. Right away the crowd surged forward, moaning at the wonderful objects that weighed in the branches—food enough for all!

Not so Lee who, in his superior reading, knew all about such things; instead, he betook himself off the trail in order to watch the women with their pots and pans and lizard (it gave Lee a rueful look), as they jogged past in the ungainly fashion of their own special kind. Breadfruit and horse apples! he could barely wait to see the effects of *this* upon these sixty- and seventy-year-old digestive systems. Suddenly he, too, began to run forward in a panic, lest he arrive too late for the show.

This cold and unpleasant land, it did have its compensations; almost the first thing he saw was the Latinist daubing tenderly with his kerchief even as he continued retching on the sand and his own two shoes. Lee gave an even higher grade to this than to the four old men who had managed to climb a certain distance into four separate trees, thence very hastily to climb down again, leaving the greater part of the fruit in peace. Surrounded by all this, Lee went into his dance, crying:

"Ye fools! Chasing after bad things *here*, even as ye did on earth!" (It delighted him beyond measure, how that the stupidest of them *went on gathering up the stuff anyway*.) "Yes!" he called. "More, take more! May I help? Pile them high, do!" And then, sidling up to the classicist:

"It surprises me, a man of *your* training. Perhaps if you had read more *deeply* instead of just *widely*. Or had been more like me."

The man mumbled, possibly in Latin. Changing into his double-pane glasses, Lee could verify the number of breadfruit seeds lodged in the man's beard. This, too, was gratifying—that whereas his own beard still had some tincture to it, the Latinist's was

"Absolutely white!" said Lee, plucking out one of the seeds.

"You're an annoyance, Pefley. A pedant, too."

"Oh? You ever seen *me* puking on the trail?"

The man hissed at him. Lee, however, in new high spirits (night had fallen), poked him twice in friendly fashion and then, probing with the longest, thinnest, and most agile of his fingers, removed another seed.

The next hour went quickly, Lee having learned by now to make very long strides and then to rest up between. He had also fallen into the unrecommended habit of counting each step he took, a tedious job that required more arithmetic than was natural to him at his age. And then, too, he was leery of setting down his leading foot just anywhere for fear that the desert's underlying "joists" and "struts" might prove unavailing, or lest time's "fabric" should break apart and lest Lee find himself in a place still worse than this—*these* were his thoughts when, toward evening, he chanced to look up and see a small but portly hermit sitting athwart a high place just next to a shack made from advertising signs. As calm as he seemed, and bald, he comprised in his own physical person the top of the knoll that, seemingly, had been sawed off for just that purpose. So at peace was he with the world and himself that he seemed unaware an entire army of egotists just then was passing beneath his hill. Instead, his gaze, full of understanding, flew to the fartherest limit of the valley, ceasing only when it ran up against a basalt rill and bounced right back. Lee signaled to him in cordial fashion, even going so far as to hold up his book and glasses to show that he, too, was a thinking person and not without some understanding of his own. All in vain; the man yawned and stretched and, rolling over onto his belly, crawled into his tiny shack. And although Lee might continue to scan the peaks, cone-shaped features that turned into hermits at 2,000 feet, yet he could not be certain they were anything but further hills with smoke coming off the summits.

It fell full dark at just before seven, the sun dipping below the horizon in order to break into a display of little silver stars. Lee didn't complain—the thing had gone all day without giving any warmth worth mentioning. And anyway he had always preferred the moon, a cipher so dear to his family that it could be found in all four corners of the armorial that had come down to him through his fathers. Because of that Lee now laid aside his glasses and offered up his smiling face for the moon's sole use and delectation. Continuing, he smiled in turn to the lesser stars as well, before then picking up his stick and swatting violently at each of them in turn, missing by somewhat.

He was cognizant that a complex of buildings was coming up quickly on the right hand side, a series of warehouses, as they looked to him, with yellow lamplight glowing faintly in several of the windows. Cheering broke out among the crowd, some of the geezers trying to push to the front in expectation of . . . What? Of an authentic meal? Of a night between clean sheets and a riotous fire giving off piney smells? Lee doubted it. Of a hind roasting on the spit? Of black German beer? Lee laughed out loud at the very thought of it. Of a suite for each of them, together with butlers and cooks with positive attitudes? Hardly. Lee was exasperated by all such naïveté as that. Of a fine dark library, well-chosen, that ran from floor to ceiling in pigskin bindings? Gold dust on the fore edges?

He was wheezing dangerously, his system under real strain as he rounded the bend at his best speed and then aimed for the nearest of the buildings, a low-lying structure, ten times longer than wide, that might almost have been designed for poultry. One could do worse (said Lee to himself), than come to a place rich in eggs and peopled by the very numerous number of hens needed for producing the same. Suddenly, the gruff man called the crowd to a halt and, turning to face them, began cautioning against one thing and another. It was, without a doubt, the most patronizing exercise that Lee had so far seen anywhere in this domain. And that was when the humped woman broke through by main force and began pounding on the door, pounding loudly and stopping only when

A man opened, a hard-looking type in work trousers and undershirt. To Lee he looked like a professional poker player, or truck driver perhaps, or something of that general kind.

"Good evening, my good man," the Latinist said, lifting his cap. "We've just come in off the highway and . . ."

"You ain't 'come in.' Not yet."

"Shore would like to though," said the humped woman.

"We can pay."

Slowly, begrudgingly, the man stood aside for them, permitting them to file past one by one as he evaluated their faces. Himself, Lee put on a cheery expression that sorted rather well, he believed, with the sort of person he might almost have been, had things been different. He couldn't sustain it. A second person, as Lee now realized, was seated at the back of the room, a harder, as it seemed, and even more cynical personality than the man at the door. Fleshy to disagreeable extent, he bore two dreadful tattoos on his naked chest. Lee nodded again in collegial fashion and went on smiling back and forth at the two men.

"Now just what in the hell are *you* grinning at? Asshole."

"Ha! 'Ass.' No, no, I was simply . . ."

"Oh shit, and what is *that*? Jesus!"

"She was born that way."

"No fucking lizards neither—leave the fucking thing outside. Don't you know what these things do to your diarrhea?"

Lee agreed.

"And I want to see some of that money you was talking about, O.K.?"

They dug for it, the engineer coming out with good decent paper bills, the others producing only coinage for the most part, together with a little silver broach of some sort with the picture of a flower on it.

"Look at that. I ought to throw the whole bunch of you back out into the road, for Christ sakes. And I better not find any *Canadian* money in all this shit!"

"What are we paying for?" asked one of the women, a former therapist and facilitator who even here remained the best-dressed person in the group. Knowing that she was still comparatively young and sexual, Lee had at all times tried to avoid drawing her attention to his own person.

"What are you paying for? What are you paying for? Well let me ask you this, 'lady,' have I ever put my goddamn gun"—he drew it now, a small black pistol mounted with a calibrator—"put it up your fucking little pussy and pulled the trigger, hm?"

"N . . . no."

"Then that's what you're paying for, O.K.?"

They were given something to feed upon—a genre of mush ladled into unclean "bowls" that originally had served quite other purposes. Lee, refusing to vomit, forced it down by aid of the "beer" or, mayhap, "wine" it was. Or possibly both wine *and* beer, to judge by how the two fluids refused to mix.

Thus, too intimidated to speak, the old people sat at table studying their platters. The harder man, ignoring them, continued to devote himself to making a tiny repair on what looked to Lee like a girdle or brassiere, or some similar piece of wear. Pornography covered the walls, no great surprise to Lee, considering the quality of the people they were dealing with. Finally, having forced down all the cabbage he could endure, he rose, stretched, and then sauntered back in lazy assurance to the hard man seated at the back of the narrow room. Here the stove had a good fire in it, with tongues of green and yellow flame; he almost wanted to step inside it and bed down for a hundred years among the warmth.

"Ah yes," (said Lee), "a goodly blaze, this. Couldn't help but notice how you carry a whip, all coiled up and attached to your belt."

The man said nothing.

"And this establishment, no doubt you're carrying on some sort of manufacturing activity out here in the desert. Good."

The man said nothing.

"Or poultry."

Now finally the man did glance up—he was chewing on something—and made a motion with his pliers, asking:

"What's the story over there, the monkey with the beard?"

"The Latinist?"

"Yeah. Looks to me like he might of been in the *publishing* business. Was he?"

"No, no, I wouldn't think so, no. No, I . . ."

The man went back to laboring on the undergarment

which, as Lee now realized, was interlaced with a network of bare copper wire. "How about you? *You* could of been in publishing, the way you talk."

"Ha! No, no, not really, no. Sorry."

"Television?"

"Please! No, actually I was retired. Still am! In fact, I . . ."

Suddenly, that instant, he was interrupted by the sound of an inconceivable screaming, a yell of hoarse agony that, after a short while, was joined by two others. Hearing it, the geezers bent still further over the table, staring in silence at the food.

"Great Zeus!" said Lee. "What in the name of . . . !"

The man glanced up again, grinning slightly. His breasts, more like a woman's than a man's, bore each a dark blue tattoo that Lee strove to ignore. Came now a whole succession of shrieks that could not have been anything else but the noise of men in unendurable distress.

"But, my God, those are the sounds of *unendurable* distress!"

"Wouldn't be surprised."

"But, but . . . But . . ."

"You *sure* that monkey wadn't in the book business? Or consultant, looks like a consultant to me."

"No, no, no, no, he was an instructor in Latin, simple and plain." (The screaming had stopped.)

"Latin. We don't get much call for that. Hey, you want to go next door, you and me? See what's going on?"

"I?"

Lee followed, stepping with hesitation into the wind and then tiptoeing hurriedly over to the adjacent warehouse construed, like all the others, of plywood painted a hue of something about halfway between blue and green. He had been wrong, however, to have believed that he could see lights glowing in the windows when in fact these had simply been painted to look that way. The man yanked open the door and nudged him inside.

He wished that he had never come. Even so, it still needed another ten seconds for his eyes to adjust to the dimness of the place. It was an odd sight he saw, most strange really; he did not know what to say. And what *could* one say about a long narrow warehouse in which so many undressed naked men were crawling about on all fours?

"Odd," he said. "No, I don't understand this at all. This is not, and I repeat *not*, pleasant to look upon. Oh!" (For it had taken him this long to perceive that each and every one of those "men" had in fact been "disgarnished," so to speak, and that in at least one instance the operation, apparently, had been carried out very recently, to judge by the several rivulets of blood still trickling down the wretch's shanks.)

"Oh!" said Lee. "No, this is outrageous! No! But why? *Why*!"

"Look, *padre*, I *asked* if you wanted to see this. Right?"

"But why are these people being treated so? And why are they wearing all those things and brassieres!"

"Them 'things' got 'lectricity in 'em, doc, lots. See? All you got to do is . . ." (He strode to the console, a complicated-looking apparatus with an antenna that reached nearly to the ceiling.) ". . . pull on this lever here."

He did pull it, a remorseless action that instantly caused two of the "men," one of them as old as Lee, to rise to their feet and begin shrieking in hideous fashion, both spraying themselves with sputum and snot. Lee thought at first their eyeballs might actually explode, so much did the current seem to concentrate in that location.

"Gad," said Lee. "The eyes!"

"Yup. That's how it's supposed to be."

"But, my God, the hideousness of it! How long do you leave the current flowing?"

"How long? There ain't no *rules* here, man, about stuff like that."

"Outrageous! Especially the mature one. But why? *Why*!"

"Feminists."

"Say what?"

"Feminists. *Male* feminists—that's what they were."

Lee was dumbfounded. And yet, the more he thought about it . . . It *did* explain much, the girdles and castrations and certain other indications explanatory of the sort of people these had been. "*Male* feminists?"

"Yeah, right."

"But what of *female* feminists?"

"Naw, they make their own hell. Look, don't be asking a bunch of questions, O.K.? I just work here you understand."

Lee stroked his chin. His natural politeness and indifference to non-aesthetic things, all that now began to ebb away.

"*Male* feminists."

"Right, yeah. You don't hear so good, is that what it is?"

"And *your* job . . ."

"Take care of 'em. Right."

Lee could not but smile. Without being fully conscious of the sacrifice, he took out his final cigarette and offered it to the man. "*Male* feminists. Hee hi ho. La dee da. No, no, I don't see why we can't leave that lever *right where it is*." (He began humming.) "But tell me this, where do you keep your *rich* people?"

"Block nineteen. Wanna see?"

But in fact Lee felt himself strangely reluctant to leave.

Of rich people, they had all been brought together in what was by far the most sumptuous of the warehouses, a five-story affair with a fifty-car attached garage and in-ground swimming pool (frozen just now) in the shape of a pancreas. Now, hauling open by main force the massive door and setting foot in what was unquestionably the deepest and most tender carpet in his experience, Lee began to make out some dozen persons seated at various places in a dimly-lit parlor. Going forward with hand extended, he shook with the head usher, an obsequious little man so adept at back-bending that his upper and lower segments appeared to have been coupled together with a hinge.

"Your reputation, doctor, has preceded you. So pleased."

Lee, who was beginning to like this person and his ways, tried to wave away all such flattery.

"And for my part, I'm somewhat pleased as well. Never have I loved the rich. And yet it *is* good, you will agree, that some are rich. It tends to concentrate the money in the already-corrupt, keeping it away from the many."

"I dare say. Yes, these people are fond of excuses like that. 'Supply and demand, rising tides,' oh, we've heard it all a thousand times. Meantime we try to keep them happy with their usual things—gems and cars and precious coffees brought from afar."

"I can smell the coffee," said Lee, looking at the man meaningfully. "Myself, I haven't been offered a decent cup in so long that it embarrasses me to bring it up."

"*Our* beans come from Indonesia. Now here"—he nodded toward the dozen sumptuaries, a sleepy-looking group, all of them heavy-lidded and all afflicted with the most appalling blisters and boils about the mouth and lips—"here we have a pretty fair sampling of those who managed to become rich without indulging over-much in any sort of toil. Bond holders, mostly."

"Thought so."

"Whereas yonder, past that door, we have some who succeeded beyond all imagination, becoming very, *very* rich while creating nothing whatsoever!"

"Bravo!" called Lee. "We don't have to ask which country *they* come from. But what of those who grew to be very, very, *very* rich while spreading actual harm?"

"Oh, them. They're with the publishing and television people." He glanced at his watch. "And now, doctor, would you care to witness the nine o'clock feeding?"

"No," said Lee, " I think not, no. Well! Well perhaps. Yes! Why yes, I really think I should."

But first they had to stand aside, the usher, the hard man, and Lee, all of them waiting in deference while the high-caste people, said to have been so good at capital formation, while they tarried over the coffee and croissants. Thus some minutes went by until at last, all patience exhausted, (and Lee saw that he was to be offered no coffee, nothing), the host brought out a little silver whistle and tooted on it twice. Instantly three workers came in, muscular men dressed in leathers and motorcycle hats and tattoos that were, some of them, quite sentimental, and others quite past describing. Between them they carried a pumpkin-sized kettle suspended by chains, seemingly very heavy. Themselves, the rich people refused to look at it, preferring to glance up at the rafters, or hum, or, in one noteworthy case, to draw out a small hand-held calculator and begin hurriedly running a sequence of compound interest rates. One youth of perhaps twenty had gone off into the corner and, sitting by himself, was bawling as bitterly as a child. Edging nearer to the pot, Lee spied down through steam and flux into the smelted contents, lovely gold, a stuff with bubbles in it, although less frolicsome than wine.

"Why, I do believe you are about to pour this molten batter down the gullets of these sumptuaries! Am I right?"

"Been here before, have you?"

"No, no. I have, however, dreamt about it."

"These are the procedures, Dr. Pefley, that were used in Crassus' time. But not even he was as rich as . . ." (He pointed to the men and women.)

Truly, it was a sloppy business, that which Lee was forced now to see. Primarily it consisted of the three workers who lifted and then pinned to the floor the nearest of the sumptuaries, an already-bloated man who did try at the last moment to put up something of a resistance, all quite in vain.

"Now here's the part I like. See? He would give anything if only he could keep his jaws locked tight. But the tongs, they're just simply too strong for him. Leverage, you understand."

"Too strong for anyone. But look, the fellow has no teeth!"

"No? Well of course those all melted away long ago. Watch it!"

Lee jumped back, avoiding the little gleed of gold that, sputtering noisily, came to rest, not on the toe of his good black shoe, but in the carpet rather, doing damage to it. The stream, meantime, was still not terribly thick, not with the gold being poured as slowly and as thriftily as it was.

"It has to be this way, doctor, a tedious job if we're to fill the awful complexity of the adult human gut with all its comings and goings and secret places."

"Yes. And it's those hooks, I suppose, that make it impossible for him to scream. Brings to mind a certain dentist that I . . ."

"Formerly we used funnels. But you can imagine our perplexity when the tin was eaten away by the hot golden stream!"

"Too hot."

"And so, we came to zinc."

"And zinc, you found, suffices." However, the process was so slow and the kettle so laden, and the room so full of wealthy people that Lee began to experience a wish to move forward to the publishers. Instead, these words came to his ear:

"Care to be next, doctor?"

Lee jumped back, dizzied by terror, which is to say until he saw they were merely teasing with him. The rich man meantime was growing plumper by the moment; in spite of himself Lee was impressed with the fellow's carrying capacity, a full four or five gallons, he would have guessed, all of it seeping ever so slowly by peristaltic movement into even the most remote, most constricted and most obscure of the person's internal whorls and tubes.

"Nothing like it, Pefley, for hunting out all those hidden places!"

Unable to disagree, Lee tapped twice with his cane upon the man's extended belly, an action that gave off a mellow sound. "Chimes sweetly, no?"

They laughed, all save him with the hooks in his mouth. Next to be fed was a terrified-looking youth, his lips already so blistered and puffed-up that it would be a problem for even the narrowest of funnels. At first Lee thought the usher might actually give up on the boy, denying him his meed of gold. His *ear*, however, that was open and, as it were, calling out for notice.

"No, we don't usually do that, doctor. They tend to faint dead away."

Lee could feel his gorge rising. "They won't 'faint,' as you call it, if you go slowly enough, giving the poor devil an occasional intermission, as it were."

The hard man was willing, he who had all the time in the world and patience without end and who, Lee divined, drew his wages by the hour.

"He craved all the wealth there was. Therefore let his hearing also be turned to gold!"

"Fair enough! But may I see the publishers now?"

"Oh now, I don't think you really want that."

"Even *I* don't go there," the hard man said.

Lee kicked at the rug, making no effort to hide his disappointment.

"But I can show you the next-best thing."

"Ah?"

He was led down and around, up and behind, and thence out into the moonlight itself where, once he had changed into other glasses, he thought that he could see some ten or even twenty acres of individual human beings lying on their backs and stapled to the field. "Gad," said he, "stapled to the field, and in weather like this. And yet, I had far more lief be here than drinking fluid gold."

"Ah doctor, it would take all night to list these peoples' sins. Main chance opportunists—that's them over there, there where the ground is a little bit smoother. And here, here we have a pair of southern liberals—look at 'em—who thought themselves too advanced for their own good land."

(Hearing it, Lee could feel his gorge begin to rise.)

"Counterculture people over there."

"Yes! Why, there must be two full acres of those!"

"Now here, doctor, here we have a bunch of women who loved their children more than their men. And there, there to your left, people who hadn't read a single book in the whole six weeks before arriving here."

"Six!" Tugging at the sleeve of the harder man, Lee whispered into his ear: "I don't know. This punishment just doesn't seem to me as severe as it ought to be."

"I heard that, doctor," said the Director, "what you said just now. In fact, their treatment has not yet begun."

"No?"

"No. It begins, doctor, when I . . ." (Again he drew out that same little silver whistle that in this country seemed always to announce the beginning of things.) ". . . do this."

He did it now, a shrill piping sound that wafted easily to the far corners of the pasture. Lee saw then a door come open in the side of the barn, and from it issue a grand mob of hogs who came boiling toward them with grunts of joy. They sorted strangely, those noises, Lee's own exclamation, and the people who had begun to scream and plead and strive with all their force, but uselessly, to pry loose the rather hefty staples that held them down. "These pigs have been sent to soil the people," said Lee to himself, still thinking that even this might not be punishment enough for the crimes that he had heard.

And that was when something happened that made him faint, or nearly, and caused him to reach out for support to the harder man, who jumped back out of his way. Those hogs, these pigs, they had not come to soil the people, no, but rather to break open their bellies and devour all the contents.

He might go on for another thousand years and never want to hear the sort of screaming that he heard just now, nor see such expressions upon living faces, nor be made to look upon organs torn out "by the roots," as it were, veins stretched to the breaking point, the sound of snapping ribs, children calling, requests for mercy. Coming nearer, Lee attested the long tapering snouts of these animals, buttered now with lymph, semi-processed excrement, and bright brilliant gore. Nearer still, he avouched that these creatures must have evolved in partnership (so to speak) with the criminals, an ingenious adaptation eventuating in twelve-inch snouts that curved to just the right extent to do just right their work. Pleased always with examples of good furrowing, Lee pointed to where one animal had probed so deeply into the miscreant's bowels that it seemed likely to burst out through the very rectum itself! "Every moment," said Lee (speaking to himself), "and every half-second is paradise as long as I am not with these."

"When does the punishment end?" he asked.

"End? I don't understand."

"Ends when you want it to end," the harder man said. "Or not."

"Well! We have to provide *some* sort of intermission," the Director explained. "Otherwise the hogs get demoralized. And then, too, we have to allow the viscera to grow back."

"How long does that take?"

"It takes what it takes." He glanced at his watch. "Anyhow, my shift is over, I'm going back. You coming?"

He felt, Lee, that he had been given a good survey of the place, leaving him with a mental map that, however, had not yet included one certain little shack that sat off by itself surrounded with high fencing. And because he kept glancing toward it and more than once lifted his cane as if to point in that direction, the Director volunteered at last:

"Yes, doctor, that's where we keep someone. You've heard of him."

"Someone famous?"

"You might say that." (He inhaled proudly.)

"Foreign dictator?"

"Why foreign? Why not one of ours?"

"Someone tall and bearded?"

"You *are* shrewd! But that's enough about him; you'll come to know him very well, if you elect to stay on here."

"'Here!' And 'stay,' you said?"

"And now let me recommend that you return to your own place, doctor—you have your blanket, we have ours—and try to get a good night's rest!"

SIX

HE WOKE IN GOOD SPIRITS TO THE AMBIENT SOUND OF calls and screams. Only a faint remembrance did he still retain of that brief disturbance during the night when certain men in motorcycle hats had come and taken away the most unlikely of all the geezers, a countryman, very shy, who departed sadly while still carrying the pail that had accompanied him in his other life. Himself, Lee kept his eye mostly upon the Latinist lest the man be summoned at the last moment and made to swallow gold, or sent to the publishers, or, or, or.

The morning meal! warmed-over cabbage served in hub caps. Lee dawdled over the stuff, almost tempted at one point to taste of it and of this morning's "juice" that smelled of toluene. It was while he was thinking of this and playing with his spoon, that the hard man came and nodded him to the filthy little office in the back. Believing that he might now be offered a cup of coffee at last, Lee willingly took up a position in the room's least uninviting chair.

"Got a job for you, Pefley, if you want it. Do you? Counterculture people. Want it?"

"Job?"

"Right, yeah. Two meals a day. Women—do anything you want to 'em. Want it?"

"Well . . ."

"You ever *gutted* anybody, padre?"

Lee thought. He was tempted to tell about his cane and what he had achieved with it. "Well, I . . ."

"Yeah, we know about the stick. Knives is different. With knives you're liable to get all kinds of shit all over you—if you ain't too *particular* about stuff like that I mean."

"No, no." (He was thinking rapidly. Two meals a day, perchance an office of one's own, countercultural people to work upon—it *was* a temptation. "*Two* meals?"

"Yeah, right. Want it?"

"And coffee? No, really, I am flattered though."

"You're fixing to turn me down, ain't you? Jesus H. Christ. So you'd rather be with that shit out there"—he nodded to the geezers—"than sign on with us—is that what it is?"

Lee blushed.

"Jesus H. Christ! What, you got something going with that whore, or something?"

"Ha! No, it's just that . . ."

"Yeah? I want to hear this."

"I'm looking for somebody."

"Looking. How d'you know he ain't here with us?"

Lee watched as he snuffed out his cigarette on the heel on his boot and then, next, took down a drawer crammed with index cards that were not always—and Lee could feel his gorge begin to rise—not always of the exact same size.

"What's his name?"

"Judy."

The man stopped, stared back at him for a time, and then pushed the drawer to one side.

"A short type," Lee went on, "and wife of mine."

"Yep. Big red ribbon in her hair."

Lee, stunned, scrambled to his feet and reached out to

grab hold on anything he could. He must *not* allow himself to faint just now, not when he had information sitting across from him in even so repugnant a form as this. He did manage to clear his throat and put on an amicable face, asking:

"When?"

"Long time, padre. Forget it. Shit, she ran by here so fast, that ribbon of hers . . ."

"Flying in the wind! That's her alright. God, God, God!"

"Hey! don't be saying that all the time."

Again Lee offered to shake, again he found his hand hanging at loose ends in mid-air. "And so I'll say goodbye."

"Yeah? When you going to say it?"

"Now."

"Well say it then! And take that other shit"—he pointed—"with you. Sooner the better!"

Lee hurried; the others had already gathered their things (one of the men going to great lengths to steal a hub cap), and had begun to stumble out into the painfully bright day. Lee sought for, and found, and then gave back to the humped woman, his iridescent lizard, now much the angrier for having been parked all night outside the door. He could hardly wait, Lee, to describe how he, Lee, had preserved the Latinist from unlimited agonies, an act of kindness that ought to redound to his credit among the geezers.

"Reckon I saved *your* skin," he said, once they were out of hearing of the camp. "Saved it from something much worse than freezing."

"Prate on. The only thing you do for me, Dr. Pefley, or *Mr.*, I should have said, is make this trip even more unpleasant than it is already."

Lee growled and stepped forward with uplifted cane. He had no wish, however, to draw the attention of the two firing squads that just now were executing each other in the open field. It chilled him to the soul, seeing how they took turns at it, the men of one party helping to steady the muzzles aimed at their own heads from two inches away by the party dressed in blue. But even more distasteful than this was the little farm boy who traveled with them for a few hundred yards carrying two buckets splashing over with disembodied eyes.

By noon they began to perceive the faint silhouette of distant spires and steeples with various pennants furling in the breeze. There, gulls floated overhead and smoke trails wended heavenward, a languid process that contributed new matter to the existing clouds. Meantime a tremendous excitement had broken out among the geezers, inspiring the worst of them to go striding forward rather *too* briskly, as if after so many miles upon the trail they had gone back to that spastic mode of locomotion so much in vogue during early movie-making days. That was when the gruff man called for a recess, addressing them thus:

"There does appear to be," he said, "a city up ahead."

"Fairly obvious, isn't it? Jeez!"

"What sort of city, you ask. Well! We just don't know, do we?"

They all now looked at one another, their faces wolfish, each man and woman of them mesmerized by thoughts of food. Came then a small voice from the margin of the crowd:

"Well what kind of city do you think it is?" And: "And is it safe?"

"It *might* be safe, or might not. We could send a scout."

"Now there's a concept!"

"Someone nondescript."

"We got plenty of them."

"Someone to 'test the water,' as it were. Sniff out 'the lay of the land.'"

"Someone good at metaphor?"

"Send Lee," Lee heard someone say, a small voice, rather nasal, that came from the back of the crowd.

"No, send the monkey. He's the smartest."

Lee could feel his gorge begin to rise. "We should enter together," he said loudly, his voice taking on an objective and fair-minded coloration, "entering in one undifferentiated lump!"

"Why?"

"Why? Tell me, do you imagine for one moment that Cyrus allowed *his* men to come in one by one, do you, on the day that Babylon fell?"

"He's right." (It was a small voice, still nasal, that came from the periphery of the crowd.)

"It *does* sorta look like Babylon, what with all them spires and such."

But at that Smathers held up both hands, large ones, an "old testament" gesture that had the effect of quieting them. "We enter," he said, "together. In one nondescripted lump!"

Arriving at the place at a little past four, they found the gate ajar, no archers on call, no toll-takers, nothing. Not extremely anxious to be the first inside, Lee took up a position in the wake of the women, there where in case of need his temerity would have the time it needed to make the best available decision. In this way he constituted a one-man rearguard, so to speak, even if equipped only with a stick. So wary was he (entering backwards), that he failed to appreciate the great thickness of the wall, nor could he immediately identify the nature of the stuff—"meringue," he called it—out of which the matter was composed. Silence now fell over the travelers, especially when they began to realize that large numbers of people actually *inhabited the wall itself*—it was that thick—in an unplanned sort of arrangement of windows and shutters and flower boxes with here a pair of trousers and there a blouse hung out to dry. Shielding his eyes, Lee found what looked to him like a child's pale face watching dolefully from one of the upper balconies. Strange was the silence and strange the four o'clock sun scintillating upon that paper-white wall. It infected the crowd with foreboding and awe, all save the humped woman who stepped forward to bawl out loud and clear:

"We know you're in there!" And adding then: "Somewhere."

"And we know the gate has been closed, too," said the widow, "because we can see it!"

Lee looked to the gate, looked to the child (who had drawn back somewhat while still leaving one paw resting on the rail), and then looked behind him to the city mews with their acute red tile roofs and tenuous chimneys plugged, most of them, with stork nests. He began to feel quite dazed. Or rather, to feel what the original Europeans must have felt upon seeing the fourteenth century developing around them from year to year and one thing to the next.

"Fourteenth," he whispered, nudging the man next to him, a former lawyer with a briefcase that contained . . . No one knew what it contained.

"Or fifteenth possibly, to judge by what . . ."

"Shut up, Pefley. Something bad is fixing to happen."

"I know."

(The gruff man had actually gone up to the wall itself and was rapping peremptorily at the casement of one of the apartments. Above, the child had come back, bringing his brother with him, both of them now looking down emotionlessly upon the geezers.) "There's a child," Lee mentioned, "nay, *two* childs, both of them now looking down emotionlessly upon us geezers."

"Quiet, Pefley! We know all about that."

Lee hummed. Something bad, it *was* time for it; they had not experienced any real badness for several hours. Meantime a curious idea had come into Lee's head, namely that his own late beloved wife might very possibly be imprisoned in one or another of the six high towers of the town, noble structures with, each, a gaily-colored pennant spiraling in the wind. Lee, changing into other glasses (and then changing back), tried to ascertain whether any of those banners bore her own personal device of a small white swan with eyes cast modestly down. He did see other sorts of birds, including most notably a ferocious-looking boar drooling drools of spit. Lee moved three steps nearer and was in process of freshening his glasses when, suddenly, that moment, the "bad thing" happened.

Later on, looking back upon it, he was to remember how the man from Alabama had thrown up both hands and then, teetering and trying to recover, had ended up on the cobblestones with shreds of cabbage besmirching his coat, vest, shirt, and pearl-gray tie. Lee at once took up his place behind the woman, uncertain as to whether it was cabbage only or whether the townspeople hadn't still heavier ammunition in store for them. Altogether he believed nearly a hundred people had come crowding out onto their balconies in order to unload upon them and to scream:

"Go back! Scum!"

"Intellectuals!"

Lee did try to respond, even going so far as to take out his book, open it to the title page and then, holding it aloft, show that it was something that almost anyone could read. But ended up using the thing for a shield. It said something, he thought, about the nature of children that the two boys had chosen the humpback for their special target.

"Blackguards!" he yelled back at them. "And *you*, mothers and fathers, for coming out with such brood!" (He then waited a few moments, giving time for the words to fully register on them.) "Why you people don't even measure up to the already rather low standard set by . . ." A cabbage hit him.

Later on, still looking back upon it, he remembered that the cabbage had been too far decayed to do real harm. The gruff man meantime—and Lee did admire him for this—had chosen to remain where he was and allow the people—and never had Lee witnessed a more perfect example of pure stupidity—to pelt him from top to bottom. Already he had endured a dozen great stains together with one burst lip. Finally, finally at last, after several useless efforts to reason with them, the gruff man turned and conducted the group into the awaiting slum.

Later on, again looking upon it, Lee was to remember the days that followed as differing in no important way from any similar number of days that had followed each other in days on earth. Certainly the people here were no better; almost at once he detected a red-faced fat woman standing in a doorway, her natural indignation turning to outright fear when Lee stopped, parked his cane, and bowed sweepingly to her. All the village dogs meantime were barking in unison at his ankles and loose socks. Twice he slapped with his cane at the most asthmatic of them, a sorry-looking runt sizzling over with anger and whose innumerable nipples were dragging in the dust. Thus far he (Lee) had seen nothing to distinguish this from any other fourteenth-century city the world over, not until he began to discern odd fragments of Greek, Roman and, in one notable example, Ottomite masonry mixed in randomly with the pabulum out of which the town was by and large composed. Nothing ever surprised Lee anymore, not even when he alternated over into his stand-by glasses and, looking up, found two bricklayers in leathern aprons working frantically with trowels and paste to make the ramparts higher. Nor was Lee surprised by the number of children, nasty-looking people who grinned and called and offered all manner of obscene gestures, some of them dating back to Greek, Roman, and Ottomite times. Nor yet was he surprised to come onto a blacksmith's stall which, however, surprised him greatly when he perceived a pair of wise-looking mules looking out at him as if in recognition from the darkness of their room. Feeling that he was home again, Lee went to greet them, the more gentle of his two hands already extended forward to stroke the more velvety of the two noses. The Latinist stopped him.

"Pefley! What are you about? Don't you irritate these people now, you hear?"

Lee had to struggle to disentangle his arm from the Latinist's grasp. Himself, the smith, a nervous quantity, went on watching worriedly, at last putting aside his hammer and coming to shut the door.

"Ah, me," said Lee to the Latin teacher. "Do you know how long it's been since ever I last smelt the wet smell of a wet mule in wet rain?"

"Madness. Very well, Pefley, we'll haul you back here first time it rains. *Wet* rain, I meant to say."

The following block was no better. A killed cat lay in the gutter, its belly exploded, while the avenue itself was filled nearly to overflowing with various animal wastes. "This," said Lee (speaking to himself and, if he cared to listen, to the Latinist, too), "this is 1530, or thereabouts. And see, there's a book-making factory!"

But he was moving too quickly to make a sharp-enough turn, and must therefore continue on for another several paces before slowing to a stop and coming back and throwing himself inside.

It was, just as he had said, a book-making factory. In a place like this he had every right, he thought, to be welcomed with warmth, the printers opening wide their ink-stained arms to receive him. And in fact they did, one after another, toss him a smile and a nod that proved they recognized him for what he was. Lee, however, waved them off modestly, encouraging them to continue with their work.

It was the best thing he had seen in his whole post-mortem career—a shop full of busy people given over to books and the allied arts. His eye came to rest with special favor upon an elfin man, older yet than himself, who had gone off into the corner with his needle and thread and was in studious process of stitching up a hefty volume in pigskin with gold dust on the fore edges. No mules here; Lee did nevertheless identify six inked cats sunning in the window sill. As to the man who was the master here and manipulated the cumbersome press, he had developed a set of muscles every bit as noble as the aforementioned smith's.

"Egad," said Lee, "but that is a *most* awkward-looking contraption you have there."

The man, nodding sadly, was resting all his considerable weight just now on the handspike that transmitted thought to paper. Lee waited for him, using the interval to take a more critical look at the rather coarse-grained paper stock which seemed still to have kernels of undissolved flax in it.

"Granulose, this! How, you use this for printing old histories?"

"Just so," said the master, revealing in the enunciation of those two words, or indeed in either of them taken singly, that Lee had here an *educated* man with which to cope. "But for literature proper, we use a more refined stuff."

"I ween. And those that are history and literature simultaneously at the same time—how *then*? And especially them with maps in them?"

"*Colored* maps?"

"Certainly."

"*Hand*-colored?"

"Just so; that makes my case even stronger."

The master blushed. It flattered Lee that he had hastened to towel himself off and get back into his shirt, a show of respect for someone who was older and better-read than himself.

"In an eventuality like that, Dr. Pefley, we would want to use our premier stock, no question about it. Pure rag and silk."

Lee was pleased. "Rag and purest silk," he said, humming. "But let me ask you *this*."

"Please."

"When comes time to rubricate and gild with gold, and time to imbrue with eucalyptus the skins themselves—how *then*, hm?"

The man no longer took efforts to conceal his pride. Lee could see in his face that none of these, neither gold nor oil nor anything else offered any hindrance to *him*. "It's right," he said, "that you should ask, coming, as you do, from the epoch from which you do. See that doorway yonder?"

Lee changed glasses. "I do."

"Know then that it is there where our gilders gild, our binders bind, and inlayers lay."

Lee looked toward it longingly. "Yes. Yes, and even now they're busily at it, I'll wager. Slaving away! May I?" He lurched forward, his longer arm outstretched to push open the door. Unfortunately in his haste he tipped over one of the machines, an archaic-looking apparatus with blades and wheel and a cat snoozing in the works.

"Don't you worry, sir," said the Latinist, grabbing Lee by the arm. "I'm not going to let him go barging in there, bothering people. Good gracious no."

There followed a space during which the three men strove to regain their balance. To atone for things, Lee now turned his attention to the three girls, merry types laboring diligently at some sort of grinding mill that had to be turned by hand. Well pleased with them, their attire and their general deference toward men, he patted each in turn, dawdling over the one whose blouse was most open and fullest. He had seen from the beginning that these were late twentieth-century novels they were shredding in order to make packing material.

"I would think," said he, "that one could also use this stuff for fertilizing crops."

"We did!" said the loveliest of the girls, "but nothing," continued the plump one, "would grow in it!" finished the third.

"It follows. And now," said Lee, "I must leave you" (for he was standing inch-deep in a pool of dye and the girls were laughing), "not wishing to impede what you were doing."

Thus Lee; nine bloody footprints he left behind while wading back in seeming unconcern to the master of the place. He found it difficult, however, to come face-to-face with the man, owing to the number of new-printed pages strung out to dry on wires that ran across the room at the level of a person's chin.

"Fine girls," said Lee, "especially the one with . . ."

"I've been watching you, doctor, and I've come to the conclusion that you definitely have a calling for this sort of work. I ask myself: Would he be willing to take a job here with us?" (Suddenly he blushed deeply.) "Or rather a *position*, I should have said."

Lee jumped back. This was a serious proposition and seriously did he consider it. "I've had positions," he said finally and with sadness. "But I found they always required such a God-awful deal of *time*."

The man blushed. "It's the same with us. I don't know why it has to be that way."

"But I am flattered. Truly."

They shook, each man exploring the other's face for the presumptive underlying integrity.

"He doesn't ask if *I* want a position," the Latinist said.

They must hasten now if they hoped to rejoin the main crowd. It worried Lee that this main crowd, which had little enough to hold it together in even the most favorable times, that it might finally dissolve in the temptations of the city. Already the whore had broken away, had gotten into some cosmetics and a skirt, and already was marching up and down on the other side of the road. Suddenly a bakery came up on the right, the mind-benumbing smell causing both Lee and the classicist to groan out loud.

"Ah, me," said the other man.

"Oh!"

"Bakery! Puts me in mind of when . . ."

"Me, too; it puts me there every bit as much as you."

"Mid-century towns! Bakeries."

Lee admitted it.

"Soda fountains. Why, we used to . . ."

"We used to, too. And ten-cent stores."

"Oh!"

But they had snapped free of the bakery and its smells. Up front Lee saw and recognized a computer outlet, to judge by the oaken sign hanging out over the door with the picture of an abacus on it. It made a somewhat anomalous appearance, squeezed in, as it was, between a rose merchant on one side and a cobbler's den the other. Lee tried to move past quickly but failed to avoid the four exceedingly well-dressed salesmen, mere boys really, who ranged up and down the sidewalk in order to shill for the things.

"Sir?"

"No, no."

"But sir! This is tenth-generation stuff! Light years ahead of the Japs!"

Came now two others, the best-dressed people Lee had recently seen. But mostly he was entranced by their faces, tanned, pleasant, and rubberized products straight off the shelf. Lee now began to feel the feeling he had felt before, namely that with this tenth generation of machines and boys, history had at last come up against a blank wall. Came now a seventh and even an eighth person, all of them dangling this season's latest instruments (tiny things!) in front of the morning glasses that Lee happened still to be wearing at this time. The Latinist himself had managed somehow to wedge past all this and stood now twenty yards further on, grinning back at Lee.

"This teeny probe," the fourth boy was saying, "we simply insert it into the frontal lobe. No, really, it doesn't hurt at all! And sir, we guarantee it, we can squirt five times more information at you than any other company in the world!"

"Five! But can that be true?"

"Sir! I swear it! Four hundred infotoids a bit-second. High resolution, too. You like Renaissance art? Football? You can do your own punting! Girls?" (He held up a capsule-shaped item of about the size of a tooth.) "They're all in here, blondes everything."

"Whew! However, I . . ."

"Sir!"

Lee ran.

Moments later, they had passed through town entirely and come again to the encompassing wall. Lee went forward to it, testing whether it really was composed of what he had thought, and whether or not the people had been able to excavate their cozy dwellings with shovels and spoons, or had needed more robust sorts of tools. Cozy, too, were the tiny square windows paned with membrane, some of them glowing yellowly in a twilight that, owing to the wall itself, consigned some of the citizenry to sun and some to shade. One cabbage only now exploded at the classicist's feet, a mere happenstance falling out of the sky with no malevolence whatsoever behind it or (they preferred to believe) those that followed hard upon.

"Brutium." said the monkey. "No, it's eerie, really, the resemblance between that place and this."

Lee, however, snorted. "Troy VI, I vote for Troy VI. The *wall*, man, consider the wall! And how the populace withdraws at twilight into those compartments of theirs, twenty, thirty, even fifteen feet above the ground!"

So they fell to arguing over it, the Latinist sneering, Lee lifting and lowering his cane, up and down. Nothing could bring them to an agreement, save only the smell of . . .

"Food! Great Jupiter, I hadn't realized just how hungry I truly am!"

"Yes? Well that's the way with you, isn't it? Me, I've known for some time just how hungry you must be."

Called by odors, they turned then and began to drift back into the maze. Onions and potatoes, Lee knew them well and remembered even better the characteristic smells that had so often before given away their locations back on earth. Meat, however, was what he craved. Craving it, his mind turned naturally to the sign of the boar who continued to threaten with ferocious mien any who at this late hour might still be tempted to try the gate. Lee, more intimidating than intimidated, gazed upon the creature's flanks and hams whereupon he, too, began drooling drools of spit.

"Roast hog—I'd give my whole library for just one such meal as pictured on that pennant."

"His whole library. That's one book, according to my count."

"Mushrooms at the side. And think of this—that the cook, an ingenious man, that he will have placed in that swine's maw a well-plucked duckling, roasted too."

"Like *that* duckling?" (He had borrowed Lee's stick to point to the remaining banner which, however, had become so entwined about the pole that the night warden was having trouble bringing it down.) "Very well, Pefley, you have the duckling and I the boar."

"That will be why you're leading us *toward* the pig, and *away* from the bird."

"Shrewd, you're shrewd. Really, Pef, you should have taken your degree. In any case, the halyards have been untethered now and the duck has flown."

And so, jesting and starving, limping and shivering, they came at last to the proper building and stood with noses pressed against the glass. Inside, the custodian, a big man with a straw toupee had fallen asleep in his chair with a comb in his lap. It appeared to be warm inside, judging by the woman in the painting behind the bar. Savory smells came through the glass. Lee focused on the watchman, using his Will to bring the man (but not too abruptly) out of his sleep.

It was a tiring exercise; even so, Lee continued to train upon the person until at length he rose and stretched and then went to the window in order to read what was etched on the award pinned to the monkey's lapel. Suddenly, he noticed Lee. "Oh shit," he said, jumping back, "I was just dreaming about somebody like you."

Lee grinned. Even now he had not completely finished using his Will. "Roast hog," he called. "Mushrooms at the side and thick dark gravy!"

"Gravy? You got money? No, no, not him, *you*. I know *he* dudn't have anything—I can tell by looking at him. And why is he wearing that little . . . ?" (He nodded at the award.) "Oh, boy."

Displeased by the man's tone, Lee plunged for his money but came out by bad hap with his Canadian penny, a pie-sized coin that carried a portrait of the Queen in what had always seemed to Lee a rather frozen smile. Seeing it, the proctor tried to close the door in their faces but proved unable to dislodge the cane.

It was in truth a warmth-filled vestibule that led into an even warmer atrium, the best in weeks. Right away Lee threw himself into one of the cushioned chairs and remained there stubbornly. Resigned to them, the host wrote down their orders and after going behind the bar and dithering there more or less incompetently for a few moments, came out with two mixed drinks, both of them floating with cherries and other debris. In no way did it surprise Lee in the least when the whore came in with a client and, ignoring them, strode past to the elevator. The Latinist meantime continued on in his flat voice about mushrooms, gravy, pigs, and the rest of it—till the bartender called a stop to it.

"Cabbage is what we've got, cabbage soup. Want it?"

"But the flag, man! It distinctly shows that . . ."

"It's a flag and that's all it is, just a flag with a goddamn picture on it. What, you want to eat the flag? And I suppose you think we've got swans running around over here, right? And all because of that flag over at the featherbed factory."

Lee sat up. "That flag has a swan on it?"

They had to bargain for their meal, bribing the man with flattery and small change until finally he let them into the foyer, a tight space with hardly width enough for the long narrow table that ran down the middle of it. One guest, one only, had arrived there before them, a Chinese in a business suit who, (the doorman explained), had been "unfolded" in time and sent off onto a mistaken trajectory. They all looked sympathetically upon the man who, embarrassed by it, slipped further down table and hid his face.

Ranging themselves with dignity, the two classicists now sat facing each other across the table, both of them still speaking in terms of food.

"I've concluded to opt for veal in lieu of hog."

"With mushrooms at the side?"

"And why not? Yes, and a fine white wine."

"This wine, it . . ."

"*Grape* wine, yes. White."

"Ah. But with wine you're liable to find little nibblets of cork floating in the wine."

"That doesn't disturb me in the least."

"No, I dare say. No, it never deterred me neither. *White*, you say."

"And I shall want a salad of course."

"I'd almost forgotten about salads," said Lee while gazing up dreamily at the chandelier. "It needs a dressing, as I recall."

"It does. *Cheese* dressing. Say it."

Lee repeated the word, doing it to the man's satisfaction. Sadly, it awoke in him memories of the cheeses he had known on earth and their variegated smells that not even he with all his magically evocative descriptive powers could describe. "Veal and cheese, pale wine and . . ."

"Cheese."

They looked at each other. Would the waitress never come? Or had they been lured to this place to spend eternity with a lonesome Chinese? Both men stirred nervously, especially the younger of the two who, however, had the more serious hemorrhoids. (The other had unstable teeth and was forever testing one or another of them between his thumb and finger.)

"I shouldn't want *that*," said Lee, "removable teeth. Not on the eve of a meal such as this promises to be."

"Oh? Actually I'm surprised you can see this far. Or have you 'alternated' over into your 'better' glasses?"

Lee said nothing.

"And tell me, Pefley, how is it this bench makes you squirm so much? Some little defect you haven't told us about? Say what?" He smiled rottenly, well pleased with himself. Soon he was chuckling as well. Lee could very definitely feel his own left hand taking a tighter grip on the handle of his walking stick.

"That's right," said Lee. "Make jest, do, if it gives you pleasure" And then, bending close: "And you, sir, are nothing in this world but a *superannuated orangutan*, and never mind what it says on the credential in your lapel. And someday you . . ."

The waitress came.

"Veal," said Lee, "but not for me. He also wants a good amount of cheese on his salads."

"Whereas God knows what *he* wants. Let me do my own ordering, Pefley, and I'll order for you immediately after."

"Yeah!" the third man said.

The woman wrote it all down with solemn professionalism and then, having finished, went back over it to make a few corrections in word order. She was such an austere and serious person, Lee was torn between his regard for her and his increasing dismay over what the chimp was ordering for *him*—chitterlings with cornbread and black-eyed peas.

A long time was still to go by before the woman returned, *too* long for Lee and the other person simply to sit and stare across at each other. After some minutes, Lee began to use his Will against both the Latinist and the Chinese—until forced to admit at last that really there was nothing he wanted from either of them. Finally, half an hour passing (and the room beginning to fill with odd-looking people), Lee opened his bundle and went scrambling through the pages of his sole book in search of where the philosopher had anticipated with uncanny prescience those modern failings that characterized so perfectly the Latinist and others of his kind. The other man had his book, too, of course, and continued to glance up at Lee from time to time with knowing smiles. Thus passed the time, the salon growing more and more crowded with stranger and stranger people whose proximity Lee was enjoying less and less with each following moment. One person indeed was perpetually brushing up against him with his elbow—till Lee turned and changed glasses and glared back with a gaze that had behind it at least five full volumes for each individual page the other man had ever read.

"Not civilized, these people."

"No. But better than the outside cold."

"No doubt, no doubt. Where the hell's our food?'

"That same question arose in my mind, too. Well! Apart from being engrossed in my book, of course."

Both men went back to reading.

He had completed his book and had started it again when, toward ten, the woman brought his meal, a thin sort of porridge in which evidence of cabbage could be found. It was cool enough to drink.

Both men gulped down their portions, doing it quickly and leaving a meager tip. Lee had no wish to tarry here and be made to see the disappointment his Canadian money must inevitably produce on his pale waitress's face. Accordingly, he rushed out the door and down the hall where, once again, the watchman had crumpled off to sleep amid grunts and moans. Working with delicacy (but staying with his present glasses), Lee was able to extract two several green American dollar bills that the imbecile had left peeping out over the pocket on the left hand side of his unclean vest. And the Latinist made no objection.

A room for the night! They raced for it, chortling, both men reading aloud the numbers as they passed down the hall. The key, it proved, turned out to be a curiosity, a thing of iron that weighed several pounds. It *did*, thankfully, fit the aperture which was nearly large enough for Lee's whole arm. Thus Lee —he was humming optimistically, his mind already gloating over the hours he could foresee for himself between clean sheets on an accommodating mattress that would know when to yield, when not, and how. Grinning, he now threw open the door, stepped inside, discovered the switch and then to his inexpressible amazement recognized that . . .

The room was full of people.

Later on, thinking back upon those days, he was to remember that the place was more than merely full. Spilling over with geezers, they sat, some of them in each other's laps even as others tried to flatten themselves against the walls. As to the bed that he had so yearned for, it had fifteen persons in it, including one who, to judge from him, had passed through a traffic accident or been murdered in war. Lee wanted to scream out loud, his ancient nightmare having finally been brought to pass in front of his eyes, namely that he would wake some night to find his chamber full of individuals whom he had wronged at some point and who craved now to wrong *him*. So many souls, so many of them so old, and so constricted the space and over-burdened the bed, and such a lot of weight upon the assumed beams and joists that supposedly held it all up. Even so, Lee quickly took possession of himself, squeezing out a smile and then, after retreating into the manners of a southern gentleman, bowing courteously to everyone in sight.

"So good of you," he said loudly (searching at the same time for Judy), "to have come," (and then experiencing something like relief to see that she was not among such company). "We thank you for that."

"Would you kindly shut it up over there for Christ's sakes? Jesus!"

And then nearer at hand: "Nobody told you to turn on that stinking light!"

Lee quenched it at once. "The light," he said darkly, "is off."

"Good! Now if we can just get *you* to shut up."

He was engulfed, Lee, by the resumption of wide-spread snoring on all sides. Gingerly he reached for the doorknob, but only to run his hand up against someone's nose. He had trod, not upon living flesh, but an individual's shirt sleeve or, possibly, trouser leg. "Most sorry," he said, aiming his apology toward where he estimated the person's ear could most easily pick it up. And then, aiming again:

"But just where, after all, *do* you expect me to stay? The bed is full."

No one replied. Outside, an advertising sign was flashing off and on and giving split-second glimpses of the room's occupants bathed in a blue-green light. Some were sleeping, some standing, and two at least—Lee pointed with his stick—were engaged in vice. He must not blink in consonance with the neon, not if he wanted to go on seeing.

In this way passed ten or even fifteen minutes of some of the most uncomfortable moments of his entire old age. As to the pain in his defect, his diurnal need to piss, the cabbage worming its way by peristaltic action through his tract . . . He refused to think about it.

He had more important things to worry about, and none more important than the very good likelihood that he would have to go all night in one unchanging position. (He knew better than to ask for the bed, even though his rank, age, and education ought to have created a demand among the people for him to have it.) Instead, he began humming, bleak measures taken from Shostakovich. Right away—and he should have expected this—someone stamped twice on the larger and more splayed of his two way-weary feet.

"Damn!" said Lee, cursing under his breath. "This is *bad*, this. Can't breathe, can't sing. Why, I can hardly afford to *itch* without perturbing someone. And then, too, there's always that neon business beaming square into my eyes!" And saying so, he hummed again, even if this time he stayed below the level of the surrounding snoring.

Many years ago he had learnt to read while walking on the march; now, by necessity, he was learning a great deal about how to sleep while standing in one spot. He could not, to be sure, snooze for long, not unless he wished to come crashing down on top of people and set off a *real* disturbance. But where was the Latinist? Lee delved for his cigarettes and then, remembering he had none, retrieved instead his little cardboard box with the Swedish matches in it. So confident was he, so absolutely certain of success that when at last he ignited the first of the matches and held it up to the face that he believed to be the Latinist's, he jumped back in great surprise, abashed to see that once more he had put the whole room into a commotion.

"Son-of-a-bitch! You stick one of those things in my face again, I'll put a knife into you! I will!"

He had still not located the Latinist. As to the "knife," Lee had one, too, although it needed longer than was good for him to get to it. Suddenly, that moment, the neon skipped a beat, a discontinuity that threatened to throw one's whole heart out of rhythm. Far, very far away, he could hear a truck laboring up a hill, or possibly an airplane sputtering through the moisture of a cloud. Also the sound of creatures howling in dismay and timbers breaking—*wolves* (according to Lee's theory) throwing themselves against the gate.

SEVEN

AT SOME POINT DURING THAT LONG AWFUL NIGHT HE had managed to place himself, not *on,* but rather *under* the bed, an undiscovered land where he could lie at full length and call up thoughts about his own previous activities considered retrospectively up to a certain point. But when morning came and he saw that his thoughts had been suspended by sleep, immediately he picked up mentally where he had left off and continued on down to present time where he began to look forward with various degrees of anticipation to days still to come. Above, those were *bedsprings* he was looking at, and four not very confidence-inducing slats. And the geezers? Gone, all of them save one who, as Lee prodded with his stick, began uttering English words in the delirium of a sleep that had perhaps been too far prolonged:

"Low!" (Lee heard him say.) "Buy low." And then following it up with: "High, sell high!"

The lobby was blank and bleak, no geezers anywhere but for the hosteller himself, a bleary man who appeared to have come through a night as unenjoyable as Lee's.

Moving into the dining area, Lee saw how on every table the goblets had been positioned upside down, a cunning tactic that forestalled dust and other small things from coming to rest in places where they were not wanted. Having slipped past the Chinese, he then took a far table and proceeded to unfold the napkin, a massive affair as large as a newspaper and startlingly heavy for its weight. Spreading it flat, Lee rose, took off his glasses, and then bent down close to the stitching in order to read again that good old story about Pyramus and Thisbe and what happened between them. Finally, after folding and refolding the thing in a bootless attempt to make it as tidy and square as when he had found it, he moved to the next table (confusing the waiter) in order to read its napkins, too. But only to have a menu thrust under his nose.

Lee used his Will upon the boy. "Wine," he said in dry voice. "Dry."

"For breakfast?"

"Goddamn it!"

"Yes, sir, I'm writing it down right now—'wine.'"

"And eggs, numerous fried eggs. Do not, however, puncture the bubble and allow the fluid to run out."

"No, sir!"

"Bacon. Coffee. Biscuits."

"*Hot* biscuits?" The boy winked at him obscenely. And then, in a voice that was nasty and low: "We have marmalade, too."

Knowing that he must be made to wait, Lee fixed his attention upon the outside world where all manner of incongruous faces were passing by in constant streams. Particularly he focused upon a certain grinning churl who appeared, judging from his rucksack, his codpiece and chemise, to have been fetched here from medieval times. Or *mediaeval* rather, as Lee preferred to see it spelt. He tried briefly to use his Will upon the fellow, but found the window just too thick. Came next a swaggering youth in leather jacket and oiled hair, one who might almost have been a contemporary with Lee's own 1950s—until he saw the flounced knickers that connected the boy to a much earlier period. That was when the waiter came and tendered Lee a rather small and conspicuously diluted cabbage stew.

Lee forced it down, saving until the end that little morsel of meat (if meat it was) no larger than an acorn. Gorge rising, Lee called for more. But instead of "more," the manager himself came and sat across from him.

"We would," he said, "if we could. Give you more. But stocks are low."

"And yet this same stuff is being used for ammunition by the people in the wall."

"That explains it then." He scratched slowly, a sleepy sort of procedure in which his lower lid was drawn down by the finger tip as if to reveal on purpose the veins and bright red mucus that one would not otherwise wish to see. "A man like you. We *do* try, for our special guests. Oh yes! I knew we had a scholar in our midst, soon as I saw you sitting over here talking to yourself."

Lee waved it away, blushing with modesty. The other man might almost have been a scholar, too, given more knowledge on his part together with less stupidity and smaller dearth of brains. "And you," said Lee, "you might also have been a .... How shall I say? No doubt about it. And now if I could just have one cup more of well-sweetened coffee."

"I *am* sorry."

Lee could feel the sources of his gorge begin to activate. Suddenly, that moment, even as he was still holding out his cup in a pleading manner, that was when the head waiter came, took up a stance in the center of the room, and then hushed everyone to silence by means of a little silver bell.

"Ah!" said the manager. "A Great One has just this moment passed over. Yes, and he'll be turning up here, I ween, in a few days from now. And us with our stocks so low!"

"You get a lot of Great Ones, do you?"

"We get them all. I myself"—he pointed—"was loitering just over by that window there when Mahler himself came lumping past in that peculiar gait of his."

"Mahler! Moving fast, I suppose."

"Very."

He did finally get his second cup, earning it with conversation mixed with flattery. Refreshed, he rose and stretched and then strode out in dignity past the cashier, disdaining to pay. His purpose on this bright day was to hie him over as quickly as possible to the tower with the swan on it; instead, he had not traveled a full block before he ran into a government building with a long straggling line of unemployed persons shuffling miserably in the wind. Nothing could have been further from his mind, nor had he ever entertained on earth any least interest in *employment* and its things; nevertheless, out of old habit, he immediately fell into line and began displaying signs of extreme feebleness, whereon a kind woman allowed him to get in front of her. She had, he noted with displeasure, a powdery look to her, and wore upon her chest an example of one of the most ostentatious pieces of jewelry he had lately seen. And yet, as much as he disliked being in proximity with such people, still he lacked the cigarette by aid of which he might have sent her off with smoke.

The next hour went by slowly as he tried without success to wheedle his way down the line. Finally, coming into the building at last, he was shocked to see that the interviewer was but a young man, college-aged indeed and so sunny in aspect, courteous and bland, that right away Lee began to feel a headache coming on. It was not in his habit to respond to questions put by a youth who, on top of everything else, spoke in the low confidential tones of a loan officer. He had seen this before, had Lee, and at a time when he had had no intention whatsoever of paying back the loan. Even so, he allowed himself to sit and then, one by one, to reveal his name, provenance, and cause of birth, all which the boy entered into his bottomless machine. It was proceeding swimmingly (Lee believed), until his interlocutor began to titter and then to laugh out loud and then, finally, while pointing to the screen with one hand, to clap the other over his mouth.

"So! You weren't going to tell us about that little occurrence of last week were you? I don't blame you!"

"'Us?'"

"But wait, what's this? Jail? And when you were only sixteen? No, no, it's all in here, everything." (He patted the machine.)

Nonplused, Lee said nothing at first. Never had he imagined those episodes would follow him all the way to the antiworld. He answered, however, in comparative dignity:

"Young I was. Long time ago. Already been punished for it. *Still* being punished. Want me to leave?"

"Hemorrhoids, too!"

Lee looked down. The mention of it had set him to itching, the itching had resorted him to his cane, and meantime he had caught a glimpse of the Latinist who, apparently, had been given a severe beating at some juncture and now was weaving blindly down the street.

"No outstanding warrants on you?"

"Certainly not! They all expired long ago."

"Social diseases?"

"Social? Me?"

"And now—God. Would you say, Dr. Pefley, that you enjoy a *personal relationship with God?*"

"Yes, I would. He hates me."

"Says here"—he touched the screen with his finger, reading slowly—"says that you have always behaved in your own self-interest, but have always expected everybody else to behave from principle. Hey, that doesn't sound too good."

Lee looked down.

"Says here: 'he continues to carry on dealings with inferior sorts of people.'"

"Perhaps. But how otherwise could I have any dealings at all? And now I wonder if you'd ask that miraculous machine of yours about a friend of mine?"

"Judy? I was wondering when you'd ask."

Lee reeled. In his dizzy state, he could now only fragmentarily hear what the boy was saying.

". . . different trajectory. *Not* an egotist. Rare, very rare, Dr. Pefley, to shift from one route to another, especially to a higher. Easier if she were to hop down to your level."

"My level! But does she know what my level is?"

"Married you, didn't she? Come now, doctor, you're not *really* looking for a job, are you?"

Lee said something or another, neither of them picking it up. The boy's machine, which held so much more than even his own ten-thousand volume head, it emitted, chameleon-like, an ever-alternating cloud of colors that fascinated Lee—which is to say until the interviewer suddenly plucked up a black velvet hood and hurriedly covered the thing.

"So it's Judy you want, eh? Judy yes, job no. Oh boy, you people. You come over here, you people, wanting everything except a job. I had a *whore* this morning, for Christ's sakes, who wanted a list of divorcés!"

"Nothing surprises me, hardly ever."

"Now you, on the other hand, you're asking for a lot."

Lee, still looking down, still said nothing.

"Oh boy. O.K., listen up, there *is* a certain man . . ."

Now Lee looked up.

"Yes, a man. Crazy, I suppose. However, he does claim . . ."

"What does he claim?"

"Ssssh! I'm not supposed to be telling about this. He claims . . ."

He ran down into the out-of-doors, but then had to come right back up and enter into an argument with an elderly man over ownership of the cane. On his next emergence he capsized a pushcart and had to waste several minutes helping to chase down the cabbages. Crossing at the intersection, he then wedged forward between the pedestrians, all times keeping his gaze a safe distance from the spackled sun that today was tossing off rather more than the ordinary number of bright warmthless sparks.

The tower, when he came to it, proved to have *two* swans, each with a pennant of its own. He knocked three times courteously and then, counting to four, broke inside and ran forward five paces to foil the six men who (in his imagination) might be lying in ambush for him. In fact, he seemed to be in an auditorium of some description, a holding area loaded to the ceiling with disused television sets, computer peripherals, pin ball machines, stereo equipment and the like, all of it heaped up high in one big mix. Lee marveled, at the same time keeping well away from the pile lest somehow he set off a landslide and end up in his old age crushed beneath an avalanche of junk.

There *was* a path, it *did* lead between the piles of stuff; following on tiptoes, he came soon to the source of the noise that made him want to hold his hands over his ears—a grubby-looking mechanic listening intently to the non-stop stupidity coming from his radio. Lee was willing to shake with the person and might actually have done so, had not the fellow been so full of oil and other stains.

"Alabama branch," said Lee, taking back his hand. "The reason I've come . . ."

"I know why you've come!"

"You couldn't possibly."

"Want me to fix your goddamn little *microwave*, right? There ain't nothing wrong with that microwave, not if you treat it right. What, you lost the instructions already? It's the *polarity*—that would be my guess. But I don't reckon that's something, polarity, that you worry about very much, right? Thought not."

There followed then between the two men an extensive conversation which the mechanic seemed almost to be carrying on with himself alone, so little was Lee allowed to participate in it. Listening to him, Lee went to examine at closer range an enormous repository of refrigerators heaped up in a most unstable-looking stack. One single automobile had found its way here, and it so small and crumpled that it nestled now in inconspicuousness among the refrigerators. He was especially surprised to come onto a hoard of old-fashioned plow shares that lay in the dark part of the building, as if there the nineteenth century was remembered still among the ambient scent of camphor and kerosene. Squinting, he probed into that direction with his stick, interrogating himself as to whether indeed *all* the centuries might not be on display just a few steps further on. That was when the other man called him back.

"OK, if it ain't a microwave, then it's got to be your goddamn cigarette lighter, right?"

"You have cigarettes here?"

"Hey! You ain't one of those *trajectory* people now, are you? Trying to get onto another trajectory?"

Lee drew himself up to full height, a process that put him a good two or three inches above the man. Never had he been able to accept the presumptuousness, the address and self-presentation of members of the mechanic class. He spoke to the man coldly:

"Difficult for me to believe that you, a man like you, could direct a man like me to a higher trajectory—I just can't feature it."

"Naw; Harrison, he does that."

"Harrison."

"Yeah. 'Course now, he don't do it for just anyoldbody, know what I mean?" (He pointed the way with a gesture of his oil-stained head, inviting Lee to proceed, not toward previous centuries and their relics, but rather in the other direction.

This "Harrison" proved a man much more to Lee's natural liking; looking each other up and down, they shook with formality, both men then coming back to shake a second time once they had realized what sort of person they each were dealing with. It cheered Lee to find that the man had brought together a small but select collection of books which, however, appeared not to have been arrayed with any sort of aesthetic consideration upon the shelf that Lee with his imperfect vision could immediately discover. Saying nothing about that, he went forward to them anyway and, nodding with an approval that was partly sincere and in other part mere decency, used his cane to nudge one of the volumes back into place.

"I've come," said Lee finally, "to ask about . . ."

"Trajectory."

"Yes."

"Sit, please. Embarrasses me that I can't offer you a cup of coffee."

"Oh, it doesn't have to be coffee."

"Myself, I've acquired a liking, or anyway a *tolerance* for . . ."

"Cabbage? No, no, thanks all the same. No, actually I could do without the coffee *if only I could be offered a cigarette from time to time.*"

They looked at each other steadily, the trajectorialist at last removing the cigarette from his own mouth and then holding it out of sight beneath the level of the desk where Lee would not have to see it. The conversation that ensued was put into motion by Lee.

"I find myself, owing, I suppose, to egotism, find myself here."

"Yes! And you don't like it very much either, do you?"

"O, it's not so awful, not so unlike what I was already experiencing back on earth."

"First time I've heard *that*! You must have been a very wicked boy."

Lee waved it aside. "It's my wife, don't you see. Can't find her—hankering for her—about 5'2"—*not* an egotist—you seen her?"

"Hankering for his wife—now it all comes out. But tell me, doctor, are you so certain *she* hankers it? After all! you've admitted to being a very wicked boy, and an egotist, too. Gives me chills, when I think of all the things you *haven't* admitted. Perhaps she fled away on purpose, scampering down through the ages, sphere to sphere. These are delicate questions, sir, eschatological really. Where *did* you get those shoes?"

"It's true that she was good at scampering away. Puts me in mind of when . . ."

"I don't want to hear about that."

". . . got clean away!"

"Please!"

"Shoes? They came to me by natural merit, I like to

believe. And yet, I'd gladly give the both of them for but one glimpse of the breathing Judy."

"The socks, too?"

He was conducted into the adjoining room and then pointed to a high throne contrived from an old-fashioned toilet equipped with bicycle pedals. Already the trajectorialist had put on a pair of earphones and was adjusting them fussily. When he spoke, his voice came through a system of speakers and echoed in the cell.

"You wish to be promoted to a higher orbit in order to join your late beloved wife—do I understand that correctly?"

"Right," said Lee. "Yes. You have it right."

The man wrote it down, an effort that caused the antennae on his headset to wriggle like a bee's. "You understand, of course, that you must describe her to me in *precise detail.* Otherwise, why you might find yourself joined, and joined forever, to an inappropriate mate! How would you like that, doctor—to wake up next to an urban girl full of a career and lots of clothes?"

Lee paled. "I'm going to try with every force at my beck to describe her, my late beloved, in the most *absolute detail.*"

"So. And now if you'll be pleased to take a seat . . . No, no, don't worry, I haven't turned on the juice, not yet."

Lee did sit, but then immediately leapt up again when he descried the tangle of transistors and wires and the steel cap that, apparently, he was expected to wear on his head. More worrisome still were the two stirrups into which (after taking off his shoes) he was invited (removing also his socks) to insert both feet. The man, meantime, was beginning to show symptoms of an impatience that Lee had not previously remarked in him before.

"Yes, yes, good, good. And now . . ."

"The details?"

"If you will."

"She was," said Lee, "shorter than commonly realized, and remained always the sort of person of whom it might be said that she grew both wiser and sweeter as the decades went and came."

"How short?"

"She was," said Lee, "five feet and two inches on the day that we met."

The man wrote it down wrongly, transposing inches and feet. A horrible thought came to Lee—that he might end up with a woman only half as tall as Judy's already rather short height.

"Hair? Eyes? Speak up, man!"

"Brown," said Lee, "and brown."

"Nose?"

"Yes. But to revert to the hair—it had that fineness, don't you know, and used to gather up the light in grains of gold."

(The man groaned and lay down his pen.)

"But by afternoon, with the light splashing upon her in a certain way from out of the West, those were the days when . . ."

"We know, doctor, that the light does sometimes come out of the West; we know that already. Did you wish to meld with the light, or with Julie?"

"Judy, the name is *Judy*!"

(The man, having climbed into Lee's good shoes, was prancing about in them with great evident happiness as he tested them for comfort and fit.) "And was she educated, this woman of yours?"

"Indeed. She had read nearly as many books as me."

"Titles, please."

Lee set off at once, listing them by the dozen. He was good at this, given his facility for getting down on his knees in imagination in front of the authors who once had filled to overflowing his cabinet and chests. Having finished with the books, he then continued over to their other furniture, a poor equipage when first they had embarked upon their astounding early marriage days. "Two chairs only," he said, "and both quite rickety. For meals, we had to hold the platters in our laps, almost afraid to lift the forks."

"Very touching. And slept of nights upon a pallet, I suppose, instead of any standard bed. Nay, doctor, I've heard it all, time out of mind *ad nauseam*, ever since I've been in this line. It's the nose *I* need. Tell about the nose."

"The nose. It were as unique, that nose, as her two thin feet. 'Duck's feet,' we called them. All in jest, you understand."

The man looked at him with new interest. "No, that's very good, duck's feet—we need unusual features like that. But of course they weren't *really* like a duck's, were they?" (He giggled. Lee, highly miffed, had nothing for it but to wait until the moment passed.)

"Duck! Thin as pancakes! Must have been droll, those times she went 'scampering' away from you on feet like those!"

Lee endured it.

An hour's worth of questions, and then Lee mounted the throne a second time and, fitting on the hood and goggles, began pedaling forward against considerable resistance.

"I used to go pedaling," he said, "but never did I face such a journey as *this* promises to be!"

"Never. And if you abandon those pedals, doctor, even for a moment, why then you'll almost certainly break the spell, you sure will."

"And go tumbling down into an even lower trajectory than this current one? Doesn't bear thinking of!" He laughed uproariously, unwilling to admit that he was exhausted already and that the pedals seemed to him even more balky than at the beginning. "To flounder forever, alone, among cubed things and squared?"

"Very probably."

Lee put on a more serious tone. He had five minutes of stamina remaining in him, no more. "But I'll not desist," he said, "not ever, not till the cows come home, the sun peters out, and all the hills . . ."

But here the trajectorialist waved him to silence. "If you can peddle as tirelessly as you rave, why you'll soon have transported yourself to Elysium and back."

"I'll churn so hard, pedaling home, and never will I stop, not till."

"The cows, yes." Again the man pulled himself to his feet and went clopping about in his new shoes, delighted, apparently, with the way they conformed to him. Lee's operations, meanwhile, had established a tingling in his extremities and his condition, a sensation so peculiar that it had him grinning into the four corners of the room. Seeing this, the man urged him to continue with it and resist the urge to remove his left hand from the aluminum "glove" that, indeed, had begun to smolder somewhat. "Faster!" he cried, and then: "Can you not feel the egotism draining all away?" And then: "The smoke!"

But Lee, racing now, thought that he could begin to see pictures of that summer-like place where his wife with her own two hands had completed by now the pebble-built house they had designed together so many years ago while lying awake in rented quarters. And where, he knew well, she waited still. Lee strove even harder therefore, pedaling and pedaling more until, suddenly, he understood that he had fouled the electricity and snarled the wires, ruined the battery and made the room's one lamp go out.

And yet even then he did not give over entirely. In his

mind he was seeing things: lake, dog, garden and—and this was the part that made him put on his ultimate burst of speed—the tip of one of the fingers of the wife who sat by the window in the cottage she had constructed for his reception. "Judy!" he called, whereupon, of course, that was the moment the contraption exploded, a terrific event that left him sitting on the floor amid large and small shards of shattered porcelain. As for the pedals, not for anything in the world could he get them rotating again. And meantime the man was yelling at him.

Later on, looking back upon it, he was to remember how uncompromising the fellow had proved in relation to the shoes. A very bad day, that when Lee, drenched in battery acid, was made to leave town without the brogans assigned to him by providence and supplied instead with two thin slices of Styrofoam held on by rubber bands. Exhausted, charred, robbed, poorly shod, yet still he carried away in memory at least a momentary glimpse of those higher domains, and that one fingertip.

E I G H T

SO TERRIBLY THIN AS HE HAD BECOME, HE MIGHT almost have slipped between the bars; instead, the toll keeper drew open the gate with an exaggerated deference and then stood back, pointing to the palm of his hand where, evidently, he expected it to be filled with a tip. Lee fumbled for his penny, but then decided the man's hand was too small and his arm too weak for the coin's outrageous size. And did not look back until he had hiked a certain distance.

Sweet weather it was, these last mornings before the coming of the anti-spring. Behind him Lee took a lingering look at the city's steep-gabled roofs all crowded with vanes and roosters and swaying chimneys plugged with stork nests. Of Judy, she lived there no longer, although he knew for a certainty that she had come this way. Accordingly Lee now hoisted his cane and pouch and, girding up his Styrofoam, turned again to face a terrain that was more unsteady, more up-and-down and cantilevered than any he had so far been made to traverse. It gave him all the right reasons for staying with his original glasses, the thickest by far of those in his keeping. Ground to the most conscientious of prescriptions, he preferred these always when passing through the more extreme regions of the color spectrum. Equipped thus, his angle of vision was continually bumping up against things, hills for example, and cows incarnadined from a diet of roses. Courteous always, he nodded to the scarecrow, in this case a living person, poorly tailored, who must go on dancing all day to warn away the crows. Far to the East he saw a ruined windmill with hanged men dangling from the paddles, and further still, there where the sun was wont to rise each day a little closer, he saw what looked to him like a giant tumulus heaped up in old days against the memory of someone once deemed unforgettable by those who had known him.

He was good at books and good with tumuli; he was *not* so good as once he was at reading those same books while striding down mountainsides. Pestered by memory, he was furthermore distraught by certain old world opera tunes. *These* were the songs that had him in thrall when, suddenly, he collided into a cohort of male feminists coming over the hill.

Lee grinned to himself. Led on by a drummer and two clarinetists, they gave evidence of extreme neurasthenia, a tremulous condition brought on—so Lee theorized—by unendurable guilt. "Ah, me," he said (talking to himself), "if only Grant and Sherman had been like these!"

"Yes, come forward, do!" he said, extending his hand to the "man" in front. "Yes, that's right, Alabama branch, that will be me. You're familiar, of course, with the Virginia Peflies, I'm sure. Now when you reach the top of that hill yonder, my advice to you is to continue forward, straight into town and out the other side without pausing."

"In other words . . ."

"Yes. In and out. Never pausing."

"But . . ."

"And once you're safely on the other side, why then just keep on continuing for another league or two, till you come to a place of warehouses—that's what *I* call 'em anyway, 'warehouses'—a place of warehouses where you'll be received in the *most remarkable fashion*, truly."

They all smiled happily, their expressions so radiant that Lee, too, began to share in the general glow. "And in times to come, perhaps you'll remember that 'gaunt old man'—that will be me, of course—who gave you this advice."

He had put gladness on every face. One by one they came and tremblingly shook with him until at last, by force of modesty, he stood to one side and allowed them to file past, their noses all pointing forward eagerly toward the place where they would at last be let to stay.

Long ago he had learned to use his cane like an oar, and longer even than that had learned how to leap over cracks and crevices in the cold hard ground. That the geezers had recently come this way (moving in starts and spurts), he knew it from several indications. But mostly he knew it from the curious marks left behind in the sand, and from the discarded tube—and he knew whose it was, too—of empty lipstick.

Slowly and slowly as time goes by, the season *was* changing over into a more propitious one for intellectuals and egotists. Smiling at the improving sun, he pulled his mouth open full wide, as if in this way to grant his soul its own due meed of warmth. Thus it was that while he was fighting to get his mouth shut again, he saw that he was experiencing a sensation he had experienced before. It forewarned him that in days to come, he might need to defecate once more.

And yet the sky was nearly perfect on this day, and offered to his eyes an expanse that was green and like the sea. But it was the sun that most intrigued Lee, a thing so thin, so thinner than thin, and so seemingly near that when at last he went storming up to the top of a hill in order to put his finger on it . . . and lo, . . . it was further than he thought.

It failed to destroy his mood. Behind him were hills, volcanoes ancienter than the world and holding large reserves of smoke; Lee saw how the gulls, fearing for their feathers, make detours in the sky. And Lee, too; he much preferred to turn out of his way by a few inches than to blunder into the termite mounds that so often stood between himself and where he wished to go. In this way (going out of his way), he hoped to forestall any unnecessary bites upon his legs, his cane, and lower person.

Mid-afternoon had come and partly gone before he hove to within hailing distance of the throng. But really, could he still call it a "throng," now that it had so thinned out and with many of the more colorful personalities having elected to stay in town? Twice he signaled to them with his staff, a heroic-looking gesture carried out with his feet planted far apart on a hilltop some eighth-mile to the south-southeast of the column. No one saw him. Cursing, it needed much effort and a considerable expense of time to oar his way back down into the valley and then up the following ridge to take up a position where he could not fail to be seen and where once again he signaled to them with more or less indifference.

Truly it was a sorry group he saw, old ones and sorry ones and all (save one) in sorry clothing. He could not but smile, seeing how the Latinist fared; to Lee he looked like a person who had spent a series of bad nights tending to his bruises. But where was the leader, that bearded man and pathfinder who had brought them to . . .

This. At once Lee ran downhill and, pointing out the way with his rod, seized the role for himself. Responsibility had always rested with amazing lightness upon his own particular shoulders; indeed, as one who cared nothing for people, he felt no weight at all. Thus two minutes went past, Lee striding forward with energy while at the same time pointing out and commenting upon interesting features that appeared from moment to moment along the line of march—which is to say until he chanced to look back and found the crowd had rejected him and had veered off down quite another trail altogether.

Good fortune did not stay with them for long; they had covered less than a bare mile when, suddenly, a chill rain began running toward them from out of the west. For guidance, they all looked to the engineer, an organized sort of person who had been drafted for the role that should have been Lee's. Stupid beyond belief, he stood now, pointing off emotionlessly toward what looked to be a tumble-down farmhouse some half-league off the route. Many times Lee had seen this in his native south—abandoned places (the paint all missing) guarded over by windmills bending graciously to earth. But had it indeed come to this, that the anti-world was but a smashed version of his own natal region suffering through an agricultural depression? Nevertheless he ran toward it, as did everyone.

It was a last century's farm, an epoch of turfen roofs and chimneys built to give warmth in winter and give shelter to swallows during the summer. But in this particular example the chimney had broken off many years before and had then melted down beneath the weather into a lump of "gold," or clay actually.

Next, he identified the smoke house and then, racing toward it, verified that it was invested still with that most tenacious of all essences—pork flitches that had been cured for long periods over coals of hickory and/or oak.

It was a two-story house; unfortunately, the staircase was missing, gone, obliterated, and had perhaps been used by other travelers as a source of fuel. Using a match, Lee probed into the four corners of the place, finding where someone a hundred years ago had parked a harness and saddle with iron fittings, all of it now reduced to a mound of putrefying leather that gave off a stink.

He was tired, tired in bone and soul. Five hours, he craved, of uninterrupted sleep, even if he must accomplish it among whores and old people on hundred-year-old flooring that might or might not rest on adequate struts and beams. No youths in *this* crowd! And for that he was truly grateful.

Having laid claim to the best corner of the house, he went and sat in it, watching with interest as one by one the others came in hesitantly and with trepidation and then selected for themselves the locations that best comported with their preferences. He observed the accountant, formerly a leading figure among them, who now went quickly into the adjoining room and closed the door. Trading glasses, he watched with especial interest as the women entered, some arriving with bleeding feet, some in tears, and at least one bending under a sullen lizard that seemed rather to belong to the crocodile species. Someone had had the prescience to bring a candle and the goodness to set it up where everyone could share in its unsteady glow. This worried Lee, as did all those communitarian and collectivistic tendencies that led to reciprocity. "Ah, yes," he said, "and soon they'll be singing folk songs together, and if not around a campfire, around a candle then. Oh, good." For even the men had taken to smiling companionably, one to another. Seeing this (and wanting to puke), Lee fled into those other glasses whose short-range lenses were good but for reading.

But instead of reading, he found that he had gone to sleep in those same glasses, only then to awaken with a start, his book in one hand and the other empty. That it was black night outside and still raining, he knew it from the way in which the geezers had drawn up in a circle around the candle, as if waiting for the thing to begin giving off real warmth. It was a sorry group; moreover, a fat man had taken a place much nearer to Lee than Lee liked to see. For some time they stared at each other, Lee toying with the man by dint of his own superior Will. At last the other began to speak:

"And so it comes to this. Tell me, friend, is this what you expected after seventy-five years of . . ."

"'Friend?'"

". . . hard work and always trying to do the right thing?"

Lee took off his glasses. "Listen, 'friend,' *you* may have seventy-five years, but that doesn't mean that *I* . . ."

"No, no, of course, not."

"And it doesn't mean I ever tried to do the right thing, either!"

"I don't know, I just don't. Maybe this is a *trial* of some sort we're going through. Yes?"

"Trial? Trial? *I've* been on trial for seventy-three years! 73!"

"I know you have, I know it; we all have. There's no need to get all worked up about it, for Pete's sake. That's right, just sit back down again, good; I'm not trying to take your cane, good, good."

Lee blinked at him. Ordinarily he might have pulled the cover to his eyes and then turned and faced the other way—save that what he saw now in that direction was worse even than in this. The candle, too, had waned down to nearly nothing and seemed poised to give up its own little ghost after a "trial" of less than two hours. Many of the people had sputtered off into unquiet sleep, two of them snoring so tumultuously that they seemed to be hurling thunderbolts at each other from distant regions of the building. Lee could not, however, without losing his location, rise and give both of them a caning. Furthermore, he could see that the man at his side had by no means finished speaking.

"And to think that I once trusted in the common theology —separability of body and soul, and all that." (He snorted at himself. Or snorted, rather, at what he used to be.)

Groaning, Lee picked up his book.

"Whereas I understand now what I could not understand before, namely that the 'soul,' improperly so-called, is simply a pseudo-entity squeezed in between the id on the one hand, and the super-unconscious on the other."

"*You* may be built like that, but not *me*."

"And lies over against the *Atman*, or ego-personhood."

Lee tried to plug up his auditory channels.

"And you, Pefley, to know that even now your corpse lies rotting on that hillside. That's sad. Was it ten seconds ago, or ten thousand years?"

"It were rotting ere I left it."

"Pefley! That was funny, what you said. First time, I believe, that I've heard anything like that from you."

"If you could, as it were, move back a few inches . . . I think we'd both be more comfortable."

"An egohood like yours, rich in self-esteem; oh, you'll go far, doctor, which is not even to mention all that wit."

"Well tell me this, since you know so much—when may I expect to gaze upon my own late beloved wife again?"

"Judy? Why I don't know."

Lee went back to reading.

"However . . ."

Lee looked up.

"Neither do I know that you *mayn't* so gaze. Have you been keeping a bright eye for clues?"

Lee looked at him.

"A dropped comb perhaps? Or even just one tooth thereof?"

Lee stood and sat, his super-unconsciousness spinning wildly at the belated recognition that he could not even describe to himself the shade of the dress that she had been wearing at the time. Accordingly he could hardly be expected to recognize random tatters of it as "clues."

"Did she smoke cigarettes?"

"Certainly not! This is *Judy* we're talking of."

"For if she *had* smoked . . ."

"No, no, no, nothing like that. This discussion is over."

"Chewed gum?"

"Jesus!"

"Sorry, no sorry, no; now don't go getting all worked up again, all right?"

Both men settled back, both meditating together on other aspects of her former personality. Suddenly:

"This 'Judy,' would she say that she had been a great reader of books?"

"Some of the books were great," Lee said slowly, "and others merely good. It's true that sometimes she opened things that *I* never recommended." And then, after thinking over in mind some of those titles: "O! And so according to your theory, I ought to be watching for scattered pages!"

The man smiled, and rather condescendingly, too, as it seemed to Lee.

"Scattered pages! But from which book?"

"Oh come now, you can't expect me to know *that*, can you? Of course, if ever *you* had authored a book . . ."

Lee, his mind running over, sat again and stood. No sleep tonight! And now, if only the other man would consent to draw back a few inches and speak no more, it might give some range to the thoughts and memories that would be kaleidoscoping for the next six hours inside Leland's head.

It was not the case that he had to go all night without sleep; on the contrary, he fell off almost at once, owing in part to the rain, partly the candle flame, and in some part a few residual old-world crickets still stridulating in the upstairs rooms. Two full hours of a fine moist sleep, deep and good—Lee considered it a reward for his recent conduct. Rising and peeing and coming back, he followed it up with two further hours of ordinary grade slumber that was the result of Will alone. Finally, at about three in the morning, he came awake to the sound of a commotion in the adjoining room.

The humpback was dying—he had been expecting this. Positioning himself just outside the door, he was able to see much, and what he saw was a woman in death's labor, together with others of her sex who were hovering and whispering and fussing and, in general, making efforts to attenuate her passage to life's next phase. Lee thought it best to leave these matters to the women, a steadfast conviction that persisted even after he observed one of them rifling avidly through the dying person's purse. Suddenly, the candle sputtered twice and expired, presumably to go forward into the next world and light the humpback's way.

Lee now took one of his very few surviving matches and, after fumbling about with the thing, managed to ignite it. Contrary to what he had been led to believe by the silence, the men had come awake, most of them, and were staring with dread at that place where shortly the miracle of death was to take place in front of their eyes. Lee, who longed to cane the lot of them, was not awfully surprised—he had seen this before, how such men could suddenly become so strangely coy and girlishly shy. Rising now and holding high his match, he waded in amongst the women, who duly gave way to him.

"Lizard," he said, "*where is the lizard?*"

"Father!"

Lee jumped back. Regrettably, she had done some vomiting and had set up a situation that made Lee feel as though he ought not come too close. "No, no," he said, "no father, I. Hell, *you're* older than me." And then, relenting somewhat: "But yes, do sleep, if you can. There'll be other lizards."

"Sleep?"

"Absolutely." (The women had moved away, content to let Lee usher her out of this world and to the next.) "And when you wake, why it will be in a place where the good things are three times better than here. No! Good things *cubed*, I should have said."

"Really, Father?"

"Haven't I just said so?"

"And bad things, Father, how about *them*?"

"Yes, those too. Cubed."

She smiled rapturously. Outside, the rain was more profound than ever and the thunder that heretofore had stayed at a distance, it was less distant now. Lee was barely able to hear the woman, who seemed to be describing an earlier time in her career.

"We so wanted to be happy, me, Andy, the children."

"Happy, yes, a common-enough desideratum. Desire, however—and I say this reluctantly—desire is not enough."

"And then he had to go and die."

"Die. But remember this, that whereas you lost an Andy, just look at what *I* lost."

"Father?"

"Hm?"

"Do you believe that . . . ?"

"Doubt it. But with Judy, anything is possible. She's just the type, don't you know, to thrive in a place where life has been carried to its next higher power." (He came nearer, looking into the humpback's eyes. Her time was nigh, her breathing weak; she had lost her ecstatic smile. Lee now went over into his other glasses, as if their more powerful lenses might let him see what she was seeing, assuming he wanted to see it.)

"Father!"

"Nay, nay, it's only the match that has gone out, not you. Already you've persisted much longer—all those miles!—far longer certainly than ever *I* would have guessed."

He could see nearly nothing now, save where from time to time a bolt of thunder granted a second's worth of light. He estimated it at about five in the morning and with a mean (mean in both senses) temperature of between twenty and thirty degrees of mercury. Winter was returning, no slightest doubt, and him with no sufficient shoes in which to stand against it. Swept with pity, he swayed and moaned, his memory running back over all the unlisted injustices that had forever been his share in this and every other realm so far visited by him anent his ten-thousand-year tour among the planets, etc., etc. November, was it? And Lee within the South? Or was this late September now and himself at hazard in the hellish north? It didn't bear thinking about.

Dawn came up like an old engraving; it gladdened Lee to see moths dancing in shafts of meadow light. Into the nearest and most luminous of those beams he now inserted (and allowed to remain for a while) (before then drawing it back out again) a portion of his own exaggerated nose.

Next, he inspected the sky. It had *not* been washed clean by rain, or not entirely so at any rate. He still could see clouds of magnesia and (unless it were a fissure in one of his lenses) giant cobwebs girdling the sun. Of the travelers themselves, most had gathered around the fire in order to compete for the nicest places. Further afield, the fuel gatherers, like so many horses, could be seen blowing spumes of condensation as they searched the ground. More experienced in these matters than most, Lee drew off toward the granary which, however, had been picked so clean that not the best glasses in the world, nor brightest eyes, could have located so much as a single unaccompanied grain. He came down therefore and, having secured the door, ambled back nonchalantly to the crowd where he loudly announced:

"Well then, gentlemen, and so what do you propose we . . . ?" His voice trailed off. No one listened to him, not anymore. Instead, they all turned to the computer specialist, an inverted sort of person who spoke seldom, but did so rationally when he did so:

"You ask about food? My answer is to steal it."

"In other words," the broker said, "we could just steal it."

"Those aren't other words. Those are the same words."

"I don't hold with stealing," the third man said.

"Ah! Well *you* can perish then."

"I did! That's how come I'm here."

"What would Xenophon have done, Pefley? After all, I mean, he had, like, *ten thousand* to feed."

Lee jumped back, gratified, amazed, and highly encouraged that a mere businessman had come to know such things.

"His position was indeed tenuous," he answered finally, giving his most thoughtful answer to this the best question he had been asked in several years. "But remember this, those were rich lands, those. Very." (He then hastened to add, his voice dark and low: "Actually their numbers were probably fewer than that, to believe the most recent research.")

"Oh, good."

That was when the accountant rose, a tall man, very morose, his pocket full of pencils. "*I'll* do it," he said, "and go for food. After all, I've had lots of experience at it, if you take my meaning."

"Shore!" said the third man. "Been stealing for years."

* * *

And so they departed, the broker, the accountant, and the literary agent, three brave men taking with them the burlap bags that had been found in the barn. Lee's hopes were high—always he had cheered for youth and bravery, and knowing that these three were by any measure almost the most-nearly youthful and experienced in the group. He waved to them admiringly therefore, glad to see the last of them, urging them on with his kerchief before then returning to the granary where, however, the humpback's corpse had begun to shrivel beneath the delicate touch of morning light. He wanted sleep, did Lee, wanted it badly and music to go with it, and in that same order, too, and wine, and *her* of course, who had been his wife.

NINE

IN THE AFTERNOON, THE RAINS CAME BACK AGAIN. LEE, thinking deeply, kept to his loft, his legs dangling over the edge. He could see far; his concentration, however, was poor. Finally he decided to shut the book and start anew with it.

He was reading, reading well and sometimes speaking out loud to himself, and sometimes listening to it, too, when, suddenly, he descried an early model car rampaging at high speed across the desert and coming toward the farm. Ought he or ought he not, sound the tocsin? While he was debating that, the car itself came pushing into the barnyard with great clatter and made an abrupt stop. The driver—and Lee had never liked these types—was a military man who was so lean and his hair so exceptionally short, and whose holster held such a gun that Lee saw right away he had no chance whatsoever of taking it for himself without at the same time alerting the man. Instead he continued to stare at it hungrily, even as the major climbed out onto the hood of his car and stood there, his hands in the authoritative position, thumbs out, two of his fingers *inside* his belt and six without. It allowed Lee to see that he had also a military watch, a dark-faced affair that was large as a Canadian coin and with all manner of dials and gauges on it.

Ought he, ought he not, ignore the pistol and go for the watch?

"Motherfuck! Now just what the hell do we got here—bunch of goddamn cold-weather geezers?"

They admitted that they were.

"And one old whore," said the whore.

"Jesus P. Christ, now I've seen it all. What, you figure you can hole up here on somebody else's property, is that what it is? Hey! what's with *him*?"

"Sick."

"Jesus! Well just keep him the hell away from me."

Lee was pretty sure the man was about to take the weapon from its holster and proceed to slay them all; instead, he reached into the cockpit of the car and came out with a full loaf of bread that was so nearly the size of a bread box that Lee was by no means certain it could have fitted inside it. He watched as the soldier pinched off a morsel of the stuff and threw it into the rather tiny crevice that was his mouth. Moaning at the sight, the egotists began to crowd in upon the car, the driver, and the bread. Soon—and everyone understood this—soon he would toss the loaf down amongst the people where they could fight for it.

What followed was not good, not in keeping with the dignity that Lee had been practicing ever since that day when first he had seen that it was more in keeping with his dignity to do so. Worse yet, he had come up with but one single crumb of the stuff, albeit a grand one of about the size of his own left thumb. He who once had believed that all of life was supposed to be like certain divine measures of music carried on to perpetuity—now he was flailing about, and none too efficaciously either, contesting for certain nibblets of bread.

"Go now," said the lieutenant, "for you have dawdled here too long already."

"But . . . But, but . . . !"

"Night's coming on!" the Latinist yelped.

"Night? Why yes, it tends to do so each and every day at just about this hour. Go now!"

Meek as kine, they set forth in single file. The women, being women, had overburdened themselves extremely, owing to their great love for objects and things and manufactured products that reminded them of the old life back on earth. Lee came last, embittered from being constantly nudged forward by the fender of the colonel's car. Nor could he think, nor sing, nor hum even, not with the horn blasting at him every few seconds. Finally, half a mile out, the vehicle turned off toward the east and left them.

The night itself was thin, blue, and strange as fluid; taking a specimen of it between his thumb and finger, he tested it for pedigree. It distracted him from his reading, especially when he saw how cluttered was the sky with so many unwonted numbers of great jagged stars. Having all but coalesced, they formed a "grid," those stars, through which only the most adept of pilots could hope to navigate and still come out in safety on the other side. The moon, too, it flirted, by dint of beauty, with evil absolute. Sadly, the thing had lost a fragment of its belly, there where it had been scraping along the western hills. Came now to Lee those intimations about his wife that so often came at times like these, namely that she, too, was watching this same demonstration and thinking the same thoughts she had so often thought before whenever he had asked what she was thinking. He knew her! And knew how for her, as short as she was, the stars appeared so much more distantly than for most people, and more faint. Lee groaned, very loudly. Except for Time, dread Time, Time that "turns wives to dust," and except for Space, loathsome Space (and Distance, too), except for that she might still be in his arms right now! But what most worried him was this—that they had come over into this awful place in such discrepant conditions, with his wife still lovely but he himself disgusting already.

He was thinking about these matters, sometimes groaning out loud and then ever and again putting on a burst of speed so as not to be altogether left behind in the dark bad night. To south, vast fires had broken out—he counted seven—where entire cities were being given over to incineration. It cast a gloom over the travelers, even if they could by no means pick up at that range the sound of the assumed screaming. Suddenly, stung into action by his hemorrhoids, Lee gave a series of little hops and then went spurting forward.

It was shortly past midnight, the mercury still falling, when they broke past mile marker number 72 and then veered toward the south-southeast. The terrain that until lately had been so full of hills, it had turned to low-lying pasture lands scattered with ruined homes, collapsed barns, and upside-down burnt-out late-century automobiles with neither engines nor upholstery nor anything else left intact. As lightly burdened as he was, he felt he might go on walking forever, snippets of world literature slipping easily in and out of mind along with certain prose contributions of his own. Books and thought—he was not unhappy. This was *his* milieu, with night and moon, always his own favorite star. Further, he was being rewarded in his old age by the sight of cities going up in flame, both on starboard and port. In that unearthly light (and while straining to catch the sound of exploding cars and buildings falling), he thought he saw something, the sort of something that he had been seeing in imagination ever since the possibility of it had been mooted to him by one of the egotists—a clean white page fluttering in the field, a hopeful thing hanging on a thorn.

Dropping his cane (but then at once turning and coming back for it), he raced to the spot, harvested the object and then, after waiting for the crowd to go around the bend, leapt into his glasses and held the sheet a few inches in front of his cleaner lens.

He thought that he would faint. For although the first lines were not instantaneously familiar to him, soon he recognized the overall quality of the language itself, a delectable stuff that proved who the author was. Lee moved nearer. By hap, he had come onto page 72, a number that seemed unaccountably familiar to him wherein the hero, a dried-up old man of seventy-two, had committed a cruel deed upon two pea-brained youths. Reading of it, Lee grinned. But where, and how far, and which winds and breezes had taken pages 1-71?

He still thought that he might faint. He wanted to fall to his knees and give praise to someone or something; instead, he simply harkened to the stars, flattered that on this one occasion at least they harkened back.

It turned cold, the weather deteriorating in their very faces. Finally, toward one, they left the path and began crowding into a roadhouse under management of a huge man dressed in bib trousers. Right away Lee began looking for, and right away found, the string that told in which pocket he kept his tobacco pouch. Saying nothing, the man gathered up that string and put it where Lee could by no means get at it.

"My grandfather was a redneck," Lee said, extending his hand, "but we always got along extremely well. May I use the toilet?"

There *was* a toilet, bright and clean; the women especially were glad to see it. And Lee had to give credit to them, too, for the way they formed up in line with no unseemly pushing. Himself, he ran around to the rear of the building.

Thus Lee—he was peeing at leisure when the big man came and, in a show of hospitality, began peeing alongside.

Lee hummed; he had not wanted to mention the woeful stink that seemed to be coming up out of the valley.

"Tires belike," he said, "rubber tires with no further use in them—it's those, no doubt, the villagers are burning for warmth."

"No, sir, not hardly. No, sir, them's just some yuppies they been burning all day over in Charlie Mason's back forty."

"Burning!"

"Yes, sir. Had me a ticket, too, but I give it to the boy. Seems like I just don't have time anymore to go places."

"Burning 'em! Where's the ticket now?" (He understood, of course, that he had finished with what he had come for, and now was standing uselessly in a certain posture.) "Don't have anything to eat, do you? I must say, even an opossum would be acceptable on a night like this."

"Don't have no 'possums. Dog got 'em all."

"Dog?"

They looked at each other.

"No, sir, I couldn't do that to ole Barney, just couldn't. Got some cabbage though."

Lee cursed. He would have given anything for a bit of meat, gravy on it. He was almost grateful therefore when the breeze brought back the smell, not this time of tires and 'possums, but of retribution plain and simple, and blew his appetite away.

Minutes later, they were on the trail again and jogging to make themselves warm. Lee, who all his life had detested haste in all its measures, cursed. The physician, a bald-headed man, was coughing as he ran. Lee managed to sidle up to him.

"Why, you run almost as poorly as do I!" (He laughed merrily, laughing alone.) "I've been meaning to speak with you."

"Medical advice?"

"Why, yes."

"It never fails. Tell me, have you ever seen me coming to you for a free Greek literature consultation? I don't think so."

"Constant pains, misery every day."

"Oh boy. He's asking anyway." (He was a sorry sprinter. And then, too, for someone who knew about health, his own health seemed none too good.)

"Do you do your own doctoring, doctor, doctoring to yourself? And if so, can you recommend yourself? Hm? No, just a jest, you understand. And yet, according to Ctesias . . ."

But here the man stopped him. "Ctesias? I'm surprised at you, Pefley, I really am. Ctesias was never, and I repeat *never*, certified."

That was true. Lee fell silent. The two men had meantime dropped further and further behind the main crowd, which seemed to be gaining both in stamina and speed as night wore on. In this province the hills were steeper and came to such sharp points that the geezers found themselves from moment to moment racing up into the sky or else plunging at horrifying angles into the valleys and awful night. It took him by absolute surprise therefore when a throng of old people, their mouths sewed tight with laces—they seemed to be sweating from some great unimaginable dread—came up quietly out of the dark and, refusing to acknowledge the egotists, raced past without a word. And what, pray, could have been *their* sin? Lee preferred not to think about it. Instead, turning back to the doctor:

"Now my own health, for example, well!, it's not everything it should be, I don't suppose."

"Health? You're three-fourths dead, man, *that's* your 'health.' What, cancer is it?"

"No, no."

"Lupus? Shingles? Glanders?"

"Ha! No, no. No, fundamentally, it's *hemorrhoids*, not to put too fine a point on it. But please don't ask me how to spell that word."

"Oh yuk! Old man with hemorrhoids. Me, I'm an above-the-waist doctor. Sorry!"

He moved off, gaining new speed. Lee was amazed to see how fast he could in fact go.

TEN

CAME DAWN, BRINGING GREAT RELIEF. AND YET, THIS, too, proved illusory, and soon it was as black once more as in the very worst part of night. Near at hand, a wolf barked twice, and although Lee waited with patience for him, cane held high, the thing came no nearer and in time was heard no more.

The true dawn also proved something of a disappointment. Where, he asked, was the flora, the glades and dells and dappled crannies of the literary South that once he had known so well? Here, the day was full of thunder with snow threatening, and naught but additional sharp-pointed hills ahead. A bad day's travel he foresaw, and then further mountains, bleaker fields, and only the remotest possibility of that roseate and pink sparkling sea of his dreams at continent's end—clear, distilled, thin as atmosphere.

Somehow they had acquired two stray dogs during the foregoing night, neither of them worth eating and one of them, apparently, a wolf. It was the other one who, lacking a tail, had attached himself to Lee. Getting down on one knee, Lee began to question whether they had not perhaps already known each other at some previous stage in their careers, when they had both been "puppies," so to speak. Lee did know this, that he would never be shut of him now.

The next town, as it turned out, was a modern city—no towers here, no archers on call, nothing like that. Here the people right away came boiling out of their houses in order to throw the usual comments and cabbage at them. Lee, hardened to it, bowed sweepingly and then, calling them "amateurs!" (in reference to their marksmanship), followed it up by offering them a rather tawdry gesture with his cane.

Four blocks they trudged, saying nothing. By good fortune they had somehow come under the protection of a constable, a portly man dressed in bits and pieces of uniform that seemed to date from previous times in history. Lee now thought seriously of breaking off and of going his own way; instead he hesitated and at the last moment entered along with the others into a government building where sat a prim-looking receptionist—her lenses were thicker than Lee's—whose two blue eyes appeared to have been drawn in by a child. Lee, having neglected to bring his Will to bear, met her gaze for but a few seconds before he began to feel quite odd.

"Egotists?"

They admitted that they were.

"Second-tier egotists? You were expected two days ago."

They apologized. As a government building, it proved full of government people; accordingly, Lee took up one of the massive questionnaires and set to work on it. It was not just information they wanted, but confessions and, in general, a discussion about good and bad attitudes. Strangely—and Lee had seen this before—the most vexed questions had been allotted the least space in which to compose a response. He solved this by writing on the obverse, his analysis growing longer and longer and his script tinier and tinier as he came nearer and nearer to the edge of the paper. The receptionist saw this, was angered by it, and got promptly to her feet.

"And just *what*, if I may ask . . . ?"

"Essay!" said Lee. "No, it's an intriguing question really, many implications."

"You people. Give me that!"

They fought for it. Once before, he had had a third-grade teacher who had treated him this way; this time, however, *he had managed to purloin the government-issue pencil.* And now she was pointing him down to an open office where sat a rough-looking sort of man tapping impatiently at his blotter with each and every finger that he had.

To be offered a cup of coffee just now, dark brown indeed and accompanied by a powdered crumpet with jelly in it—he would have accepted that, Lee would, without demur; instead, he waited respectfully while the man finished off his own cup and crumpet and then began extracting one by one some of the larger crumbs that had lodged in his foot-long mustache.

"Egotist?"

"Yes," said Lee.

"Yes, *sir*, don't you mean?"

"Yes, sir."

"Ego people. You come in here, day after day after . . . got any money?"

Lee, nonplused, went at first for his penny, but then quickly changed his mind and came out instead with two individual dollar bills that were dark green on one side and had previously been silver on the other, before the stuff had mostly flaked away. They did seem to soften the man, but only by a little.

"We don't need this, do we? Playing games, you and me?" (He nodded toward the dossier that lay on his desk.) "We're grown-up people, aren't we? Give me a hundred and I'll tell you where your wife is."

Lee, reaching out for support, very nearly fainted. The dossier was thick enough to hold all manner of information, and more importantly, had half an inch of bright red ribbon sticking out. Heart pounding, Lee grabbed for his wallet and counted out . . .

"Twenty-two! I have twenty-two—you want it? Heck, *I* don't need it."

The man corralled the money with a hand that had four rings on it and drew it softly to his side. "Twenty-goddamn-two—that'll get you a cup of cold tea and a stale croissant. What it *won't* get you is no goddamn wife."

Lee pulled back the money and again counted through it at high speed. "I could give you . . . twenty-two."

"We've already been through that! What, you want I should give her to somebody else? You'd be surprised, the people who come through here, what they want."

Lee stood, and his dog stood with him. It was true that he possessed a further seventeen and some odd dollars kept in various places upon his person along with certain small coins, all of which he now began to lay out upon the table, a tedious process that forced him to get half undressed. Seeing the bills that continued to appear, the man rose suddenly, tiptoed to the door, and shut it.

"Lordy! How much of that stuff you got, hidden in different places?"

"No more, nothing, this is all, everything."

"You sure?"

"Quite sure." They stared. Too late to bring out his Will and use it, Lee allowed his gaze to drift to the portrait of the newly-reelected President, a smiling youth famous for his tender philosophy in regard to policy and girls. Finally, reluctantly, Lee took out the last money he owned, a five-dollar piece that looked as if it had been nibbled about the edges by numerous small mice. "All that I own," he said. "Forty-four American dollars."

"Yeah? And how's about that little *pouch* you got there, the one that hangs from that stick?" (He pointed to it with a finger that was blunt and short and bore much dirt beneath the nail.) "What you got in *there*, hm?"

"Nothing, nothing at all, loose change and nothing more, that's all."

The man held out his hand for it.

And so thus Lee—he had put together forty-four old-world dollars and a few pence more. Of his book and knife, his blanket, dog, penny, and matches, the man demanded none of those. Finally, proceeding with timidity, Lee stretched forth his hand for the dossier and, with the bureaucrat watching all his moves, drew it ever so cautiously to himself.

"Judy's in here? No, I mean the maps and directions telling how to get to her— are *they* in here?"

"Did I say that?"

"No maps?"

The man shrugged. Now that the interview was over, he was continually glancing at his watch and giving other signs of conspicuous impatience. And still Lee could not bring himself actually to open the folder that he had so dearly bought. Most likely, he thought, it might contain an 8 x 10 glossy showing her in her present condition.

"You going to open it, or not?"

"Certainly I'm going to open it!"

"When?"

Lee opened it. Right away he saw no glossies, no maps, no pages from his erstwhile book. As for that red ribbon, it was less than two inches' worth, a mere "lure" that had been pasted to the underside of the cover. Frantically he splashed through the contents, finding nothing but coupons and receipts, a report card that dated back to her seventh year together with a mess of correspondence from the I.R.S. And when he looked up, hand trembling and heart making a fluid sound, the man was grinning.

"But . . . But, but . . . !"

"Hell, ain't it?"

"Why, there's nothing here but . . . !"

"You people, always so surprised about everything. Why is that?"

"But, but . . . You couldn't have done anything worse than this!"

"Thanks."

Lee thought that he would faint. Too late in the day for him to take out his Will, he began to rise and then, in another such movement, to lift the cane. Only now, when it was no longer possible to do anything about it, only now did the government man begin to remind himself of just what sort of history Lee's had been. At one moment he made as if he actually believed that he could arrive at the door and open it, and actually escape before Lee's massy rod came crashing down on top of him.

"What a mistake! And to think that I was the one who closed that door in the first place!"

Lee smiled.

"And now you'll be able to . . ."

"Beat you to death." said Lee. He knew so well the choreography to come: lifting his wand and lowering it, lowering and lifting it again. He rehearsed it now, the stick producing a whistling noise that seemed to entrance the man.

"Gosh, how it sings, slipping like that through the air!" And then in darker voice: "I've read your book."

"Notice how even now I am in process of propping this chair against the door."

"I saw that. No one will be able to get in."

"Not immediately anyway."

"And when they do get in . . ."

"For who would dare to disturb government property?"

"As I was saying, when they *do* get in, they . . ."

"But wait—there's no real guarantee that it'll be as noisy as all that, no. No, I can make it go forward in complete silence if I want to."

"Do you? Want to?"

Lee thought. The door was invested with a pane of frosted glass. And although someone *was* standing just without, yet Lee felt he had little to fear from him (or her) since she (or he) was conversing very animatedly just now with a second such person whose silhouette largely resembled that of a duck, owing perhaps to the cap the person happened to be wearing at the moment. Ascertaining all of this in one quick glance, Lee began next to hum at high volume, hoping to use the music to cover any cries and shrieks that the man in front of him might happen to give off.

"Ready?"

The man flinched and threw up one arm to protect, not his head (always Lee's favorite target), but rather his underbelly, as puffy as it was from too much soft living and croissants.

"Ready?" Lee asked again. (It was, of course, a perfunctory question, rhetorical in nature. And yet, having asked it, he felt obliged to wait for the answer.)

"'Ready?' You *know* I'm not going to answer that! Would you? Answer, I mean? What, you'd say: 'Sure, I'm ready, go ahead and beat me almost to death?'"

"'Almost?' No, I can't expect that, not really. Ready?"

Again the man flinched, again showing partiality to parts that Lee had no intention of targeting. Now, lifting high the cane (and finding that the ceiling was rather lower than he liked and problematic therefore), he came down with it, catching the man a fair-grade blow on his, indeed, solid-looking head.

"Christ!" he yelped. "How it stings! Bam! Crash!"

"And this?"

"Yes, that too! Ouch."

Now, getting into it, Lee smote and smote, and each smite he smotted, he smitted it on behalf on his own late beloved mate. The twelfth such stroke snapped the longest finger the man's left hand could claim.

"Finger! Finger!"

"Yes! But you have others."

"But, my man! You've gotten blood over all your dossier!"

"Aye, the dossier is mine. It's the blood that's thine."

And so thus again Lee—even while humming he had not lost his fencing skills. Backhands and parry, the man would never be the same again. At one moment Lee saw that he had peeled away a length of scalp that, as it lay yawning and curling on the tabletop, looked relatively like a wedge of pork. These government types, would they *never* fall unconscious? And that was when Lee, blushing at the oversight, admitted that throughout the whole time he had been using the wrong end of the cane after all! The *other* end, the more hefty one, it would put the man to sleep at once.

ELEVEN

HAVING FOULED HIMSELF WITH GOVERNMENT BLOOD, he carried out his departure with perfect aplomb. To be sure, dignity was much easier now, now that he wore a pair of government shoes. A strange smile came over him, making his lips quiver and eyes sparkle. For he was thinking forward to that moment when the bureaucrat would be found "sleeping" in his office, his two feet, poorly shod, propped up on the desk in Styrofoam soles. Thus, thinking and sparkling, Lee came out onto the street and, having searched in both directions, chose the better of them.

As always when in big cities, he liked to brush the storefronts with his *right*-hand side, thereby giving leeway, a word derived from his own first name, to the stronger of his two arms, the one that kept the cane. And then, too, he highly distrusted the joists and struts that supposedly under-girded the sidewalk, itself a mere crust that might at any time begin to break up beneath his well-shod shoes. Suddenly, jumping back, he saw what at first looked to him like an ash tree that had burst through that all-too-thin pavement—until forced to concede that it was simply a potted plant set out next to a lamp pole.

By ten-fifteen he had managed to worm his way between the closely-set buildings and then come out into a reeking alley bestrewn so with many neon advertisements that he could almost believe that he was back within his own late beloved 1950s once again. And yet the next person immediately made him change his mind, especially when she floated up near enough to let him read the expression on her face. Lee groaned. Nay, this was twentieth-*first*-century material—he knew it from the way in which she shuffled instead of walked, and from the mouth that dangled open and off to one side, as if to vent the vapor that filled her head.

He turned in at the first restaurant and then, seeing what manner of place it was, came out again. He had to travel three blocks further, stopping here and there to press his face against the windows before finally he was able to identify an establishment in which trash music wasn't playing. Once inside he aimed toward a table that seemed almost to have been designed for him, judging by the silverware, the golden napkin and fresh-cut flowers—that is to say until he saw that it would have put him in a position where his back would be exposed. Far better adapted to *his* requirements were the several empty booths. He chose one near the rear, abandoning it when he realized it would leave him too near the kitchen. Finally, after trekking up and down—he was tired and his cane was dragging—he arrived at last at the proper place and stood there resolutely until the couple brought a quick end to their conversation, stood, and gave over to him. The waitress, of course, was not anyone *he* would have employed—too tall, too gawky, red elbows. He said nothing about that however, contenting himself with hand signals to call for his own cup of coffee and then, with the signals becoming somewhat complicated, a pack of cigarettes and fresh matches. He would tip this woman, when the time came, with his Canadian penny and let *that* suffice to tell her what he thought about her.

Thinking of it, his odd unbidden smile came back again and played about his lips.

It was a garish place with walls the color of paint, a room in which a man could die or go insane. He had no respect for the clientele, however, save possibly a man in a yellow beard who sat two tables away with an easel and other artistic equipment strapped to his back. It *was* quiet here, and Lee did give thanks for that. He might almost have taken out his book, but for the lout at the pool table who continued to make a pestering noise with the stick and balls.

He had come, had Lee, to expect all things to be bad, and badness itself to be carried to higher powers. The stew, however, was good; he sipped at it suspiciously at first, but then soon enough surrendered unto the aroma, the cabbage, and the economical little shreds of meat. No one complained about his manners, or that several lengths of cabbage had ended up caught in his whiskers. Having also swilled down four cups of high-grade coffee, dark brown, he even began to experience some fellow-feeling for the other customers, something that only very rarely happened between himself on the one hand and ordinary humanity the other. Generally he was thrifty in the extreme with such feelings, and tended to bring them out only for those who were constantly striving after high things and constantly failing, the minimum pre-condition, in his opinion, for spiritual development.

He signaled for further soup but then had to wait a great while before it was at last fetched out to him in a bowl much smaller than the first and holding many fewer shreds of meats. The dog had made no demands thus far—Lee admired that—but instead had remained at attention throughout, waiting for commands. That, too, Lee admired, and wished only that the whole world had taken a similar approach during his time on earth. Outside a derelict had come up and, pressing at the glass, was pointing, first, at the food and then at his own opened mouth, which is to say until Lee glared at him severely for a considerable time, sending him on his way. Changing glasses, he managed just then to let fall the little tin box that contained his extra pair. Lee groaned, laboring to gather them off the floor.

Later on, he was to remember the shock, the sense of recognition, the dread that *this* page might not derive from the same novel, or that perhaps some other party was disseminating things that had nothing to do with Judy. And yet, the page was folded neatly enough and fixed to the table leg by means of a scarlet ribbon that he seemed to remember from the old days.

For she had left a clue behind. Quickly he scanned down the perfect prose wherein Judy herself, or one just like her, was adoringly described. Three times he read it through and having done so, turned and again evaluated the people here, the pool player, the dog, the painter and the bartender. It worried him to think that ever she had dined in such a place.

He paid and came out (snow was threatening), and then opted for a side street full of red and yellow neon signs bearing emblems representing well-known trademarks. Bars and taverns, whores and drunks—he had expected it. At one time such visions had set his heart aglow, when he was young and had believed that wickedness could be interesting. But what most attracted him now was the sight of a tidy-looking little book shop with some dozen leather-bound volumes set with unashamed cunning in a bay window of tiny square panes. Immediately he threw open the door and jumped inside, startling both the proprietor (a pale-looking and rather tremulous sort of personality) and the store's one customer, who seemed to have been standing in the corner facing the wall. Here was warmth and books were here, and there on the opposite wall an array of paper-bound volumes in such artful jackets that for a moment Lee almost forgot how that in modern times the world had become so much better at jackets than at English prose. Now, going into his other glasses (and allowing the cane to dangle from his belt), he stalked toward the shelves.

He was in a mood just now for some good reading and was prepared to be tolerant of most any style of writing provided only it had some style to be tolerant of; instead, after three paragraphs, his hand began trembling. Quickly he checked for the photograph of the author, wanting to be tolerant of her, too. And now *both* hands were trembling and his cane, hanging from his belt, had begun to describe broader and broader strokes as his indignation grew and his palsy became more and more serious. Ah yes, it had turned into an *empira feminina*, this new anti-domain of "literature" and books, a congeries of snotty-looking authoresses making plaint about something or another. Taking off his glasses and coming nearer, he believed that he might actually have been able to insert the end of his cane into the left nostril of this particular photograph and then, drilling slowly, very slowly but very diligently, ream out the contents and throw it on the floor and jump on it. But all this was as nothing when compared to the writing itself, waste material that sounded like lazy conversation spoken over the telephone by a woman lying half-asleep among the bubbles in her tub. Surely this *was* that awfulness squared, stupidity cubed, self-satisfaction reaching to the stars, against which the better Greeks had warned.

Grabbing up two of the books at hazard, both with snotty photographs, he ran with them to the cashier.

"Blackguard!" (His cane was raised on high.) "And so *this* is what you're foisting off onto"—he nodded toward the one customer—"innocent people!"

"Wait! Don't hit me, OK? Just don't! OK? Good."

Lee lowered the cane. He had not, after all, come over into

the anti-world in order to do hurt to the sellers of books.

"I just give people what they want. Free market, you understand. Don't blame me."

Lee raised the cane. "Free market? People? Want? Why, you little son-of-a-piece-of-shit! We're talking *literature* here, L-I-T-E-R-A-T-U-R-E, not 'people.' And certainly not 'market.' And *never* 'want!'"

The man grinned weakly and then, after thinking over the possibility of going for the pistol that no doubt lay in the drawer to which his gaze continually reverted, said: "Don't hit me, OK? After all, *I* didn't write that shit."

It was true. For the second time Lee lowered the cane. "Yes, there is some validity in what you say. Very well then, why don't you just read a couple of pages for us, if you will. So as to remind us of what we're both fighting against, what?"

The man seemed to look upon this as a bargain as compared to the cane. And although Lee took it upon himself to choose the book, basing his selection upon the frightfulness of the photograph, yet he left it to the man to read any passage that he would. As to the customer, a worried-looking entity who twice had tried to take his leave, Lee pointed him back both times to his corner and glared at him severely.

His voice was good, the cashier's, full of resonance and theatricality accompanied by meet gestures. The book itself, this week's most successful, was pure swill of course, and amounted to but little more than a list of approved sentiments of which the authoress seemed inordinately proud. Lee could feel a headache coming on. Minute by minute the man went on reciting, his once-strong voice melting down page by page into a kind of goo that sorted very well with what he was reading. Lee left.

He traveled far, tiptoeing past factories, past empty places, past densely occupied apartments where entire families could be seen huddling in mittens about the television set. Ignorance he saw, and a degree of poverty that almost (but never quite) satisfied what he wished for, for people of this sort.

Thus, speaking to himself (and taking care not to entrust his whole weight to the middle part of the sidewalk), Lee plodded on. No one offered to give him trouble, not even the nasty-looking little children who were so much better than their parents at reading the danger that resided in Lee's sly smile. *Their* necks were thin (and they knew it), whereas Lee's cane, ah, that was thick. They knew it.

Chill night it was when finally he had disentangled himself from the outer slums and had stepped over into the encompassing countryside. Here, vast numbers of anti-stars could be seen jubilating through the pines, as if the trees were adorned with a new sort of fruit that could gleam like these. And now for the first time in weeks Lee was able to speak out loud and in candor while at the same time dredging up favorite lines from world literature. Listening to it, his dog already had become better educated than seven-tenths of the anti-people that Lee had so far met, and at last was beginning to show promise of becoming a fit companion for such a master as he had.

But first a fire. Lee was good at that, owing to his past work with matches, and shortly enough he had made a noble blaze, yellower than sunlight. Hypnotized by it, he brought together his usual pallet of leaves and, stretching out at a judicious distance from the flames, went to sleep.

He woke twice during the night, each time finding that the dog was studying him astutely from four inches away. "Ha!" (said Lee), "I know your type—carnivore, abbreviated brain. And you call those 'feet?' Why man, I've seen ungulates in hooves that could put all four of yours to shame! No, I go further—you're nothing in this world but a . . ."

Lee stopped. The animal was looking at him beseechingly, desiring a halt to all such characterizations as these.

The third time Lee awoke, lo, it was morning. At once he leapt up in great alacrity, impressed in spite of himself by the character of today's sun. "O ye great star!" he hailed—but then had immediately to admit that another writer had used that line before him. Even so, nothing could abate Lee's gladness on this day, and especially not so once he realized that he had camped just above a clarified pond that glistened and beckoned and seemed to invite him to a swim.

And yet even here, a full mile above the city, he still hated to draw off his clothes and expose the repellent corpse that in his old age he carried with him everywhere he went. Seeing it, the sun threw up both hands and ran behind a cloud.

Really, could anything be more strange than water? Too blasé were humans, or otherwise the amazement of it had been unendurable. (Lacking integrity, it was only by the grace of something that it was able to hold together at all. The little share of it that he held in his hand sparkled at the whim of the sun.) Suddenly he yelled out loud, baying with great noise into the valley when he saw how cold this puddle really was.

Half an hour went by, Lee stranded up to his elbows in the stuff. As to the dew that had lain all night upon his head, it had blown away by favor of the dawn on this most splendid day. And when he questioned himself about his spiritual condition, that, too, he found to be good, the best in days. It also flattered him that the valley magnified the sound of his singing. Anyone traveling past at just that moment might have taken his song for that of a certain locally-remembered hero, awake again after all these years.

He hiked for miles, singing still—until persuaded by circumstance to come back again and get into his clothes. This was *his* milieu: field and woods, dog and a vermiculated countryside rilled with bright blue brooks. Behind him were hills, fog and smoke contending for the summits, and on both sides wasps in such number that they filled the South with a throbbing distinctly of its own. Was spring coming in? Certainly he very much wished for it, spring, Lee did, wishing. He had given his penny for but one single hour sans chills and shivering.

It was close to three in the afternoon before he saw that spring *had* come in, having chosen a certain niche in the western hills for its point of entry. Grinning, Lee got into his warm-weather glasses and beckoned it nearer, quite prepared to receive the brunt of it on his own wasted face. One final spring, the last in the world, let it come *now*, now when he most hungered for it. He knew, of course, the danger, and that he need only to sample the first faint smell of it in order to be sent running off down the hill with his head full of memories, memories of Judy on the day that they met.

He moaned, very loudly. He had grown so tattered, his hair so grey and split that it gave off spores each time the wind whipped about his head. "Ah me," he said, "I have been transported into a legendary person. And to think that it would come to me!" He could not but smile. Seldom had he felt more legendary, and never mind whether the world was ready to concede it to him. Never more free and never more sly, and never such a breeze from out of a climate never so recently arrived—he had been sent forward specifically to greet it. He bowed sweepingly therefore, following it up with courtly gestures. Next, he bowed again, and then slapped on his hat and strode off down the hill.

He found little that was good in the days that followed, and soon was reduced to feeding on flowers. Now that the nights were warm, he liked to position himself under the sky and lie for hours, examining each star individually as he shifted back and forth among his glasses. Each such sphere held some dead friend of his, or wife, or favorite author. But when the emergent *Dog Star* began to move into ken, and Lee had to endure the prodigious commotion that came therefrom each night (his own dog answering back), and especially when the moon was bright . . . Well! Then Lee rolled over, stopped his ears, and tried to think on other things.

It was during the afternoon of the ninth day that Lee, progressing inch by inch, suddenly uncovered a farmstead sheltering at the edge of the forest. The people themselves had gone for supplies; even so, Lee did not immediately stave in the door or destroy a window, not until he had circled around to the barn, a lipstick-colored structure, very old and full to bursting with tenants of all sorts. Once again he was reminded of the strangeness of things, and of how these simple creatures—cows and whatnot, mules and hens—of how they could be so wildly dissimilar when compared to each other in point of size, rank, cost, and underlying personality. Some had wings, others not, and still others were extremely short. That was when Lee first set eyes upon the horse.

He dashed to its side, whispering endearments into its foot-long ear. Many long years had gone by since last Lee had been privileged to gaze for any length into the eyes of one of these, in this case a roan who was looking back at Lee with but half its attention while reserving the other half for memories that dated back. Coming nearer, Lee saw wisdom of a sort, and gifts of prophecy.

"Woman called 'Judy'—hast seen her?" Lee asked. "And loose pages blowing in the breeze or hanging on a thorn—have you never come across any of *those* while on your excursions and exercises?"

No reply. Lee, unable to remove his hand from the muzzle, as soft as it was and as much like foam, believed that he could see something of a smile in the animal's amused eye. And that, of course, was when they were interrupted by the hogs. Cynical beyond belief, these had chosen to go through life with two little round holes in the most forward part of their faces. In spite of it, Lee did go to the bin, did shovel out a spade full of feed and then, changing glasses, stayed long enough to watch it disappear.

It needed some effort but finally Lee was able to coax the horse into harness, blanket, and saddle, and then guide him out into the light. The hens he left behind, but for the one he crammed into the saddle bags.

The house itself was devoid of anything that was interesting. It was when he searched out the "library," and saw what it contained that his gorge really did get the better of him. For each worthless book, he levied a penalty of one broken dish, window, or other glass thing. (They possessed, of course, far more dishes than books.) Television! He lifted high his cane, aimed, but then turned his back and walked away from the thing when he recollected that the best punishment would be to let it stay intact.

The roan was waiting. Lee leapt to saddle and spoke, pointing to the west. And although his mount might be ever so young, and the driver obviously so old, yet they harkened to each other. He would have to stay awake, Lee would, if he could, in order to keep this animal's enormous spirit under control. He could foresee a tumultuous ride coming up.

But because it was spring and sometimes chilly still, he had wrapped himself in his second-hand blanket before hoisting himself athwart the roan. Right away his thoughts flew back to Alexander and all those others who had made their names on the backs of horses. So far as he knew, none of *them* had been endowed with hemorrhoids. Nevertheless, as old as he was, he still thought of himself as the hero of his own situations, and never mind that he had to stand in the stirrups to keep from shrieking out loud. This much he felt quite sure of, that even though his wife might have a twenty years' start on him, yet she had never been able to run as fast as a horse.

All day he drove forward, the hound sometimes following, sometimes moving out ahead, and sometimes (once), making an unexpected appearance on a hilltop several miles ahead. Lee knew nothing of the names of plants, though it did please him to see the efforts they had made to find a footing in a soil that was looking more and more like sand. His steed, too, had to step with greatest care to prevent himself from being stymied in the stuff. Once only was Lee required to use the cane.

He had suspected that they were moving down into a coastal region but nothing could have prepared him for the shock when, in early afternoon, he rode up over a final hummock to descry for the first time the great green ocean itself, an unsteady terrain with froth in every place where swells were breaking. How Lee groaned, having to endure beauty like that too abruptly brought on! Behind him were hills, castles on the summits, and here in front (so near that he could almost touch it), a boat of eleventh-century type moving haltingly on the tide. There was no doubt in his own mind but that he composed a forlorn sight to the rowers on board—a tall person, noble in manner, Lee on shore.

And so thus the man—he had come after all these days and travels to the end of the land and with nothing now but pure salt sea between himself and the continents that might, or might not, extend on to perpetuity, crisscrossing time, mind, memory, and everything.

TWELVE

DAY BY DAY HE TRAVELED AND, GAZING FAR, MOANED along the sea. It was on the twelfth day he descried a little paper ship made from a book's white page tumbling in the surf. Plunging direct into the waves, he raced for it, but in spite of being on horseback failed to retrieve it. The dog barked, horse neighed, and then the current took it far away.

Already, three days earlier, he had ventured up to his waist in that strange and unevenly-pigmented surf, but only to come flying out when he found that the fluid, crowded as it was with schools of delirious minnows and some other things, was simply too thin for ordinary water. Clouds of tincture drifted this way and that, catching up the sun in glints of highly various colors. And then, too, he was appalled by the crabs. Such was their confidence and unlimited folly that they had cast aside their shells, making it all the more tempting for man and horse alike to feed upon them.

Lee's beard, meantime, grew apace, right up until the day it fell out. He had hung onto but six remaining teeth, none of them any good. And what *now* would his wife think about this, and would she still recognize in him the young and/or middle-aged man that he used to be?

Strangely, his intellect had continued to improve, and these days when he scanned the heavens, it was not just Confederate generals that he saw, but Grecian philosophers turned to clouds. Yes, it was a calm and solemn region here by the sea but already he hungered for the next world, which summoned and tempted him, and promised to free him from having continually to send back mental reports that no one wanted to read.

Indeed, there was no accounting for the thoughts that came into his head. Just now he was imagining himself across the sea and onto that successive continent where, mayhap, his wife and friends and favorite composers were waiting with a patience that could *not* endure forever. Twice he called, getting no answer but from the dog who in turn set off other voices from a certain star.

Day by day. His pants were rolled, they held seaweed in their cuffs, and sunburnt now was Lee all about the ears and neck. And then one day while pushing forward at high speed in the bent position, he happened upon an exploded corpse that was being shoved further and further ashore with each following wave. Easy to diagnose, the fellow was dead and had been treated atrociously by the same band of snails that Lee had been tracking since dawn. He could see enough, Lee could, to understand that somewhere across the sea a war had broken out. No books, no coins, though Lee searched each pocket thoroughly. Discouraged by that, he arranged his blanket and went to sleep.

Dawn, when it came, came up goldenly, but not without some blighted spots in the equation. Coming nearer he thought that he could make out a "hatch" in the sky by means of which the gulls were arriving and departing and, indeed, sometimes taking leave of the world entirely. Suddenly he ran forward, convinced that he had seen a page blowing down the beach. It was, of course, a crab.

His beard did eventually come back, even if it now bore a greenish cast bestowed by favor of the sea. Sorting through it with his fingers, it disconcerted him and hurt his feelings to find that a genre of tiny crustaceans had made a habitation in it. Day after day. Already his theoretical perspective had told him that this was no "after-world," no, but rather the same planet he had known, albeit set back a few millions of years to a point in time. But then this theory, too, fell all apart when on the twenty-third day of his so-called "Sea Coast" chapter he came onto a spit of land that extruded a full quarter-mile into the gulf. This was not in itself so remarkable a feature—he had crossed greater spits than this one. This one had a building however.

He strolled around three sides of it, noting for future reference that the windows all had bars on them. Finally, on his fourth pass, he stepped into the shade of the structure and began to translate for himself the well-known but also very dubious apothegm of Aristotle's that ran around the architrave. Having finished, he was about to go on to the other inscriptions when, that moment, a smallish man, largely bald, emerged from the front office and, using a bit of soft cloth, proceeded to erase away the "NO" in the "NO VACANCY" sign.

Lee entered, scowled, coughed, slapped his cane down across the counter and bawled out:

"Room! Fresh sheets. Adjoining toilet."

"Yes, sir!"

"And fodder for my mount."

The baldish man, largely small, nodded eagerly and then went splashing through his register. It afforded Lee a glimpse of the signatures of those who, presumably, had come this way before him. He held up his hand.

"Just one moment please—I'd like to see those names. So as to know just exactly what sort of . . . Goddamn it!" (He had to fight for it. No sooner had he seized up the ledger than the man had gone for the cane, whereupon Lee had to fight for that as well.)

"They're just regular people!" the baldish man cried.

"So I see. Second-tier, most of them. Yes, I should have expected it—you come to a second-tier hotel and the egotists are liable to be second-tier, too."

"Not all of them," the man said sullenly, nursing his wrist. "No, certainly not all." And then, as Lee continued to stare at him through his glasses: "No, not all. *I*, for example, was sitting just here"—he pointed toward it—"when old Wagner himself, the music writer, came floating past. Moving with great power, too, let me tell you, pushed by Will."

"Wagner!"

"*Those* were the days! Sign here, please."

Lee did sign, using for that purpose one of his favorite names from Grecian philosophy.

"Well then, Mr. ———, if that's what it really is. No luggage?"

"Dog."

"No dogs." (A second man, Lee now realized, had turned away from the television [which in any case was inert] and was peeking back at him over the top of his chair. Lee asked for the key.)

"No key."

Discouraged also by that, Lee nevertheless followed up the stairs and into a corridor lit only by the glow of the man's cigar. He had hoped for a normal hotel; instead, as he now attested, the doors were of iron and looked more as if they belonged to crypts or vaults than to the sort of place to which he wished he had come. Saying nothing, he stood by while the man, still very angry with him, went on dithering with the combination, a complicated maneuver that required him to refer several times to the code that he carried in his wallet. Further down a disturbance had apparently broken out behind one of the massive doors, creating a tumultuous noise accompanied by rifle blasts. Nor did Lee enjoy very much the looks of the two young bellhops who stood grinning at him from the head of the corridor.

Later on, looking back upon it, he was to come to the belief that everything that followed was the fault of the name he had given in his application. In any case, Lee now found himself standing in front of, and then, next, actually shoved inside of, the so-called *Ionian Room,* an airy place (no roof) tenanted by some two score of *Ionian men* who now came scrambling forward to take a look either at Lee, or Lee's thick glasses, of which the latter seemed to them far more fascinating than the first. Dumbfounded by that, Lee put out his hand to shake with them, saying: "Alabama branch, don't you know."

He fully expected to enjoy this encounter, having visited so often before with these same people in books and dreams. Some moments having gone past with no one agreeing to shake with him, he decided to speak up more forcibly, punctuating his remarks with small movements and facial expressions.

"Very good!" he said, "Ionian men. Nothing could be better. Myself, I've always had the most enormous respect, all those islands and so forth. 'Know thyself!' Right? Wonderful stuff, wonderful. However, in *my* case . . ." (He had started to say that he was a twenty-first-century man, catching himself just in time to carry out the necessary mental calculation.) ". . . 696th Olympiad man."

Two philosophers, unclean ones, were blocking off any further entry on Lee's part. Altogether he saw perhaps thirty such people, the majority of them seated on a narrow bench that ran down along the wall. All were in Greek dress. Smiling at them one by one and seeing that they were looking back with growing interest and high expectation, he now drew himself up to fullest height and, enunciating slowly, addressed the whole group:

"Yes, we've always had the very highest regard for all of you—the world's first thinking men!"

Silence followed, which is to say until one of the more belligerent-looking thinkers suddenly left the bench and strode forward, shouldering everyone else aside. Lee guessed that this one had gone a long time without sleep, judging from his mood. His voice was ragged, hoarse, and tinctured with an accent that tended toward the Arcado-Cypriot.

"Earth?" he asked. "Or water? Or is it simply fire?"

Lee thought about it. "It surprises me, how we're able to communicate like this, you in your tongue and me in . . ." But was he? It came down on him like thunder that perhaps he was conversing in original Greek! Enjoying it, and wishing to practice, he said: "Neither earth nor water, no. No, we've gotten past all that. No, in *my* century we've broken down even water itself into all manner of multifarious little constituents. Sorry."

The man, who was perhaps the most unwashed person in the room, began trembling with indignation and two red eyes that inspired Lee to step back a few paces. There came then into his mind a certain witticism that he could not even with all his Will forebear putting into utterance:

"And yet, assuming all *is* water, that would explain why some thinkers don't consider it needful ever to bathe."

There was a momentary silence followed by an explosion of laughter and wheezing and outright applause from all corners of the room. Several Ionians came pressing forward to shake his hand, but meanwhile the water philosopher had gone off mad. Lee knew enough to know when he had made an enemy. And knew, too, that the man had friends, students, allies, not to mention whole relays of biographers and popularizers waiting in history's wings.

But he knew also when he had made a friend, in this instance a thin man with a too-large nose who came equipped with his own set of "glasses"—two discs of wood with slits in them and held in place with rawhide laces. Always he had had the greatest respect for such people, the earliest physicists known to literature, and yet—he had to say this—he would have preferred a *fifth*-century hotel with its even higher thinkers, its better mathematicians, its more craftsworthy "glasses," etc. Of course, being second-tier himself, he must take what he can get. And now his friend had locked arms with him and was leading him away.

"Ignore this trash," the man said. "'Water,' my ass! Why some of this filth is straight out of Caria! Look at that one. Catamite. Been lying with Medes. Now you and me, *we* know what's right. *We* understand how the world and everything is composed mostly of . . ."

"Piss!" said a third man, a mischievous-looking quantity, eighty years or more in age, who had been trailing along behind them.

"Nay, *quicksilver*," said another who, however, appeared to be serious.

Lee stopped. It most certainly was *not* quicksilver—he knew that much about chemistry and never mind how beautiful the theory. Finally, after drawing out his last cigarette and igniting it (a procedure that seemed to astonish his friend), he said:

"Ah yes, quicksilver. This is perhaps the most beautiful of all the Grecian theories. And therefore, being beautiful, it must also . . ."

"Must be true!" said the quicksilver man, finishing for him.

* * *

When night came, Lee found himself trapped between two philosophers snoozing heavily on the bench. But to him the most compelling person in the group was Parmenides, a stubborn-looking sort who sat at all times in perfect rigidity, unwilling even to bat his lids. These were thoughtful people, all of them far more engrossed in memories of their own little long-ago lives than in Lee's current and on-going great one. One man indeed had snatched away Leland's cane and was using it to draw (wrongly) portraits of anti-atoms in the dust. Lee remained silent even as two of the thinkers rose suddenly, went outside, and then came back a moment later carrying between them a giant urn in which a man was dwelling. For when it rains, it's only right to fetch inside all those who reside in uncovered pots. And it *was* raining, profoundly so, with the Lord of the gods proving himself profligate tonight of thunderbolts.

Lee went on meditating deeply, side by side with the Ionians. There was no illumination of any sort, save from one weak lantern held aloft by the philosopher who had at last come out of his pot and now was going from sophist to sophist, inspecting each several face. Lee, not daring to breathe, waited as the man drew close and, bending near, brought the lamp up to within an inch or two of his face before then turning sadly away and padding off in disappointment and then again turning and coming back—Lee could feel his gorge begin to rise—and again thrusting the flame direct into Lee's line of vision, shutting off the night. By no means was this that "small world of fine people" for which Lee had been yearning all his life. Dismayed, he watched as the man with the lamp went a brief distance and then, hoisting his chiton, manured in full open view. Even so, Lee, who always had the greatest respect, was not prepared to give up on such respect at this time.

In truth, he was beginning to have some theories of his own, highly original ones about a whole raft of things. By now the serving girl had come and gone, leaving behind rather meager helpings, as it seemed to Lee, of mallows and asphodel. The stuff was simply no good and Lee put his own portion aside. It displeased him that one of the youths, a mere stripling indeed, was sitting in the lap of, and being stroked by, one of the "sea and smoke" thinkers, the very lewdest man that ever Lee had seen. Always he had had the highest respect, even for second-tier Greeks, but now he began to draw a line against certain of them. More than for the others, his admiration went out to Empedokles, a morose individual lacking one of his slippers. Apparently he had passed through a tremendous ordeal, this one had, and had come away badly scorched about the head and shoulders. For him Lee conserved an especial regard.

Dawn was near and coming closer when one of the "smoke" conjectorialists—and Lee had seen how a knot of them had been conferring excitedly—came up and challenged him to a trial.

"You be so clever," (the man said), "for one who comes from barbarous parts. Possibly you'd like to engage in a knowledge contest?"

"Please!" said Lee. "You fellows are *Greeks*, whereas I . . ." (He *was* intrigued however.) "Knowledge contest?" And then: "Naw! Besides, I'm only second-tier material."

"In sooth. But then you have the advantage of all those generations of men between thee and we. That ought to be worth something."

"You might be surprised."

"Your 'microscopes,' your 'computers,' your 'ball point pens and ink.' Great Pan, what couldn't *we* have done with these!"

Lee, who knew what *had* been done, looked down and blushed.

"Contraceptive devices."

"Corn-fed beef."

"Glasses made from glass."

"Ocean-crossing vessels pulled by whales."

"Self-knowledge made complete."

Lee tried to hold up his hands and stop them. "Gentlemen! You're simply hypothesizing out of all control! No, in real actuality, things now stand much worse than when you-all were tinkering about with simple instruments and drawing triangles in the sand. No, I must tell you that . . ."

They didn't believe him.

"Beauty!" said the man with the large nose. "A civilization given over heart and soul to the pursuance of divine Beauty itself! Oh, oh, oh, why could not I have come forth in *your* time, instead of merely in mine?"

"Gentlemen!"

But it was too late. They were dreaming now, dreaming Grecian dreams which no one must impede. It gave Lee time to do some dreaming of his own, about Greeceland and its things.

They breakfasted on mallows and cabbage and then immediately went back to thinking again. Finally, at about ten, a sunbeam pierced through the tangle of vines that served in lieu of a roof. At once the thinkers arose and came forward, marveling at the ray and even, some of them, sticking their fingers in it. Lee, who had the advantage of modern science, did *not* go forward. On the contrary, he was gazing up at the top of one of the columns where once many years ago someone had rolled up a milk-white page and nudged it amid the blossoms.

When noon came (pushing the sun to its apogee), Lee looked for, but could not find, the "night" philosophers, who believed all things were composed of dark. That was when the serving girl returned, unlocked the gate, and led them down to shore. Fifteen minutes they were allowed, fifteen only, and yet they were grateful for even so little as that. From many indications, it looked as if a group of modern Americans had only just retired, leaving behind all manner of wrappings and aluminum cans. The Greeks, of course, were interested in this material, but especially an empty shotgun shell which touched off all sorts of speculation. Here in bright sun, Lee's respect put on new growth. To be sure, some of the smaller thinkers continued to plash about in the sea like children, crying aloud whenever one or another of them got nipped by a bream. Suddenly, just then, Lee's dog came bounding up, his tail wagging at both ends and his face all covered in smiles—the varmint had not run off and left Lee after all! Unhappily, the quicksilver man had no liking for dogs.

"What? Be you Cynic then? I've been deceived."

Lee tried to protest. From where he stood, he could see Greeks up and down the coast, many of them flat on their backs as they gazed up in rapture at the anti-sun. Heraclitus, meantime, was hopping mad, though Lee knew not precisely why. Always he had had the greatest respect and had so still, but was he, really, *learning* anything? He had wanted a higher grade of wisdom, *fifth*-century stuff, and with it books, books and music, books, music, and a stone-built house with Judy waiting in the door; instead, he simply turned and strode off down the shore.

THIRTEEN

DAY AFTER DAY, HIS HORSE NEVER RETURNED. THE spring weather had also abandoned Lee, giving way to a summer so normal and nice that his powers of egotism began to recover and then, shortly thereafter, to burst out cubed and squared. He was, in short, once again that "legendary person" who used to rise each morning at a certain hour, go forth and pee and, seeing that the sun had turned beet-red already, used to shake his stick at it. Or, he might stroll a mile or more down the coast, still calling for his horse.

And so it was one day that while talking to himself with more than the usual bitterness he set eyes for the first time upon a little islet not far offshore that gave every suggestion of being inhabited. He could not know, of course, that this was to bring him to yet another adventure, dangerous in the extreme, and yet covering four pages only.

He still did know how to swim, did Lee, in spite of his ailments, his years, and the heavy cane that had to be transported in his teeth. Soon he had crossed the greater part of the distance but only to be subjected to the most intense disappointment when he saw that the dog had lost courage and was turning back for the mainland. Lee was devastated. Himself, he had always preferred to drown or die than to fail in any undertaking, and now the beagle and he could never be colleagues again.

No dog, no horse, Lee pulled himself out onto dry land along with his cane, his book, his penny, and his government shoes, now so much the worse for the soaking they had endured. He was too exhausted to give much attention to the women, one of them black and the other, seemingly, a Filipino (she was weeping) who had come down to give him help.

"No, this is *outrageous*!" said the first woman. "And at *your* age!"

No, this is just one more example of it, gerontism, and with the whole world watching, too!"

"And yet I used to swim so well."

"They should *do* something. The government, I mean."

"*Those* pigs?" (Filipino speaking.) "Ha!"

Lee looked at them. "Actually it's my dog, you see—he turned out to be a *real* disappointment. The devil with him."

"No, no, no, you shouldn't say that. I mean, like, you're not a *speciesist*, are you?" They were leading him on compassionately, the Asian woman now and again daubing at him with the hem of her skirt. In front, he could begin to see the settlement itself, a congeries of tiny huts fabricated primarily out of driftwood and palm fronds. As to the villagers, Lee saw some two score of them seated in a circle, hands enjoined, singing folk songs. They greeted him with warmth and salutations, more indeed than he had any right to expect. His tendency was to remove his hat, but then, remembering he no longer had one, he turned instead and bowed with deep courtesy to each and every woman in the circle.

"Oh look, his glasses are all wet!"

At once two men ran to fetch a towel for him and meanwhile a third person was tendering food of a sort, a paste-like material served in a coconut shell. They were *surviving* here, but by no means *thriving*. Lee asked:

"How long have y'all been camped out here, I wonder?"

"Oh, years."

"Years! But I would have thought that by now . . . Ah! No doubt it was a typhoon or tidal wave that took away your houses. Yes, and carried off your agriculture along with it, your science, your opera houses, and the rest. Yes."

They laughed. "Oh heck no, we don't need stuff like that, man! Not *here*, anyway."

"How do you figure?"

"Imperialism, man! And inequality and stuff—that's what stuff like that does."

"Ah! No doubt, no doubt." (The man had come to his feet and was watching Lee narrowly. It gave Lee the strangest feeling, namely that his safety was in danger.)

"You don't *approve* of that, do you? Inequality and stuff?"

"Certainly not! Poof! What do you, like, take me for?"

They looked at each other, the people and Lee.

"It's like this, doctor, in your day a person had to, what, *measure up* to stuff? But now we treat everybody the same, no matter who."

"'No matter who,'" Lee repeated slowly and thoughtfully, his mind rummaging out over the implications of that philosophy. "Yes, I've heard of this. Beautiful, beautiful." And then, seeing that they remained skeptical of him: "Certainly that's the best attitude with which to greet someone of *my* sort! Ha! Ha!"

They didn't believe him. Lee hummed. Unfortunately, he had been staring too much at one woman in particular.

"What are *you* looking at?"

"Me?"

"Because I'm a lesbian?"

"She may be a lesbian," said another, "but I'm just as lesbian as she is. And *I'm* black!"

It was true. Lee went back to his food. It was then that one of the children succeeded in burning himself on the knee when a spark jumped out of the fire. Immediately some dozen adults came clustering around, soothing and compassionating in a way that would not have been thought possible just one generation earlier.

"Oh! Oh! He's burnt!"

The whole circle began to moan and sway. Seeing that, the boy commenced to cry even as the two lesbians went on smearing his injury with cabbage paste. It needed six full minutes for the commotion to die down again, for a song from the 1960s to be sung, and for a hollow voice to be heard from one of the huts:

"O.K., you may be a lesbian, and you, O.K., you may be a lesbian *and* black, but me, I'm black *and* a lesbian, and *I've been raped*!"

There followed a long, deep, awed silence, each man, woman, and lesbian waiting to see if this could be bettered. One of the Choctaw women had meantime taken out some half-dozen bleached vertebrae and was throwing them over and over, like dice, as if to read the future in their permutations. Again Lee erred by turning to look at her.

"What's *your* problem, asshole? You some kind of *chauvinist*, or something?"

"*Fascist* is what he is. I knew that right away, when he tried to take off his hat."

"Hardly! No, ha, no, I just . . ."

"Now listen here, 'sir,' we've tried to be caring and diverse, but if we start getting any more of that race, gender, integrity shit . . ."

"Look at that! Why I don't think he has any compassion at all! Kill him."

It was too late to kill him however. For already Lee had arisen and, holding to his hat, had run off as fast as his legs could carry him and thrown himself into the sea.

FOURTEEN

HIS TIME WAS DRAWING NIGH. AND IF AT NIGHT HE still sometimes did think of self-murder, and if by day he strove continually to get beyond hearing of the folk songs, yet there were other occasions when he might clamber up to the crown of one or another of the briar-covered hills, there to spy down into the tremendous city that glowed and pulsed with an opaline sheen that called and fascinated and made him tremble. He knew what he knew, and what he knew about cities was not good, not when it came to cities. And yet, his appetite for news continued unabated, as did also his craving for one last night between ordinary sheets on a flat bed with blankets, pillow, and adequate slats, a medium in which he would lie him down and "go swimming," so to speak, in that most to be envied of all estates, called "non-existence."

Day after day, and then one day he came to a coconut tree with numerous great nuts in it. He had heard mention in books about the "milk" such nuts had been shown to contain, a beverage so much the better by far (the book had gone on to say), than the green salt sea that he had actually been consuming over the past thirty-four days. And then, too, he faulted his diet for the insidious little crabs (larger than fleas but smaller than cats), that now infested his beard and sent him into rages six times per day. No scissors. For if he had had a scissors—but he didn't—he might finally have been shut of the things.

He came stealthily toward the tree, approaching it from the rear, and after hurling his cane direct into the foliage, held out both arms to receive some nuts. But so far from "receiving" anything, he began slowly to realize that he had lost his cane. Even then he did not lose hope, not until the dog began barking at him, as if to notify the world of how foolish Lee looked with both arms held out, eyes squeezed tight, waiting for things to drop.

He cursed and stamped and kicked up clouds of the fluffy yellow sand. Nothing could bestir this tree. And yet, in younger days, he could have climbed easily all the way to the top, there to spend an entire afternoon smiling and swaying quite mindlessly, gloating over the tremendous number of years that still lay before him. But now in these latter times, he cursed and whined and swore, and then finally whipped out his thing and peed on it.

He knew this, that he had more lief go unclothed into the anti-world than to continue without benefit of cane. Already the anti-sun had burnt him down to but rind and pith, and had given him the color of old Ramses III when after that one had lain for thousands of years in bandages and unguents. Finally he (Lee) *did* try to climb, one inch per moment, but only then to come sledding back down again to the great prejudice of his rectal condition.

It was close to twilight when he descried the cold weather egotists (the few that remained) migrating forlornly down along the borders of the sea. Lee hid. They had not prospered, no, and it was in vain that he waited for the Latinist who, however, never appeared. Lee let them pass by, waiting until they were out of view, or nearly, before yanking out his handkerchief and using it to wave them on their way.

With darkness now so near, Lee took up his precious book, kissed it twice, and then sent it flying and flapping after the cane. Let him lose this volume, the only one he had, and his continuing education in the Greeks would have come to a premature end; instead, the cane did fall, the book, too, and several nuts as well. What he had *not* expected was that sixth item, a thing that fluttered and hesitated and proved hard to catch in mid-flight—page 189 from a certain book authored by its writer.

Night after night, he read the page until daylight came. For he had reached that point in his exertions where there was no further help for it than to gather up his objects and, slowly and reluctantly and with many a backward glance, turn his gaze, not indeed to the distant jagged mountains endued in smoke and haze, no!, but rather to the city itself, and all bad expectation.

F I F T E E N

HE CAME BY WAY OF THE SLUMS, PASSING IN AND OUT of a crowd of poor people who, apparently, had not had their fill of poverty while still on earth. It was, of course, the children who worried him most and made him nervous; twice he had to spin and face them, fixing them with his 17,000-book glare.

In matters of poverty, he considered himself a connoisseur. Lucky to be Lee, he could actually see into several of the apartments where here a widow was knitting by the window and there an old man was coughing himself to death on a worn-out mattress that had lost the major part of its cotton. Not that Lee wanted anything to do with these people—quite the contrary! Say rather that his sympathies had mostly dried up, and he no longer had feelings except for those who were continually striving and always failing, the aptest of all conditions for spiritual development. And then, too, he could not but feel himself flattered when he saw the expressions on people's faces as they scurried to get out of his way. Poltroons all, all of them exhibiting poltroonery squared. "Troons!" he yelled, grinning at them far and near. And that, of course, was when a powerful-looking car (*three* axles), truly an enormous thing (it needed two drivers), came and stopped and threw him in the back seat and—and Lee screamed—carried him away.

He was transported straight down into the city's business district, a beige-colored section flanked on both sides with flat-top sandwich-shaped office buildings with walls of glass. It must be noon, Lee calculated, judging by the pedestrians, a fast-moving population, enviably shod, and dressed for camouflage in beige-colored suits. He had seen this before, this late-century amalgam of hurry and prosperity and . . . he didn't really know what to call it. Pressing at the window with palm and nose, he tried to overlook the fact that he had been made a prisoner by four youngish-looking men (*extremely* well-dressed), whose faces showed no expression of any kind that he was able to read. Nodding to them one by one, he held out his hand, making it available to any who might wish to shake it.

"Pefley," he said, "Alabama branch. And yes, I plan to do something about it as soon as possible—my appearance I mean. Shave, etc. And the rest of it. So!"

None answered. Just now they were running through a neighborhood of superb homes, structures of four and five stories with balconies and fountains with sculptures in them. The youngest of the men noted his amazement.

"You approve of those homes, Dr. Pefley?"

Lee admitted it. "Gosh," he said. "And just look at that one! Why it must be the post-mortem residence of some great philosopher or composer. Melville's house, is it? Poe's?"

"Who? No, actually that's the summer place of one of the finest strong side tackles in the country. Hell of a nice guy, too."

"And *that* one! Moses!"

"I can see you have good taste. That one belongs to a really great man, doctor. He picked just the right time to unload half a million contracts of orange juice futures. Two lovely children, too."

"And there! Happy the man or woman who dwells in that!"

"Lottery winner."

"And yonder!"

"Rock singer."

Lee gaped at it. He had subscribed all his life to the meritocracy theory, and now he was being vouchsafed a look at one of the meritocrats himself, a fat man in an undershirt snoozing by the pool.

He went on gaping as they drove into the city proper, a blistered area of asphalt, glass, and federal buildings flying the beige flag. He felt quite sure, Lee did, that he was being taken off to jail, a proceeding familiar to him from boyhood days; instead, to his perplexity, the car ran down suddenly into a basement so dark that it sent him scrambling for his other glasses.

The elevator itself, the hugest that ever he had seen, was provided with armchairs, a bar, and two large televisions connected umbilically with a computer, or similar machine. Seeing all this (and dizzied by the too-rapid ascension), Lee began to experience the sort of fear to which he had thought himself immune. For in his thinking, terror was much more associated with luxury than with even the most austere austerity, not to mention common poverty.

Pulled from the elevator, he was led forward at double pace to a sumptuous office wherein half a dozen secretaries and receptionists (snotty-looking types!) glanced up at him fleetingly with that impatient boredom that he, as an old man, knew that he deserved. Fashionably thin, their peevish little faces all showed signs of annoyance mixed with various amounts of discontent. And yet, given just five minutes alone with them, Lee felt quite confident that he could have taught them everything they needed to know about respect, trembling, astonishment, and bright red *blood*.

He was given no such opportunity. Instead he was immediately prodded forward into an inner office where a certain man—Lee jumped back—sat waiting in bandages and plaster casts and a brace of some kind that kept him looking up into the sky. They knew each other well, even if, in Lee's opinion, the man was supposed to be dead.

"Alabama branch," said Lee, drawing back his hand and allowing his smile to fade away naturally, as it were, and with no untoward haste. Not once did he laugh out loud, despite the man's rather ludicrous way of peering out over the top of his desk from what appeared to be an orthopedic chair of some description. And then, too, one of his eyes, ingeniously contrived, seemed made of onyx. They looked at each other, Lee using *both* his eyes.

"Very good!" said Lee. "Sorry about the eye. But such nice furniture you've got here! And just look at those drapes!" (He went toward the drapes but then stopped abruptly when he discerned what looked to be a milk-white page pinned to the sun-facing side. That ever *she* had been in this place, and with an interviewer like this one . . . It didn't bear thinking of.)

"You did this to me."

"Say what?"

"You, it was always you. Reactionary snob. Why, I ought to have you beaten to death with your own rod!"

Lee hummed. The man, deprived of all pleasures except cigars, had taken into his mouth a good three or four inches of the detestable thing, putting himself in peril, as one would have thought, of choking on the cabbage shreds. Seeing that, Lee could feel his own left hand tightening about the cane.

"Yes, 'doctor,' I've thought a lot about you, and what I would do. Got any money?"

Ruefully, Lee took out all that remained to him, a leaden penny of grand size that chimed and clattered and seesawed back and forth ringingly before agreeing to lie flat on the person's therapeutic desk. Twice the man counted it, finally forcing the coin down deep into the genuine briefcase of leather that, in the event, seemed to have been designed for it. "Fire?" he asked. "Or water?"

Lee thought. "Water, the Smyrneans say. Me, I tend to quicksilver and the dark."

"O for heaven's sake, I'm talking *punishment* man! Not philosophy."

"Ah! Well then, water I reckon."

"Fair enough. We'll make it fire."

Fire. Of all the ways of dying, Lee had wanted this one least, based upon his familiarity with matches and southern heat. He could feel his Will getting smaller at the thought of it, his stamina and uncommon qualities all undone in the face of a jeopardy so awful. "Will it be quick?" he asked.

"Well of course not. Oh no, no. No, I can make it *very* tedious."

Lee began to weep. "Maybe if I could just have one more chance . . ."

But here the man began to snort and giggle, a rollicking interlude that had him bouncing in his various slings and casts. Outside, meantime, the afternoon sun had coagulated by now and was foisting a most gorgeous afterglow upon the cloth-of-gold curtains. But not for one moment was Lee able to take his mind off the burning.

"There *is* one possibility . . ." the man said.

"One!"

"But no, I don't think so. Forget what I said."

"What? What, what? What?"

"I was about to suggest . . . Naw!"

"What, what? I can be *very* coöperative."

"Postponement."

"Postponement!—sounds good to me; I'll vote for that. In

fact, you can postpone it for *years*, and still I won't complain."

"Six months. Of course, you'll have to show yourself worthy of it."

"I do, I will, I agree to all those terms!" (He stuck out his hand for shaking.) "Six months, that ought to give us time to clear up this whole misunderstanding."

"You'll have to meet all sales targets of course."

"I can do that! I who once wrote a full book within an only slightly larger block of time."

"Perfect attendance. Positive attitude—can you do that? Good grooming?"

Lee looked down at his grooming. The man, meantime, was suffering from his inability to scratch in places that were deep within his casts. It inspired Lee to offer him the cane, an unprecedented loan on his part to someone like that, who was slow to give it back.

He was conveyed down posthaste to the haberdashery at the bottom of the building and made to stand at attention while two fashion specialists meditated on his appearance. To win success it was necessary to have a suit where the pockets slanted like *that*. Lee so wanted to do right, he who once had thought that all of life was to be like certain strains of fine music infinitely prolonged. Just now the foremost of the experts, himself wonderfully groomed, was striving to match a shirt to Lee's blue-grey beard. Lee, meantime, was reconsidering the fire, and wondering for how much less than a full hour he might have to put up with it.

"Oh dear," said the clothier. "Goodness! No, you just *must* be more cheerful than that, doctor. After all, a thousand units isn't all that easy to sell."

Lee now put on what was probably the most affirmative smile that ever he had worn. He couldn't hold it, of course, not when he had never been able to do so while on earth. His teeth, their color, number, and placement, it all worked against him.

"Whew! No, better *not* to smile. Look, I can only do so much. Come now, try it again, that's right —bland! bland!"

Lee did try. The second man, knowledgeable about socks and ties, had moved in close and was struggling to form Lee's lips (badly split after seven weeks in the salt sea breeze) into an expression that was not absolutely typical of him.

SIXTEEN

WITH SUMMER IN THE CITY AND LEE WORKING harder every day, he came at last to believe that even fire was better than to go on practicing for much longer as a businessman. Nor could he count the days since last he had read a page, or thought a thought, or scrutinized even the nearest stars. But all this passed away into entire inconsequentiality when set beside the *people*, a tanned species, vacuous beyond description, who came together three times each week in order to talk about the units.

Lee looked at them. Out of all that crowd, none were better groomed than the boy seated just next to him. Coming nearer, Lee stared at the side of his face, a sheet of latex, as it seemed, but supplied with the usual orifices. Just then the woman who was the leader of them all burst out into a laughter that was so sophisticated, the notes so clear and the woman herself so good at units that she had been made the leader of them all. Divorced but twice, she was understood to be carrying on with both district managers at once. Suddenly Lee pulled himself up—he had been working until 3:00 am in the morning on his marketing report and it needed all his great Will to keep from dozing off in this luxurious ambiance. The table alone, he reckoned, carried a higher price than his grandfather's best team of mules added together, even with a cow thrown in on top. So bright was that table, it reflected back with fair accuracy the features of the company's founder, a far-seeing man whose massy portrait was fixed to the wall. No one dared place his or her cup on *that* region of the table. Again Lee looked around at them, baffled, as he had always been, by people such as these. And now did he in truth begin to regret his Ionian men, thinkers all.

Probably he slept. In any case, looking back upon it later on, he was to remember being nudged awake by the boy next to him and then invited to stand and give his report. He did so hate it, having to clear his throat and then, furrowing his brow (already furrowed sufficiently by age), having to confess that he was still very far from having sold his thousand.

"I see," the woman said dryly. "And exactly how many *have* you sold, yes?"

Lee strove to make himself look more or less like the founder. Twenty units he had sold, no more, and even those had been a piece of generosity on the part of the not unkindly boy who sat at his side. Again Lee furrowed, saying:

"Schopenhauer tells us that if . . ."

"Again with that? How many *units*, doctor, that's what *we* want to know."

"Well! After all, it's not as if I haven't sold *any*," he laughed, "good Lord no! Why one could almost say that . . ."

"You're not going to tell us are you?"

"Certainly I'm going to tell! Certainly. But just now I need to go to the restroom."

"Restroom again. You're sick. But you *will* tell us, doctor, sooner or later. Because if you don't . . ."

Suddenly a great clamor could be heard coming from the street below. They rose at once, all of them, and went hurriedly to the window, arriving in time to see a band of ragamuffins filing past, their appearance alarming the dogs, exciting the children, and bringing out onto their balconies the usual bawds and scolds with their cabbages. Lee, too, joined in with the others in throwing things down on top of them, recognizing at the same time the Latinist (whom he had believed extinct), and other former companions from his "second-tier" days, a sorry-looking crowd reduced by now to scarce a dozen souls and one—he knew not whose—new born baby girl.

"Just look at that garbage," the Vice-president said. "Why oh why do they do it I wonder, all that marching back and forth, poorly groomed."

Lee hurled an ashtray but then took it back when he recalled that he was himself the only smoker in the organization. Among the confusion, a wonderful notion had come to mind, namely to flee this room as quickly as he could and go at once to his favorite toilet, all of which he actually did. No report today! They would simply have to go on without him.

Thus passed the days. Or passed thus, rather, half an hour on the toilet during which his powers of anticipation carried him forward through many more days than just this current one. Compared to what he knew about the city and his position within it, the nuisance in his hemorrhoids was as nothing, a mere quirk, almost indeed a relief. Never would he sell a thousand units, nor understand how modern people had come to care about such stuff.

Truth was, he regretted the pre-post-modern world, obsolete these seventy years. Regretted his wife and regretted his youth, and regretted the discontinuation of moonlit walks through pines and kudzu. Yes, and how he did so abhor the modern regime, a life of enterprise and so many units that he could not find an unencumbered place in which to rest his head.

Nevertheless he emerged smiling affirmatively and then headed quickly for the next toilet, his third-favorite, on the forty-second floor. Already he had resolved to ambush the first man who might dare to enter what he now held to be his own private quarters—ambush, slay, put the cane to him and then down the hole with all such types forever! Instead, he slept.

S E V E N T E E N

DAY AFTER DAY, HE NEVER SOLD A THOUSAND UNITS. His noontide now approached, the moment of his punishment. And although he might give every evening to his wardrobe and whole days to meetings, and further days beyond that to working on his marketing analyses—strange rapture, that!—yet never did he come to share in the new world's enthusiasm for such matters. *His* admiration (which he kept under lock and key), flew back to his own dear dead grandfather who had labored himself to death while striving to plow in red clay, and oftentimes when it was raining. And did *that* one's ghost now look down upon *this*, a congeries of extraordinarily well-dressed people who had fainted at the mere mention of the wet smell of wet mules in damp weather? Truly, men "without qualities" were these, whileas for the "women!" . . . And in short, they could have all exchanged relationships, one with another, and never marked the change.

Day after day, and then one day, after having been sent to stand in the corner, even his great patience began to wane. The dog was better at it, standing in corners, but after some hours he, too, began to whine. At one moment Lee was actually on the verge of turning and yelling out some unfavorable comment about the units, or reveal that one of the salesmen was wearing a last month's tie; instead, he went back to humming.

"Pefley!"

Lee hushed. "Ma'am?"

"We're trying to get something done over here, *capisce*?"

"Yes, ma'am." He was standing so near to the wall, even his best glasses were unavailing. Accordingly it was only when he took them off that he was able to discern a rather faded drawing of a page with one or two still-legible words—words that he seemed to remember from the old days—inscribed in the picture of the margin. It hurt him, knowing that *she* had stood where he was standing, and that such a one as that had been made to share in this anti-post-normal way of life. Gorge rising, he hummed again, louder than before. He was aware that the woman, a stern-looking exhibit in boots and yard-broad shoulders, had come to her feet and was standing, hands on hips.

"Pefley!"

But Lee, too late to halt, was already into the final measures of his favorite aria. Never yet had he thrashed a woman to death, although he could remember nothing in his philosophy that seemed to prohibit it.

"Oh, you're a fine one!" she said. "Three weeks, right? And how many units, if I may be so bold?"

"Twenty. But they were good ones!"

"Good? What's 'good' got to do with anything? This here's a *publishing house* for pity's sake, not some little hoity-toity oh la la something or another what can't pay its own bills!"

Lee turned. There was a largish man at the table who, having done 3,000 units in one four-day space, had been given a place near the woman; apart from him, Lee saw no one who could offer much hindrance to what he planned to carry out within the next few following moments. He said:

"Yes, you're an aggressive and highly strong woman, very diverse and the rest of all that. And yet, within the next few following moments, I'm going to be doing something—that's right!—and doing it with . . ."—he displayed the cane—". . . cane!"

In the beginning, she simply threw back her head and laughed at him. Lee, meantime, continued to unsheathe the stick, an evolutionary procedure that seemed to entrance the members of the committee. Lee winked at them, grinning at the one or two who appeared to understand what was coming up. Now, with the woman laughing in a somewhat less confident style, the largish man arose and relocated to a more distant region of the room.

It had taken a long time but at last the cane did come free and, leaping up into the air, seemed to burnish there. The dog barked, the men of the committee cried out in admiration, and now was it the woman's time to hide *her* face in the corner. And where now, pray, was that strong and highly competent person of just six seconds ago? Upper body strength!—even at age seventy-three Lee still had more of it than she. Yea, and planned to use it, too!

"Pow!" he said, fetching her a medium-strength blow across the shoulder that immediately snapped the bone. "Bam, crash!" (Again he came down with it, only distantly aware of the applause that had broken out along the bench. He had no determination to murder her all at once, not while she had so many other bones still intact.) The fifth blow brought her to her knees.

"I can't believe this," she said, "really. I don't know, it just doesn't seem *realistic*."

Lee agreed and then, using this interval to address the men said: "See? *You* could have been doing this all along. And even now it's not too late!"

They nodded slowly, some of them showing evidence of understanding.

"But *will* you? Take back the mastery into your own hands? You, for example, you with the tan, will *you*?"

"I might."

"No you won't. And never will."

The largish man now slowly raised his hand and then, getting Lee's permission to speak, grew suddenly uncomfortable with the whole topic and sat back down again. The woman meantime—and Lee did not fail to see what she was doing—was trying to crawl away. He followed courteously for a certain distance, even at one point removing a chair from out of her line of march. His legend was growing, his whiskers, too, and these days when he brought his rod into play he did it with power and style and a pattern of strokes too complicated for any ordinary eye to see.

"Bam, pow!" And then: "Nay, but those bones of yours be frail! You should be more like me." And then again: "Smash, bam, pow," all through the rest of that meeting. Yes, he did have to pause once (to get into other glasses), but shortly he was back again, wanting a nearer look at what he had achieved. And each smite he smote, he smitted on behalf of the resurrection of the Male.

EIGHTEEN

HAVING RETREATED TO THE MEN'S ROOM AND HAVING locked the door, only then did he begin to appreciate how great was the damage he had done to his career. Thinking on that, and knowing that shortly he must wend his way homeward in blood-stained trousers through crowds of city people, he was flooded with an anxiety for himself that, together with an outbreak of coughing on his part, put in peril his hiding place. Home, he said? He had no home, not with the authorities having no doubt already invested his rented quarters. Accordingly he rose now and went where he went always when in similar exigencies—his *real* habitat in the slums.

They hit the street and came into the worst of the neighborhoods at just after four, the dog running on ahead. Thankfully the people in this district were too engrossed in their troubles to give heed to an elderly man in unclean clothes. Lee bowed graciously therefore, putting on his most gentlemanly manner, a sight so seldom seen in these parts that the ruck parted for him voluntarily and kept out of his way.

At his favorite tavern he entered and changed glasses and made a tour of the place. Ignorance he saw, whole mountains of it, futility, self-loathing, alcoholism, illiteracy, and the rest.

Nevertheless, and because they had been good enough to fall silent at the sight of him, Lee decided to remain here for a time, a concession to the people, the dog, and to his thirst. He needed a period of calm and reflection, even a glass of spirits perhaps; what he most certainly did *not* need was for a representative of the local fauna to come and sit next to him. For he had measured this crowd, Lee had, and knew that he could not and never would be able to thrash the whole bunch of them together at the same time. Instead he hummed, drank, smoked, and then ordered the dog to the opposite corner where, in case of problems, they would have the room "surrounded," as it were.

He was doing well, Lee, thinking and drinking. The beer was dark enough, the place sufficiently gloomy, and the people habituated to speaking in whispers only. He turned to thank them for that, using a gracious movement of head and hand. And that, of course, was when the social worker came and sat next to him.

He seemed a cheerful person, friendly to an extreme fault. Lee, groaning, moved away a few inches and when that failed, relocated to the end of the bar, which proved likewise unsuccessful. Impossible not to shake with the man, who insisted upon it and smiled continually as he nudged Lee in the ribs. Lee, however, pointed to the sound of the five o'clock whistle, saying:

"Such noise! And soon now, I suppose, the roads will be full of traffic. We won't be able to hear each other anyway, and so there's no use in . . ."

"What?"

"Won't hear."

"'Beer?'"

"No, no, '*hear.*' Won't hear."

"What?"

Lee looked to the dog, who got quickly to his feet. The noise had stopped.

"It's stopped now," said Lee, "the five o'clock whistle."

"Pretty obvious, isn't it? Cheez! There's not a man in this room who doesn't know that. And what's that goo all over your pants?"

"Look, all I ever wanted from you . . ."

"I don't know. To me, I don't know, I figured you for an *educated* man. But now . . ."

Lee could feel a headache coming on. His stool, far too tall and tenuous and with a stem that was too flexible by much and liable at any moment to snap off—it was bad both for his condition and his old-time fear in the face of heights. Finally he offered this:

"We could go sit in one of those booths."

"No, I don't think so. Old hound sitting over there—see him?" And then:

"Say, what *is* it with you—some kind of *rectal* problem or something?"

Finding impurities in the beer, Lee had called for another which, however, the social worker considered a gift for himself. It was the last of Lee's money; he watched enviously as the fellow drank triumphantly and then washed it down with ale. He was a competent drinker, quite pleasant really, and had no sooner finished with the tankard than he began nudging and smiling, as if expecting yet another boom of the honey-colored stuff, as good as it certainly was.

"No funds," said Lee. "Or, we could sit at that table."

"*I* have funds."

"Oh? How much? Altogether, I mean."

"Hey, watch it! Jeez, you almost fell off onto the . . ."

"Floor." He transferred to other glasses. Already he had caught sight of himself (with long grey hair) in a mirror that itself had also greyed very badly owing to the wear and passing of time. Strangely, the mirror was focused in such a way as that only his own face and no one else's stood out sharp and clear. But as to the nude whose portrait ran the entire length of the already very long bar, it made his gorge rise. He demanded more lushness than that in women of his, "meat and potato girls," and mature enough to have remembered the 1950s. The man was saying:

"Consultant, are you? Or barrister? Surely you aren't going to tell me that you dress like that, with customized lapels, just to come to a place like this!"

"Ph.D," said Lee. "Before I died, I mean."

"'Died?' You won't be dead, not in the real sense, not until your author has died. Surprises me you didn't already know that."

"'Author?'" (It was the first Lee had heard of this. A look of frank amazement passed across his face.)

"And besides, we don't use that word, doctor, not here. We just don't. Sorry."

"Ph.D?'

"No, 'died.'"

Three beers went by, Lee paying for none of them. The man appeared to have all manner of coins and paper, coupons and cards, wherefore Lee determined to absorb as many dollars worth of fluid as he could against the hard times still to come. But first he must listen to the man's life, a useless one in which Lee was able to detect that he was actually more interested in the history of his own small doings and former wives than in Lee's current on-going great one, or in Judy. Right away Lee wrote him off, just as he had always off-written such people, and such wives.

Even so, Lee permitted him to go on at length, until at last he came down to telling about his social work career.

"To *lift* them," said he, his face all smeared with compassion, "and give them at least a chance to . . ."

"A strange thing, you and me. For my part, I had far rather push people *in* than to lift them *out*. Deeper, deeper. *Greater* poverty, lovelier, too, and more intense forms of stupidity!" (For in spite of himself, Lee had consumed too much brown beer. Now, coming down off his stool, he stood, well-positioned, emphasizing with his stick each new idea that came into his head.) "Take away their poverty, man, and you take away their glory!"

"Damn right!" (Lee could not see who had said it. It seemed to come from the dark part of the room.)

"I do wish you wouldn't poke me with that thing. And so you want to make life even more difficult for them, is that what it is?"

"It is. I have been places and seen things and I know what they are, they who never have tasted poverty. Come on, give it back man, and let them have at least *some* chance for spiritual improvement!"

"Yeah! Give it back!" (The customers were becoming agitated and—Lee could not but feel flattered by this—were taking *his* part in the quarrel.) The welfare worker, meantime, seemed to be mulling over what Lee had said, the expression on his face showing that his whole philosophy had been put at hazard. Lee made a concession to him:

"But I wouldn't worry overmuch about it. After all! You don't seem to have had any effect on anything, not even after . . . What? Twenty years?"

The man nodded.

They strolled for blocks, the social worker never leaving his side.

"And when you navigate through crowds, never, never allow your gaze to become entangled with that of others. It leads to conversation."

The man noted it down.

"And when you feel yourself most exhausted, that's the time to put on your most aggressive airs. Otherwise, they're liable to choose that moment to make their pounce." And then: "You have a salary, I suppose, for all your hard work? Yes, I hadn't thought of that."

The man admitted it. Lee could not, however, guess how large that salary was, not until he should have a better look at the man's apartment with all its rooms and things.

NINETEEN

He hurried to get out of his business clothes. But then had immediately to climb back inside again when he remembered he had no others. The welfare worker himself was in the kitchen putting together a good hot meal to be served with coffee and, if Lee were lucky, a decent grade of chinaware with clothen napkins at the side.

"Coffee," said Lee, standing in the door. "Well-sweetened. Also a suit, if you please. Mine has goo all over it."

It was a commendable apartment in many ways, a place in which a man could sleep for days among food and supplies and a hoard of medium quality books that ran from floor to ceiling in a cabinet that, however, was too narrow and the shelves too few to hold all the volumes that Lee would have wanted in any home of his own. To atone for that, the apartment did look down obliquely into the putrefying core of the city, a benefit of significant value for anyone wishing to observe conditions conducive to spiritual improvement.

They ate in silence, a gloomy ceremony that gave Lee the feeling they had been transported back into a late seventeenth-century French-Canadian fortress with savages lurking up to their waists in the snow that lay about. No light must be permitted to escape to the outside world lest they be discovered at their cabbage and all three of them trundled off for burning. In truth, the broth *was* good, and had in it certain cloves and so forth that had been added purely for the effect of it. To give voice to his appreciation, Lee wolfed it down with speed, smacking at the stuff and belching betimes, a procedure that seemed to grate on the social worker's nerves.

"So?" said Lee. "I'm an old man! And someday you'll be old, too. Or perhaps you'd prefer it if I retired into the next room?"

His host had nothing to say. With Lee, there were but two dimensions to the eating process, namely *quantity* and *speed*. Yes, quality was a consideration, although he put that at a distance when compared to the foregoing speed and amount. Finally he pushed back and borrowed a cigarette, quite certain that he would never need to feed again. Came now the annoying part—that of cleaning his dentures with cloth and thread. Of the host, *his* teeth were apparently his own. Lee envied him that, saying:

"You, too; someday your teeth will also be a manufactured product."

"How long will you be staying I wonder?"

"What? What's that you said just now? Look, I wouldn't be here now, would I, if I knew how to find my late beloved wife."

"Late beloved . . ."

"Wife. Just so."

"Oh. And how long were you . . . ?"

"Married? Always. And even before that. Children we were."

"You mean to tell me you spent all that time *with just one woman*?"

Lee blushed. The man had hit upon his secret shame, namely the great waste of years before his marriage had taken place. "But even then we suspected about each other."

"Oh goodness gracious, why you're nothing but an old-fashioned romantic!"

"I know that! *Reactionary* romantic, to be precise."

"You're an old man!"

"I know that! Look, my 'friend,' it takes years to become a *real* romantic. It's hard!"

But here the man merely laughed at him. Lee, too, was in good spirits, pretty good, owing in part to the food.

"Ha! And at *my* age!"

"You with your teeth in your lap!"

"I know!"

It was a good moment, pretty good anyway. Lee liked him better now. Finally, with the laughter having run down to a few occasional giggles, he asked:

"And *your* wives?"

"Three."

"O ye moderns! Tsk, tsk, tsk. And how is it ye cannot hold onto your women?" And then: "Ah yes, truly it must be a perfect hell, when both sides wish to play the male." Again he laughed. It was a good moment, very good, but the host was not even smiling. "*Three*," you say? Hee! And how many of those had done for you what Penelope did for *hers*? Not one."

"Now just hold on! Regina was a fine woman."

"Until she got her second promotion, hm? But tell me if I'm wrong."

They played chess, playing until late. Knowing nothing of this game (save what he had seen in a certain old Swedish film of sixty years ago), he must depend—and this had forever been his way—upon dash and pure audacity and nothing else. Finally, toward midnight, his patience at its end, he came out with his most serious complaint yet against the man.

"You sit here hour after hour without music. Never, *never* will I understand your type, half educated."

"Your move."

Indeed the game was lost. His audacity—and this had forever been his way—was not enough. In any case this "chess" business, so-called, was by no means the noble endeavor that formerly it had been, when men wagered for their souls. And in short, he considered it beneath him.

"No wine, no music. You might as well show me your books."

The man brightened. "I do have a great many books."

Lee snorted.

"No, actually I do read quite a lot."

"I'm talking *quality*."

"That, too."

Lee doubted it. Nevertheless he allowed the person to lead him back through three successive rooms, each decorated in the style of a different wife (each wife sappier than the one before)—Lee could feel his gorge begin to rise—and thence into a fourth chamber that, in truth, did have perhaps six gross of books in it. Right away Lee realized that the things were not organized with any due regard whatsoever for size, color, width, or anything. All his life he had had to endure this—of artifacts arranged pragmatically instead of aesthetically, a leading deficiency, he said, of this all too demotic age. However, even so, he was not prepared to condemn out of hand a reader of even so sloppy a collection as this one.

"I see. Fat ones and thin, all of them jumbled up together quite irresponsibly. But let us approach nearer, you and I, to see what the *quality* is. Ho! Medieval church philosophy? Now that's a bit much, isn't it? For someone like you?"

"Hey, those are *my* books! And I reckon I can read whatever I jolly well please!"

"Do you? Read them?"

The man said nothing.

"Do you?" Lee iterated.

No answer.

"Do you?" Lee *re*iterated.

The man made no answer.

"Do you?"

"Hey!"

"I'll ask again: Do y...? But wait, what's this—a whole shelf of novels writ by girls?"

"They belonged to my wife. If you must know."

"Third wife?"

"Second."

"Better you had thrown them away. Along with her. But where do you keep your Greeks?"

"No Greeks."

"Oh boy. No music and no Greeks."

"No wine."

"No wine, no music, and no pie. Hell, I might just as well go to bed."

Lee followed him back through the three rooms and then into a musty place used mostly for storage where stood an iron bed that appeared to have a pretty good length to it while at the same time lacking the depth and polished headboard that could have been wished. It did have a quilt on it, an affecting relic with a pattern of stitchery portraying the seven agile-fingered women who presumably had coöperated on the thing. Coming nearer, Lee traded glasses in order more closely to examine the workmanship.

"Very well," he said finally, trading back again. "But tell me this—are the linens as they should be?"

"How do you mean?"

"Taut, and freshly ironed."

"God!"

At last he was left alone. Habituated to perfect solitude, it irked him to have a semi-literate roaming at freedom through the house. Thinking deeply, and sometimes speaking out loud to himself, he pulled off his clothes one by one before then putting them back on again when he saw that he had brought no sleeping apparel. And yet the sheets *were* taut; it puzzled him as to why the man had not wanted credit for that. Ten minutes he lay quietly, listening both to footsteps overhead and the sound of an insect cursing in his beard. Suddenly he rolled out, lit a match, and then peeked beneath the bed to see if the assumed slats were numerous enough and rightly organized. Tomorrow, as he knew from experience, would be another day. And now he must sleep, if only he but could.

In fact he did sleep, an amazing boom that brought him awake much too early from excess of self-congratulations. Far away he heard shots from at least two different guns firing in rapid succession in the still-dark slum. Fascination of evil! it fascinated Lee no longer. And sometimes he yearned to get him back into youngest childhood, before the question of the knowledge of the worthlessness of the nature of things had been mooted and confirmed. For although he had listened all night to foghorns, yet that did not prove there had to be harbors in these parts, no, nor boats at sea, not properly speaking, though he might lie for hours waiting for his favorite sounds.

Never yet as an old man had Lee been able to come awake with a clear head and then go back to bed again without first passing through eighteen hours or more of increasing tiredness and gathering black mood—such was his reward for having won his way to age seventy-three. And then, too, he was no more able to get the man's book collection out of his head than that he could read those same books, every one of them, while lying three rooms away in dark night with eyes firmly closed. Accordingly, he now took one of the candles, the dim one, and used it to start the other, the bright one. Holding aloft this source of illumination, he proceeded through the three rooms, delaying briefly at the headboard of his host, who had reserved for himself what was distinctly the better of the two beds and who was in the habit, Lee saw, of sucking all night on the tassel of his night cap.

Lee had at best two hours before the arrival of dawn and must therefore work at top speed if he hoped to put the man's book collection into any sort of decent order, which is to say by color and size, and do it before the cock could crow a second time, ushering in a Wednesday morning.

When came dawn (oozing out of the fissures of the East), then did Lee rise up and go to the window and stand there blinking. Five minutes he stayed, listing dangerously from too much beauty too suddenly revealed. Because dawn, having touched down first upon the hills, was intent upon destroying everything that stood against it.

At six-forty-five, with the social worker still snoring, Lee micturated into his drinking glass and held the product up to the light. Swarming with flukes in a state of high excitation, it confirmed Lee's dwindling opinion about the condition of his health. Next, he found that he *was* able to manure, an unlooked-for concession in his old age, a gift from the stars. Nor was it *too* grotesque an operation—not until he stood and tried to walk away from it, soiling himself, his under things, and socks. Ten further minutes he spent in cleaning up the mess, a tedious job that consumed all the paper and depreciated two fluffy towels as well. Pain, too, he experienced, although not in such quantities that he couldn't simply ignore it.

For as long as his patience endured, Lee allowed his host to go on sleeping. And although he opted not to say anything about it, the coffee, when it came, was weak. There was to be no breakfast, not in any real sense. Instead they shared the last of the cabbage and then, with Lee disagreeing as to whether he could properly be said to have lost last night at chess, or to have won, they hit the street in bright sun.

Today the masses were in a testy mood—baseball was over and football not yet begun. He must be careful, Lee, about what he said and the expression on his face. (For he had no wish whatsoever to be strung up at this late period and left to dangle where anyone who wanted could confiscate his shoes and go rummaging through his pockets.) Accordingly he adorned himself in his most idiotic smile, even at one point rushing up to an appliance store in order to gaze upon an important hockey game being played out on a giant television screen. It put him next to a youth of perhaps twenty, a moron with earphones, peculiar haircut, and a T-shirt with a crapulous slogan on it. Turning from the game to the youth, Lee whispered gently to him:

"Pearls and swine, swine and pearls; when the ratio reaches 10,000 to one, the Republic flounders."

"Yeah?" (He lifted the left ear of his apparatus.)

"Yes, and if you want a capsule history of degeneration, think of it like this, that whereas in the beginning the best were thought to be best and then, more recently, all were equal, now it has come to . . ."

"Worst are best, right?"

Lee was absolutely delighted with him. "Why, you're doing very well! Two days in *my* company and you'll . . ."

"Naw," he said. "Anyway, I gotta go," and did.

They formed a notorious pair—bad man with a stick and a good-intentioned former bureaucrat. This bureaucrat, he seemed to know everything about the bureaucracy; accordingly, Lee allowed himself to be led four blocks, wending in and out of a crowd of shoppers and fat people too lazy fully to lift their shoes off the ground. It was a slovenly gait practiced here, much like skiing. Falling in behind one of the fattest of them, Lee began skiing, too. His companion was displeased with him.

"These are poor people, Dr. Pefley, *poor*."

Lee stopped. "Well certainly they're poor! They *should be* poor; look at 'em. I had my way and everybody would be poor, especially the rich. Poor and poor; poor, poor, poor, and . . ." (But here the man slapped him on the back, bringing him out of what was threatening to become a trance.) ". . . poor! For otherwise how can they hope to achieve that stately quality, joined to Will, that you see in me? See it?"

The man looked. He could not, however, bear up for long under Lee's 12,000-book glare.

"Who *are* you? I mean really?"

Lee grinned. Toothless in Gaza, or in gazing rather, it was perhaps the least appealing smile that he had recently produced. Seeing it, the host backed off a few inches, preferring to walk behind, as opposed to side-by-side with, the older man. And if Lee saw dozens, yea thousands needing the cane, yet he had not time enough for *all* of them. Suddenly he winced (hemorrhoids), and then went racing forward. There *was* poverty here, and yet he verified no actual starvation taking place. This troubled him, knowing, as he did, that no authentic civilization was possible where people were denied any meaningful starvation opportunities. "For Greece," (he said half-aloud), "had no dole. Rome did."

"'Rome?'"

Lee nodded. Always he had wanted a small world getting smaller, a fine people getting finer, all of them dwelling far apart in hand-build cottages on a glebe getting gorgeouser.

While as for the poor, the rich, the rotten, for sports fans and Philistines . . . Over the edge with them!

"Careful! Don't you realize these people can see what you're thinking?"

Lee stopped, went back, picked up his "street face," (which he had so wantonly discarded), and put it on again.

They climbed the stairs, Lee having to abandon his ski gait at the very first step. Everywhere he went his long grey hair called down hard looks upon him. Once indeed he found himself in an eye contest with two turd-brained youths whose effrontery gave him almost more than he could manage. How he longed for a longer stick, smaller youths, or that his own upper body strength might still be cubed and squared! Instead he began making the first moves toward undoing his pants, as if he thought to pee on them, and never mind that they were thirty yards away.

The corridor itself, seemingly without end, stank of sour milk (so beloved by babies), and giant cigars. These were the precincts where, in one room, executions were carried out, and in the other the government cheese was stored. As by old habit, Lee, too, fell into line, falling by habit into the wrong one. He had nothing to say against the government clerks, hundreds upon hundreds laboring at tasks beyond the imagination of his grandfather on his most imaginative day. Nothing to say, that is to say, until he was ordered into a tiny office and then motioned to an armchair that, from the looks of it, promised considerable comfort. Even then he had nothing to say, not until the rather harsh-looking woman turned on her computer and began scrolling up and down at high speed.

"Ah yes," he said, speaking to himself only half-aloud,

"another one. Highly competent and extraordinarily well-dressed, and the rest of all that. Sure would like to cane her."

"What?"

"Carry on. By all means."

"You seek your . . . ?"

"Wife, yes."

"Name."

Lee gave it, giving by error his own (chosen from Greek literature). The woman laughed out loud at him, a highly sophisticated laugh that proved she knew how to toss her head and that her hair had been done up in the mode.

"Hardly! No, your *wife's* name. She does have one, doesn't she?"

He could feel the fingers of his left hand tightening, relenting, and then tightening even tighter about the cane.

"Any peculiarities of dress or manner?"

He began to unroll the list of his peculiarities, beginning with his "condition" and continuing on down. This time the woman seemed more irritated than amused.

"No. Let's start again, shall we? Your *wife's* peculiarities."

"Ah! Divine she was, and stood five full feet on the day that we met." He went further, describing in detail her major and even some of her ancillary characteristics. The smell of her hair, for example—he told about it, holding nothing back. "And then at night . . ." (He hushed, a far-away look having suddenly come over him.) "Four degrees, each from a separate university."

"I see!"

"Pretty to the end."

"'End?' We don't use that."

"People like you—you can't begin to conceptualize about people like her."

"Really! Well let me tell you, 'doctor,' that I . . ."

"Bitch. Why my own sick grandmother could have thrashed *you* to death with her Sunday bonnet! Or I with my cane!" (He stood and showed it.) "Or *him*," (he nodded to the former social worker), "why I believe even *he* could do it!"

"Not me."

"Bonnet, hm? Well then, 'Dr.' Pefley, perhaps you won't mind answering just one question?"

"One? Very well."

"Those knickers you're wearing, how did they come to be drenched in blood?"

"Blood? Ha! No, no, these pants of mine"—he pointed to them—"these pants are stained in *wine*, that's all, just wine. Red wine."

"Wine. And yet, according to my records, you're almost due for burning."

Lee got up and ran.

Ran and ran, covering one full block before exhaustion stopped him. And when he looked back—and must this forever be his fate?—his host had *not* come with him.

TWENTY

WHEN NIGHT CAME DOWN INTO THE CITY, HE BEGAN to feel that indeed it *was* his fate. For he had been strolling for hours, even at one point taking up his mistreated book and reading for perhaps the twentieth time about how the reprobate Alcibiades had done some things that, really, he ought not have been allowed to do. There was no doubt in Lee's mind but that this whole chapter offered some very important guidance for contemporary times. He was musing on this, humming, when suddenly he pulled up just in time before colliding into yet another surly-looking youth who stood stunned to silence by the length of Lee's long grey hair.

Night in the city, must it *always* be his fate? He was *so* tired, so very so, he craved to get him down on the pavement and sleep for a few thousand years; instead, that was when he came to his fourth youth of that night, a thirty- or, possibly, a forty-year-old in a business suit who lay face-down in the gutter saying bitter things to no one in particular.

"Drunk," said Lee, pointing at him with the cane.

"You got that right!"

"Feeling bad about himself too, I'll warrant. Poor little wight."

"Bastard."

"His heart all laden down with rue."

"Bastard, bastard, bastard!"

"But remember this: the rue shall pass. After all! this present moment is such a wee and tiny thing, a mere mite, as I usually call it, all squeezed in on both sides by the mastodons of the future and the past. No, no, I put no credence in it whatsoever, this present time. Nor this conversation either."

"Then you might just as well leave, in that case."

"Or be silent." He sat at the curb. He could not in this meager light make any progress with his book; he could, however, take out his teeth and work on them. "And so thus ends one who might almost have been a man," he said, addressing himself again to the drunk. "Certainly you'd never catch *me* lying all exposed in a city where any miscreant who wanted could run away with my book and teeth. Weakness for alcohol! Never had any use for it myself, not with a brain like mine to keep me amused."

"I'm tired of hearing about that brain."

"Nor hemp, nor powder, nor glue, not with . . ." (Again he pointed to his head.)

"Go! Just *leave*, O.K.?"

"And you, could you have a brain like mine? No, the answer is no. No, for you it's simply too late. Too many baseball scores, too many votes for specious men. Admit it! And so thus ends a people who might almost have been like Grecians." He hummed. Tonight the moon was ample enough but hedged around with turbid clouds. Now, availing himself of *both* sets of eye wear (and finding their virtues doubled thereby), he trained upon the calm and temperate face of his favorite constellation, called "Arsinoë in Heaven" after one of the most beloved of Hellenistic queens. Of course, that turned out to be the moment when the whole vast formation split open into a whorish smile culminating in a horrendous vomit of billions upon billions of tiny white grains of "sand," each grain a star.

"Marry!" said Lee. "Surely this portends something, although, God knows, I wot not what."

"You're not going to, are you? Leave?"

He marched by moonlight and neon, moving in circles through the concrete maze. Ubiquitous was the dereliction here, nor could he bear to look for any length into these faces, as frightening as they were, as blank as paper beneath a tremulous pen. He went rummaging back mentally through his collection of old opera tunes but could not do so loudly enough to defeat the trash music that spilled from each and every doorway and every passing pair of earphones affixed to each and every hapless head. This "music," it was as awful as anything well could be, which is to say the very voice of stupidity made manifest. Never could he pee on *this*, mere vibrations that refused to stand still for it. Instead, he lunged wildly with his cane, hitting nothing.

He continued in a foul mood, his twisted face illuminated by a flashing neon sign announcing the most up-to-the-minute changes in prevailing interest rates. Better, far better seemed it now to him to have remained with his Ionian men, thinkers all. Lee was thinking about them, thinking about thinking itself as he moved past a pornography shop, sun tan salon, video store, rape center, government cheese, and a specialist in rubber and leather. Behind him, interest rates had cooled, promising good days ahead for the makers of consumables. Lee kept silent. For a long time he had known it, how that this was *not* a country with an economy, no, but rather the other way around. And yet his Ionian men had thrived, thrived well, thriving on but figs and asphodel.

He trudged on, thinking more bitter thoughts than ordinary people would have believed possible. "Thus ends," he said, "a lengthy civilization, ending in a consensus that economics is *all.*" Certainly *he* had no economics, not even so much as a farthing's worth in his wine-colored pants. With this in mind, and ignoring for the moment what was happening with interest rates, he turned in at the first restaurant, thinking to order a full meal of figs and flesh and then to run away without paying—until he realized, almost too late, that the place *was full of turd-headed youths!*

He came out at once. Rather than for such company as that, a reasonable man might well prefer burning. How he did so abhor the young! Nor could he pronounce the word "youth," or "young" without at the same time envisioning thousands of the things all grinning and laughing, chortling and scratching, a people given over to the *body* and its things. And in short, he wanted to consolidate the whole class into one big ass for one big caning. No, his real desire was much more gruesome than that, and not to be described where even one such youth might read of it and tell.

He moved on, his nostrils testing in all directions for the scent of food and his two eyes flaired wide for a quiet place, sedate and dark, appropriate for mature persons. Finding it, he entered in dignity and bowed sweepingly to the cashier, a plain woman who, to judge by her, had not probably been offered any very great number of bows during her days on earth. Suspicious at the beginning, she blushed and smiled and then broke out giggling.

Many times Lee had experienced some of his most memorable adventures in places like this. Across from him just now was a still-attractive woman of a certain type who seemed disconcerted by the length of his fog-colored hair. He winked at her twice and proceeded then to lift his cane slowly, an outrageous gesture, lewd in the extreme, that had the woman blinking, the cashier giggling, and the husband displeased.

Such antics came quickly to a halt once Lee had taken up a nose full of the magic aroma of food. Lacking funds, he saw no reason to economize. Accordingly, he ordered for himself an entire rinktum ditty, a remarkable concoction that had some of everything, most of it cabbage. Hot biscuits he also demanded, together with various kinds of preserves which he ate with reserve, using the napkin to capture what fell from his beard. He was grateful that music was playing, even if it were but a wretched little horn concerto from his least favorite of centuries, said to have been a time of "reason." The waiters, meantime, were beginning to show real respect for him, the result no doubt of his customary dignity, his reserve, and the way he deployed his napkin and teeth. Never were there fewer than three of them hovering behind his back where he could not always keep an eye upon their activities. Finally he summoned one of them to his side.

"Good, good. Now listen to me, my man, you've been playing that cheerful little jog for longer than the eighteenth-century itself. You read me?"

"Yes, sir! I do."

"Good, good. Then let us have some . . . Argento, yes! Argento's *Poe*."

"I don't think we have any of that. Sir."

"Goddamn, goddamn it, goddamn, goddamn it."

"Yes, sir."

"Well let us have silence then."

Having victualed and feeling himself now more sweetly disposed, Lee pushed back and lit a cigarette. But where, pray, was Judy, now that he was in such sore need of her arms in which to snooze away the night? Yes, there *was* that woman just across from him whose own arms, however, bore too much jewelry to offer much comfort. He watched sleepily as at last she arose and tiptoed toward him.

"Ah . . . ?"

"No," said Lee. "I'm loyal to the memory of my wife."

"Are you that same *Leland Pefley* whose life has been so fulsomely described in all those unsalable books?"

Lee could not but smile. Soon the waiter would be asking for his money wherefore Lee now drew out his wallet and demonstrated to the woman how empty it was, with no funds anywhere to be seen. This, too, had ever been his way—to trust not merely to the "kindness of strangers," but more accurately, kindness of women.

Two hours later, with midnight fast approaching, he discovered himself in the city's most insecure region. Dogs barked, his own dog retorting back. Far in the distance a riot had broken out—or was it a sound that came from a radio, or bad weather, or fleets of aircraft searching for harbor? Lee hurried. He could predict for himself a long and exhausting hike before old Orpheus—and Lee could see him now, a black person standing in a doorway with a guitar over his shoulder—before the ancient singer could cajole the sun into yet one more summer day, and this time perhaps, one more only.

TWENTY-ONE

HE WOULD HAVE PREFERRED TO BE SLEEPING. INSTEAD, he needed three hours before at last he was able to shake free of the outlying slops with its warehouses, dead cats, and disused automobiles turning back to rust. And then, as if to make *all* things perfect, he was chased for half a mile by a man who appeared even older than himself, a resolute sort of person who never gave up trying to gain on him, not till the sun itself sprang up suddenly and blew away both man and the dark together.

It also brought forth the gnats, entire nations dashing themselves to death against Leland's glasses. It was all very well that *Zarathustra* knew to converse with insects; these here were not the talkative kind.

And so thus Lee, who toward noon came finally to that line in the sand known to history as "The Line in the Sand." Here, in windless conditions, he could still make out most of the inscriptions and anti-signatures left behind in the powder by those many generations that had come this way before him. All those in French, for example, he read easily, together with some in German, and one (incommensurably famous as it was), in Greek. Getting down on all fours, he scampered crab-wise across the terrain, reading at hazard. One man had actually written down curses against the ruling family itself, though the engraving itself was of course somewhat faint after the passage of two thousand seven hundred years. And there, not twenty yards away—it flattered him greatly—someone else had quoted quotes from the book that Lee had writ himself.

He pronounced out loud perhaps two score of the signatures, pausing when he came onto an essay that covered a full quarter-acre of that barren landscape. No doubt about it, the males were prone to expressing themselves more vehemently, their styluses biting much more deeply into the clay. But as to the women, they *never* gave up hope, not even here at the edge of the world where they continued to wheedle and flatter and only indirectly and after many irrelevancies coming down to their own small requests. Women! Perhaps if he squinted (scanning the horizon), perhaps even now he might spot one or another of them writing thoughtfully on hands and knees, using lipstick in lieu of anything better.

How to find Judy among this mess? *Her* message, of course, would be subtle in the extreme, the most timid of all who had come this way. And yet her penmanship would be as clear and normal as on that day when first she had learned to form letters, bending near to the paper as she worked. No need to look for her among Asiatics; accordingly, he crawled forward in haste, obliterating a significant portion of that rather hieratic-looking script that persisted, seemingly, for miles, even unto a grand-sized termite column that, it too, was inscribed up and down. So much the greater therefore was his surprise to find in that place his own name in English lettering set just next to a sketch of his stooped silhouette dressed in thick glasses with book and cane, all of it drawn with great carefulness in his wife's well-remembered hand.

He moaned and wept and then went trundling off furiously a brief distance before turning and coming back. Could anything be more awful than this? To know that she had been traveling with Hittites while carrying a book without pages, and after she had deserved so much better than that? He howled, called, spat, and then smited three times at a low-lying cloud with the flat of his cane.

"Blackguard!" he yelled, aiming the comment heavenward. "Hound!"

No one heard. All around that lone and colossal void the signatures and broken styluses stretched far away. He felt indeed that he had arrived at the very lowest point in his whole nadir, he who had thought when he was young that all of life was to be like certain exquisite measures of the very best music continued on to perpetuity. "Judy!" he called and then, given no answer, hurled the cane as high as he could, hitting no one. He saw no Judy anywhere; moreover, he had now to pull himself a good forty yards or further over deep incisions in order to fetch back his cane. Finding himself then in *Slavic* lands (which he could by no means read), he set about erasing as many of the names as he could, a wicked deed designed to put the last touches on his already very questionable career.

The Greeks, of course, he left intact, while peeing on the New York names. But not even with all his huge Will could he hope to erase *everything*, and especially not so when at last he hoisted himself to the roof of the termite column and observed the immense expanse of writings that opened into endless vistas toward south and west.

He marched north and east therefore, and in time the epitaphs began to fall away. He had now to worry about the day's hotness, and whether he might not dehydrate before he found shade. Changing into other glasses, he saw how the sun, green about the edges, seemed actually to be *feeding on itself*, a repugnant business, quite barbarous really. Nor could he look upon a thing like that without experiencing a strong desire to cane it.

He hated to perish in this way, he who had died already, to expire from too much summer. Even so, he limped on stubbornly, excerpts of world literature running backward and forward through his head. It seemed to him that he had been excellent from the beginning, the sole representative of his generation to have measured up so closely to his own requirements. And now that he stood in sorest need, where *were* those authors of his, and why had they not already flown to his side, those whom *he* had heeded when the need was *theirs*, hm?

And so in this way Lee went on conversing with himself, sometimes napping, sometimes inching forward, and once (once only) scrambling to his feet and racing forward toward a fresh green brook made manifest, he liked to think, for his sole use alone.

Evening did come but still Lee refused to leave his brook. Probably he was waiting for the sun to drop and wanted to hear the tremendous hiss that it must make at the world's edge when after a long and very hot day it flings itself gladly into the annealing sea. Night, certainly, held no fears for *Lee*, he who once had thought that all of life's business ought to be conducted only then. No, rather it was his anxiety about this stream, and whether it too closely resembled that same "River of Forgetfulness" against which Plato and Lucien had warned.

TWENTY-TWO

HE AWAKENED EARLY, LEAPING UP IN HUGE APLOMB and then setting out in improved spirits for the village that he had first descried on the previous afternoon. He could see far and what he saw was the village itself with gates opened wide, and behind that, mountains of royal blue where shepherds were harassing one another with trumpet blasts.

He emerged from the desert with his cane over his shoulder and a book under his arm. His next task was to set foot in the village proper without exciting the dogs and children and being identified for the stranger that, of course, he was. No one observed him, not until he passed the candy shop. Lee sped past, moving at good speed and continuing on for another fifty yards before curiosity and perturbation brought him back again.

He burst inside, the indignation showing in his face. "Do you *know* me, or something, that you should wave to me like that. Why, I might have been any sort of person!"

The confectioner, however, went on smiling in the friendliest way. Lee could not but notice the array of candies and chocolates and, indeed, mints on display. Most alluring to him were the pastel-hued wafers, things so thin that he could point to where the nuts were hidden. He had been wrong, Lee, quite wrong to have imagined at the time of his last dinner that he would never be hungry again.

"Egad. Might I . . . ?"

"Please do!" (It was a clear voice the man had, and cheerful, too.)

"I don't have any money."

"I know!"

"I'll just take this blue one, if I might, yes. No, this is good. *Real* good!"

"Try the . . . No, no, not that one. Try the . . . That's right, yes, try *that* one."

"Jesus!"

"I thought you'd like that. Pefley, is it? Yes, you've come far."

Lee reeled. And dropped both cookies.

"And suffered greatly, too, I'll warrant, judging by the looks of you. Are you disappointed?"

Lee gaped. Always he had flattered himself that he would recognize quality when he saw it; here, the quality was conspicuous in the Man's eyes especially, and His impeccable wares. For a moment Lee thought that he might actually faint; never had he expected to find This One dressed in an apron and yard-tall baker's hat, flour-white in shade.

"'Quality,' you say?" (Lee had said nothing.) "Very decent of you to say so. And you—disappointed, are you?"

"Well shoot yeah I'm disappointed! How would *You* like it? It's bad over here, *bad!*"

"Ah! But then I'm not a second-tier intellectual."

"And that's another thing—how come You're so hard on us brain people all the time?" (He could feel the fingers of his left hand tightening about the handle of the cane.)

"Now there's gratitude for you, really!" (He came nearer, resting His elbow on the counter and His chin in His hand. As heavyweight as He conspicuously was, Lee feared the glass might not support Him.) "You think you can indulge the highest pleasure on earth and not have to pay a price for it?"

"Oh."

"Try one of those green ones. And you can just lower that stick of yours, too; I want to see the tip touching the floor at all times."

"Yes, Sir." He tried another green one.

"Heavens! Anyone who enjoys my cookies as much as all that . . ."

"Can't be all bad, right?"

They laughed, both. Lee liked Him better now. He watched as the Man took up one of His own mints and tossed it down.

"Just love the way you dealt with that degendered CEO. Swish! Bam!"

"You're not mad?"

"My dear man! *Temerity*—can you realize how rare that is?"

Lee grinned. "Yeah. But heck, I didn't know *You'd* like it so much."

"You're not supposed to know. That's why it's temerity. Try a yellow one."

The yellow ones were not nearly so good, although Lee decided not to say anything about that.

"Me, too, I love best the blue." (Again he went forward with that lip smacking that Lee didn't much enjoy watching.) "And now, 'doctor'—and now you *are* a doctor truly—(for I have said so)—and now I recommend you continue your stroll about the town. Proceed on down to the river. And all about the Courthouse Square—it will appeal to your sense of things, I do believe."

"It *is* a pretty town."

"Should be. After all, I've put some of My best stuff into it. A reactionary like you, you especially ought to love it."

"I love it already."

"Care to see the recipe?" He went to the desk and, after fumbling through a mess of papers, candles, and beads, came out with a crumpled page filled with a script that looked uncannily like that same Hittite that Lee had lately been trying unsuccessfully to read. Now, holding it to the light, He began reading off the ingredients in a booming voice that made the windows tremble and the cookies dance.

"For farms," he said, "and the life of farming, I picked 1910 once again. Railroads enough to be picturesque, but not yet so many as to interfere with sleeping. Red barns and cowscapes. Unfortunately, I couldn't find *anything* in the late part of that century."

"Me neither, I never found anything."

"But for flora and vegetation, I chose Silurian times."

"Silu . . . ! Why You're an even greater reactionary than me!"

"Films and music? Your own late beloved 1950s."

Lee clapped hands and spun around. "And novels?"

"*Pre*-postmodern. That's what you wanted, isn't it?"

"You did well! But what about love and romance?"

"Ah. Well I thought a certain *mélange* might be in order. An amalgam, shall we say, of War of Northern Aggression times and your own 1950s once again."

"Oh!"

"He likes that, does he? But hurry now and go about the town. You're allowed just an hour, you understand."

"Just one?"

"Yours is the only soul coming through today—is that what you think?"

Lee hurried, but then came back in time to prevent the door from slamming. Already he had espied a woman in crinoline, a demure one with parasol and her head full of wifely thoughts—they passed without speaking. Said Lee to himself: "Perhaps we need another Aggression, if that's what it requires to eventuate in women like these!" So intently was he thinking about it, he scarcely noticed the little red-headed urchin who, drowning in freckles, now came whistling toward him dragging a string of fish. It came down on Lee that this might be his own father who, he too, had done much fishing in 1910.

"Catfish!" said Lee.

"No, sir; them's perch."

"Perch! That's a mighty fine-looking dog you've got there, too. *He* wouldn't turn back, never, not if *you* were caught in choppy water."

"He ain't worth much."

"No? Does that mean you want to sell him?"

There was a long silence while the child scribbled in the dust with first one toe and then the other. "I reckon not."

"Ha! Well then, you run on along home now and do your chores."

"Yes, sir."

Lee moved on. It was a lovely summer day from out of his father's age, no asphalt anywhere. Now and again he could spy flashes of the bright blue river that ran behind the houses, and at one house in particular three little girls swinging in a swing while screaming screams of joy. It was a place full of cats, a washtub in the yard, flowering plants hanging from the porch alongside birdhouses made from gourds.

He had wasted his life, had Lee, having come into history when he did. His father, on the other hand, having come when *he* did, *his* life had not been wasted at all. It took all that Lee had to stand up to it and to accept it, and then force himself to spy into the open parlor of the following house where one of the local girls, this one almost, but not quite marriageable, was playing yearningly on the piano. Here again all sorts of flowers and roses were running up and down the columns and even sometimes getting into the fretwork. Finally, he saw a small boy hiding in the corn and refusing to come out again no matter how many times his mother called. Lee laughed. It was nostalgia for days that he himself had never seen that would prove the second death of him. And what a lot of cast iron weather vanes in the form of roosters! Came next a buggy pulled by mules. Suddenly he checked his watch.

He went quickly now, skipping past the churches, the livery, the half-dozen grist mills and glowing forge of the town's one smith. He understood this much, namely that it was highly propitious here for literature and love alike, and yes a very Golden Age for mules. He had no right to expect a bookstore here and yet, coming nearer to a truly adorable one on the next corner, he found that he had to work his way through a disorderly crowd fighting over his favorite author in what, admittedly, were very attractive copies indeed, with gold dust on the fore edges.

Clearly this was a world for Lee's own heart. No cane here would ever be needed, and for a moment he almost thought of casting his away. (He did not.) Nor did he see any of the three Graces of his own day—neither Atrophy nor Entropy, not yet even Anomie in her mannish suit. These faces of 1910, they lacked that sleepy film, those extinct eyes, those mouths that dangled open in the lax stupidity that the late century was to look upon as normal.

The river, when he came to it, was as blue and brilliant as molten gems enriched with sunbeams, a place of ecstasy to eels and migrating things. Lee marveled at it, craving to step across and set foot upon the Silurian Shore with its rouge-colored barns and calico horses romping in fields of umber. Here, a man might fall in love in surroundings like these, or dream of prophecies, or write a strange wild book. He had wasted himself, yes he had, the fates having set him down so regardlessly into the leeward side of the century, the tawdriest in fifteen hundred years. Cruel it was, to be shown what life *might* have been. The Greeks knew it. "O ye . . . !" he called, and fainted then.

He woke, changed glasses, and then suddenly leapt up in great alarm. "No doubt He despises tardy people," said Lee. Even so, he had never been one for hurrying, having learned long ago in the South how never to hurry. And anyway he had six minutes left, and the town was small.

"Here I am!" said Lee. "Yes, it's me. One hour and no more."

"Ah." (The Man looked tired.) "And did you enjoy your little jaunt in circa 1910?"

"I did, yes, oh I did. In fact, I'd like to extend it to perpetuity."

"Girl in the parlor—did you like that part?"

"Very much!"

"But you're not satisfied even now, are you? Even now you want something more. Don't you?"

Lee looked down.

"And I know what it is, too, don't I?"

Lee nodded.

"So. And do you think you'll ever get it?"

"I don't know."

"Alright, let's phrase it like this: Do you think you *deserve* it?"

"I do, yes. Remember that CEO? And the 9,000 books? How many others have read that many?"

"Seven, actually. Thousand. They were, however, good ones—I grant you that. Ah, well. Now what was it you wanted? I've had a long day you understand."

"You *know* what I want. You've always known."

"I don't hear you saying 'please.'"

"Please!"

"Again."

"PLEASE!"

"*Now* I hear."

"Please, please, please, please!"

"S'blood! Enough already. Lord! Very well, if you must have it so. I suggest you just turn around now and go back outside, that's right. And then *behind* the shop. Go there."

"Behind."

"And I think you might just find a little path that leads through the woods, you might. Take that path."

"Take it."

"But you mustn't be surprised at anything, not even if you were to encounter your long-regretted . . . Whatever it is you most regret."

Lee went and did not look back. Deep were the woods and dark, albeit splotched with occasional wild flowers. His eye, of course, was eager for long-regretted things, and although his heart was smashing so loudly that he daren't even listen to it lest it explode, yet he was also thinking about other things as well. And what he was thinking was of the possibility of a certain personality waiting in a doorway, someone with outstretched arms waiting in the doorway of a home that would have been builded by herself pebble by pebble . . . He dared not think about it.

Instead, he was thinking of a moment from out of old days when they had both been young, children really, and both filled with the most tremendous enthusiasm for the world and the achievements to come. He could not but smile, remembering how in those times he used to return home to find her waiting for him, Judy glowing in the door with arms outstretched.